THE
ESCORT DIARIES

Survival of the Lingerie Girls

ROSE BURKE

Novel edited by Sarah at
Irrefutable Proof
http://irrefutable-proof.com

ISBN-13:
978-1490386508

ISBN-10:
1490386505

www.roseburke.com

For Lawrence

DAY THIRTY-SIX

EVA PALMER fell to the rigid hotel mattress, forcing her eyes shut as she waited to feel the weight of her client on her chest. The aroma of the bed sheets consumed her immediately, reeking heavily of mildew and cigar smoke. She cringed as his whiskey breath began warming the side of her face, and his lips found her neck. He crawled drunkenly on top of her, forcing her frail body up against the bulk of his massive gut as they sank into the bed. She felt his hands on the inside of her thighs, spreading her legs apart. Eva closed her eyes even tighter, her nose scrunching up in obvious disgust as the client thrust his hips towards hers. She tried to drive her mind to take her somewhere else, anywhere else.

His name was Allan Schaener. Eva had never let him fuck her before, but he was a regular at *Slayers,* the hotel bar where the girls in the club often met their clients. Anyone could tell he was extremely wealthy, as were most of the men who had come in and out of her life recently, but Eva would never accept Mr. Schaener as a client. There was nothing particularly attractive or intriguing about him, and she simply wrote him off as a pervert.

This night was different though. Mr. Schaener had approached her only twenty minutes earlier with a whiskey sour and a gin and tonic.

"Hey there sugar tits, you givin' discounts for first timers yet?"

Eva giggled innocently and took the drink he handed her. Laughter was one of the many things she had learned to fake.

"I only give discounts to my regulars Mr. Schaener, you know that."

"Oh, so I'd have to buy you a condo or a car to get at your pussy for a smaller price?"

"Actually you would have to buy me both, Mr. Schaener." She sipped on her drink and smiled cunningly.

"Do you accept credit cards? I'd gladly swipe it for you," he said putting his hand on her thigh.

She gently swatted it away. "You know the rules Mr. Schaener, no touching unless an agreement is made."

Ignoring her wishes, he put his hand back on her thigh. He leaned in and whispered in her ear, "Come on gorgeous, let me swipe my card in your ass."

Eva motioned to push his hand away again, but paused to take a second look around the bar.

"Well, Mr. Schaener, it appears that my client for this evening is over an hour late, making this your lucky night." She downed the rest of her gin and tonic before asking, "Shall we go back to the hotel then?"

He grinned and downed his whiskey. "Yes, however, I've arranged to stay somewhere else tonight. My driver can take us."

Twenty minutes later, Eva found herself in a disgusting cheap hotel room being demanded to get on her hands and knees. He pulled her hair so hard her head nearly touched her shoulder. With her neck exposed, he took the opportunity to bite into it, hard enough to break the skin. Eva knew better than to object though, and gave in to his dominance.

"Do you like that, sugar tits? Do you like when I bite you there?"

"Mhmm, yes Mr. Schaener." Desire was just another thing she had learned to fake.

He slid himself inside of her, keeping his lips next to her ear.

"Do you like my cock inside you sugar tits? Does it feel good?"

"Mhmm, yes Mr. Schaener. It feels so good!"

"Do you want it harder, sugar tits? Do you? I'm gonna fuck you so hard you'll be outa business for a month!"

He grabbed her by the back of the neck and shoved her face into the bed, thrusting harder than any man his age should.

Eva threw in a few moans and an, 'Oh, you fuck me so good!' to speed up the process, but it was hardly necessary. He finished with an 'Oh, oh fuck!' and a chuckle.

"Is there anything else you'd like me to do for you Mr. Schaener?

"What, the $300 doesn't include cuddling?" he asked playfully.

She let out a short laugh and collected her belongings.

"No, Mr. Schaener. Cuddling is extra."

By the time she had her clothes back on, he had the money ready for her on the nightstand. She scooped it up muttering, "Not bad for a 'first timer'."

"Until next time Miss Hannah," he said taking her empty hand to kiss it.

She smiled politely and responded with,

"Goodnight Mr. Schacner." In her head she screamed that there would be no next time, and cursed him for being a cheap prick and bringing her to such a horrific hotel.

As she walked the seven blocks back to *Slayers*, it hit her that it was Day Thirty-six. *Tomorrow will be Day Thirty-seven.* Would the Eva Palmer from Day One recognize the present-day Eva Palmer? *Absolutely not,* she thought. *Eva doesn't exist anymore, I'm Hannah now.*

DAY ONE

BEFORE THE SUMMER OF 2011, no one knew me as Eva Palmer. To everyone I thought mattered, I was only known as 'his girlfriend'. Even when I introduced myself, I would eagerly point him out in the crowd like the devastatingly naive schoolgirl I was, head over heels for some douchebag that most people couldn't help but adore. I was blissfully unaware of how great I was at being anyone he needed me to be, other than myself of course.

Day One was the day that all changed. Little did I know when I woke up that morning that I would soon encounter my final moments with the label I had unintentionally created.

The sun was scorching my back as I walked home from what my small Long Island town liked to call 'the beach'. However, the lack of waves, goose shit infested water, and rocky sand made its title laughable. Still, that was the place to be on a summer's day. It was barely eleven-thirty when I left, but I had lounged by the water for over an hour and my fair skin couldn't bear the heat any longer. I recall the hike back to my apartment being excruciating. Sweat dripped from crevices I hadn't even realized existed and man-made sand ground against the skin where my sandals met my feet, making them raw and blistered. My decision to wear a sundress was one to be regretted as it caused major chub rub on my thighs. It had turned into one of those summer days you shouldn't even consider stepping out of the luxury of your air-conditioned home. And if you weren't lucky enough to afford such luxuries, you parked your ass on a bench in the nearest mall with a book or magazine with the intention of staying until sundown.

I was relieved when about halfway through my walk I spotted my boyfriend's truck heading my way. He had one of those oversized black SUVs with tinted windows and chrome rims that looked like they should belong to Puff Daddy. It was a spontaneous gift from mommy and daddy of course, following the trend of most wealthy Long Island parents. I guess it's their ass-backwards way of teaching their kids 'independence' and 'responsibility'. Giving kids everything they want usually does that.

Either way, in that moment I saw his ridiculous looking truck as my liberation from the sweltering heat. Waving my arms frantically over my head while shouting his name, however, was not enough to grab his attention and he continued to drive by me.

Looking back, I should have noticed his windows were wide open and it would have been impossible for him not to have heard me. I should also have realized that the shady looking white van that passed me first belonged to his equally shady friend Stephen, and that both vehicles were stuffed with boxes and furniture. But I didn't. Even when I walked into a nearly bare apartment twenty minutes later, my denial was so overpowering that I proceeded to invent explanations for the missing items. *He must be putting things in storage to paint the walls...I guess he took all of his clothes to the cleaners...Maybe his parents are buying us new furniture...* It wasn't until I found a note taped to the living room wall that I understood what had happened.

The note briefly informed me that I wasn't 'right' for him and that he would be back soon for the rest of his things. It was signed 'Love [*The Douchebag*]'. Like 'love' was always a thoughtless addition, and never an actual emotion.

As I read the note over a few more times, my heart pounding so hard I could feel each beat in my damn earlobes. My body became overwhelmed with anxiety as his words set in. *Not right for him? That's it? That's all I get as an explanation?* I let [*The Douchebag*]'s heartless note fall to the floor as I felt the heat of a panic attack spread across my chest. My body dropped to the couch, and I began rocking myself back and forth in the hopes of regaining control. Gasping for air as my breathing became short, I struggled to prevent the physical reaction I was having as the realization seeped into my heart that the person my whole life revolved around had just left me. Tears streamed down my cheeks and onto my bare legs. I lifted my head in one last desperate attempt at resistance, hyperventilating as I tried to fight off what was taking over my body. Finally my frame shook with submission, and I let my head collapse to the couch cushion in ruin.

It was sometime during the next fifteen hours spent sobbing on the couch that I finally realized [*The Douchebag*]'s window had been wide open, and that his dumbass friend driving the van had helped him move out.

DAY THREE

MUCH TO MY SURPRISE [*The Douchebag*] didn't come crawling back to me with a pathetic apology, and I found myself waking up on Day Three to discover the rest of his belongings missing.

With eyes half open, I first noticed that the muffled voice of Bruce Willis had gone, and when I was finally able to prop myself up on one elbow, I could see why. All that was left of our reasonably sized entertainment center was a cable wire and my Die Hard DVD placed carefully among the pile of shit left on the coffee table. I had popped it in around seven that morning hoping that the sounds of Mr. Willis' rugged voice and nonstop ass kicking would sing me to sleep. That and the fact that the sight of any middle aged man glistening with sweat and covered in blood usually put a smile on my face. Well, I had apparently not only managed to snooze through most of the movie, but also the entire four hour window [*The Douchebag*] decided would be best to remove the rest of his things. Other than the couch I was laying on and the coffee table, everything in the living room was gone.

I shot to my feet, still wearing my now sweat soaked and tear stained sundress from Day One, and sprinted through the apartment. A large part of me longed for the chance to speak with him. *Maybe I can reason with him... I'll promise to change and beg him to stay.* But all I found were empty rooms and bare walls. He didn't even leave me the fucking bed. There were no missed calls or texts sent to my phone. He came and left, and there was no note this time. *How could I have slept through all of this?* I didn't make it to the couch this time before collapsing in defeat. My heart was broken.

When I was finally able to pick myself up, I practically crawled back to the couch. Sadly, I spent hours staring at the ceiling that day, drifting in and out of consciousness, hoping he'd come back. It was pathetic. The couch became my safe place. Every hour that went by made it harder and harder to leave the vicinity of my comfort zone. It wasn't even a great couch; in fact it was pretty dreadful. The color resembled something you might find in and around a toilet after a long night of whiskey shots and beer chugging. There were a few minor tears, and the cushions were definitely worn in…but it was mine.

I bought the couch with some of the money I got back when I dropped out of school. Technically, I suppose, it was purchased by the relentless student loan company – the one that calls me nonstop to remind me of what a sucker I am for signing their contract. Either way, it doesn't belong to [*The*

Douchebag], and he better fucking remember that.

Later that night, my phone chirped from the bedroom. *Can it still be called a bedroom if there's no bed?* My phone was lit up, resting on the single remaining piece of furniture in the room – the nightstand I had grown up with. It was pretty much the only thing other than the couch I was able to contribute to the apartment when we moved in. My phone lit up again, chirping three times. *Two new Facebook notifications. I guess* [The Douchebag] *changed his relationship status to 'single'.*

I was wrong. Both notifications were from the same person, a girl named Jillian I had gone to high school with. We hadn't spoken in about a year, but I guess she still felt the need to write on my Facebook wall...twice. 'OMG! Eva, what happened!?' The second one read, 'Call me ASAP!' *Ugh, you nosy cunt.* I remembered her as being the kind of friend who was always giving 'mother knows best' speeches, but never seemed to follow her own judgmental rules. Meaning, it was only slutty to make out with a random guy in a bar if anyone other than herself did it. Even when she went as far as to go home with some guy, she claimed he was 'special' or 'the one'. *Cuz you're really gonna meet your 'soul mate' while he's grinding his dick against your ass in a club...idiot.*

I couldn't help but take the opportunity to peek at [*The Douchebag*]'s Facebook page and search for some clue as to why he left. With one click, I got more than a clue. Instead of the expected update of a 'Single' status, I was smacked in the face with [*The*

Douchebag] is now 'In a Relationship' with Brianna Lexington. *Who the fuck is Brianna Lexington?* One more click and I had my answer. [*The Douchebag*] had posted thirty-four pictures of him with the new me. *Shit, she's so pretty…*

Tears fell as I scrolled through photos of *our* kitchen table, *our* entertainment center, and *our* fucking bed…all in this girl Brianna's new apartment. No, scratch that. An old status update let me know it was *their* new apartment. *What was the date of his* 'Moving :-)' *status? Two days ago…the same fucking day he walked out on me with no explanation…. Day fucking One.* The anger took over and before I knew it my fingers were dialing his number faster than my brain could catch up and tell me it was a shitty idea. *He can't do this to me and expect me to just sit here quietly! Not a fucking chance!* 'Leave a message after the beep….*BEEP!*'

"Wow, too pussy to pick up the phone huh? Okay, well I guess I'll say what I gotta say to your fucking machine then. You are a pathetic excuse of a man. How dare you walk out on me after all the years I devoted to your stupid ass without an explanation! And to let me find out you're fucking someone else on *Facebook*! FUCK YOU! I hope she enjoys your tiny cock and three pumps of love every night because few women can put up with that for as long as I did! Don't you dare come back to me when you regret this! I hope you fucking get herpes…"

After I hung up, my eyes swelled with tears. I thought it would make me feel better to let it all out, but my irrational outburst only made things worse.

He couldn't even bother to pick up the phone, and every minute that passed without a response to my voicemail added to my misery. *He doesn't even care what I have to say, and he's not coming back.*

Seven hours after leaving what later became known as 'the legendary message' among his friends, I began to accept that my relationship with [*The Douchebag*] was over for good. A few clicks and I no longer existed in the Facebook world. The last thought in my head before falling asleep that night was revenge. Not literal revenge on my ex, but the kind of revenge where the good guy pulls through in the end no matter how much bullshit is thrown their way. *I need more than to pull through this; I need my 'Yippee ki yay' moment.*

DAY SIX

IT WAS ONE of those days you simply regret waking up. You spend all morning rolling around in bed (or on the couch in my case) cursing the sun for rising before you eventually suck it up and find the energy to start your day. You reason with yourself, saying you'll save your sick days at work for nicer weather, or you can't miss another class without lowering your grade point average. So you get your lazy ass to wherever you need to be, and immediately wish you hadn't. Something always happens, like you get stuck doing double the work at your job because your co-worker was smart enough to call in sick. Or, after getting to class, you find out it was canceled but your computer-savvy professor couldn't take thirty seconds to write an informative e-mail to the class because they never think of the students who have to haul ass across campus to get there or the commuters who sit in traffic for an hour and fifteen minutes. You usually end up wishing you had just followed your first instinct and never got up in the first place.

Being both unemployed and a college dropout, my reason for getting off the couch that day had nothing to do with a class or a job, but the combination of boredom and the curious looking envelope I spotted out of the corner of my eye. The letter had come three days before Day One; Day Three B.D.L. (Before Douchebag Left). I found it already opened, among miscellaneous bills and old mail scattered across the coffee table. It stated that our rent was over a week late, and in the nicest way possible it informed me that if I could not pay up by the end of the month, I would be evicted. The letter also kindly educated me on how to add an extra hundred dollars to my payment for every week the rent was late, signed [*Asshole Landlord*].

It was exactly two weeks since the rent was due, which meant I only had two more weeks to come up with the rent money and the late fee. That wasn't the first thought that consumed my mind, however. It became obvious to me that for at least two weeks [*The Douchebag*] knew that not only was he going to leave me, but intentionally stick me with an unpaid rent bill. As I continued my search through the massive pile of junk on the table, I also found late notices for a few of our utilities. So, it turns out that I had more to deal with than overdue rent, but also a late electric bill, cable bill, and no fucking furniture. My mind was spinning as it searched for answers. *How could he do that to me when he knows I don't have a job, and barely an education? Why would he sign the lease for another year with me if he didn't plan on staying here?* We had signed on for our third year in the apartment on Day Twenty-Six B.D.L. *What changed?*

It was slowly coming together, but not nearly soon enough. Before we met with the landlord that day, he had suggested I put the lease in my name this time, to help my 'credit score'. And that's exactly what I did. *I'm an idiot.* I let out a furious scream that could have brought down the whole damn apartment complex, and threw the only thing in sight that was breakable. My Die Hard DVD shattered against the wall. *Sorry Bruce.*

How long has he been fucking this bitch and coming home to me at night? He looked me in the eye every fucking day telling me how much he loved me when he knew he was leaving me for her! What a fucking dick! How long did it take him to come up with this genius plan? Wait, fuck that. There's no way he came up with this on his own. I bet that slut thinks she's so smart fucking me over like this. And I fell for it... I fell for all of it... shit.

I was pacing around the living room when inspiration took over. *I need a goddamn piece of paper.* Nothing could have stopped me as I exploded through the apartment ripping empty draws out of cabinets and slamming doors to empty closets until I finally came across what I needed. Instead of bringing the notepad I found back to my safe place, I forced myself to sit on the floor of my bedroom. That room had been the heart of our relationship, and I needed the images of my missing bed and half empty closet to leave scars. I needed to ensure that I would always remember feeling weak and abandoned. And so I took a deep breath and wrote:

Dear [The Douchebag],

It's over. I'm done with you. I've finished your tacky and pointless novel and shoved it back on my shelf. It didn't have the conclusion I expected, and to be honest it still hasn't set in yet. So much love… so much potential… demolished by your selfishness. So now your book can collect dust on the shelf of my past. Perhaps one day I'll pick it up again, read a chapter here and there; skim a page or two. But I will never again read it cover to cover. Books don't change. When you pick up an old book, you welcome the familiarity of each line like a childhood friend. It's essential to reread the books that are unforgettable; the classics… and you my dear, belong in a bargain bin. So for now, I've started a new book. It's titled Eva Palmer, and your chapter in her book is short and insignificant. In fact, your name isn't even mentioned.

After reading it over a few times, I felt empowered. I was ready to take on my new life and leave the past where it belonged. My hate had turned into motivation, and I knew the perfect place for my letter. I taped it above my temporary sleeping, eating, thinking area – the couch, my safe place. It quickly became daily reading material, always giving me the boost I needed to keep my mind in check. Or at the very least, get my ass off the couch. Surprisingly, that last part about getting off the couch became quite easy after Day Six, the day I wrote that letter. I put off letting the landlord know what my plans were, mostly due to the fact that I had no plan. For the first time in my life I had no one to fall back on. No one would be there to catch me. I was on my own.

DAY EIGHT

THE APARTMENT PHONE rang for what seemed like the hundredth time since [*The Douchebag*] left. Everyday I hoped the phone company would finally disconnect the phone due to lack of payment. But still, it rang and rang. As usual, it came up as a random eight hundred number on the caller I.D., so I neglected to pick it up. *Fucking bill collectors.*

It was time to venture out into the world, figure out how a twenty-two year old with very little work experience and no college degree could possibly make enough money to continue residing in a gorgeous living space most adults couldn't afford. So I threw on my sneakers and left the apartment for the first time since Day One, determined to come home with a job.

Little did I know, it wasn't even necessary to leave as long as I had a few free hours and access to the internet. Most people, in fact, have quite the attitude when you go into their place of business in person inquiring about available job positions. You ask them for an application, and they act like your question just ruined their day. The response is always in the same 'how is it possible that you don't know what I'm about to say' tone of voice. 'Applications are available on our website.' Okay then. It took about nine or ten of the stores in a nearby mall to turn me away that afternoon before I picked up on the new trend. Obviously it had been a while since I applied for a job.

LATER THAT DAY, I found my laptop leaning against the back wall of my closet collecting dust. It had been a high school graduation present from my parents, whom I haven't heard from since I dropped out of college my second year and crushed their dreams of me becoming anyone worth keeping in their 'family circle'.

To my pleasant surprise, my prehistoric laptop not only turned on but also connected to the web. *I wonder how many days we have left until they turn off our internet… no, wait. Rewind. There's no we anymore, and it's not our internet. It's* your *fucking internet Eva, get real. Hopefully you have a week. Will all the electricity be turned off too? Is electricity included in the rent? Shit, I should know this!*

Four hours of job applications and 'personality tests' later, I realized my search was going to be more difficult than I had anticipated. Many of the places I had applied to weren't even hiring but 'accepting applications', and my lack of vehicle narrowed down my options quite a bit. *No, this isn't going to work.* The stress of the large sum of money I owed was starting to get to me. [*The Douchebag*] had handled all of the bills with his parents, and left me with nothing but a stack of papers to figure it all out. The fear of losing the apartment was of course at the top of my list.

I don't have time to sit around waiting for these people to call when they aren't even hiring. And if I have to answer one more goddamn question about whether or not I'd make a trustworthy employee, this laptop is going to end up in a pile next to my Die Hard DVD. 'Is taking a pen from work considered stealing? Is it wrong to smoke marijuana at work, even after one is clocked out?' Who writes this shit? Or, better question, who's dumb enough to get these questions wrong? Moving on.

I typed in a new web address. *Craigslist, land of the weirdos and the oh-so-infamous Craigslist Killer. I have no degree and no experience, who the hell will hire me? How about bartending.* Click! **Bartenders Wanted, EXPERIENCE A MUST!** *Nope, next.* **Bartenders Needed, minimum one year experience…** *Nope.* **Female Bartenders Only! Must send a picture along with resume….** *Yeah, that's not creepy.* **No Experience Necessary!** *Nice!* Click! A second window popped open. **Bartending School! Only $250 to Start!** *Ugh, seriously?* I went back to the search box, and typed in 'nanny' instead. Three postings caught my attention.

Looking for a highly energetic, creative babysitter for our children. Ages 2 and 5. Light cooking and housekeeping required. $8/hour. *Babysitter and housekeeper for only eight dollars an hour? No thank you. Next.*

Full time early morning sitter needed. One child, age three. References and experience a must. *Hmm…references and experience? That's easy to fake. And one kid should be easy enough.*

I typed 'teacher resume sample' into Google, clicked on the first link, and copy/pasted it into the reply box for the early morning sitter position. It was an act of desperation. I deleted all of the references except one, kept the fake name but changed the phone number to the apartment number. *If she calls I can do a great menopausal/neurotic motherly impression, and pretend Eva was an old sitter of mine. 'She's reliable, and extremely playful with the kids…'blah blah.* After editing a few obvious things such as my name and contact information, I sent it to the mysterious owner of the post. Worst comes to worst, they realize I'm a fake and don't respond.

The third posting was a similar posting, with little information. It did, however, give their exact address (*fucking idiots*) which I knew was across town. Much too far to walk. *So, now I just wait.*

DAY NINE
PART ONE

"GRAB ME ANOTHER BEER while you're in there!" I shouted into my apartment.

I had spent my day trying to piece together my bills, patiently waiting for a response to any of my job applications, and failing to avoid Jillian's nagging text messages. She was ruthless. I eventually gave in and invited her over just to get my phone to stop vibrating. It's not like any of my other friends were dying to hang out with me, but who could blame them. I never made time for them after I started dating [*The Douchebag*], and I hadn't heard from a lot of them since graduation.

Jillian and I were having a few drinks outside on the deck leading to my second floor apartment, pre-gaming before we went out. The deck was one of those things we thought we'd use all the time for barbeques and such, but in actuality we maybe used it twice. Of course it was an extra three hundred dollars a month, but [*The Douchebag*]'s parents paid most of our rent anyway. He shrugged off the extra three hundred like the arrogant twat he was.

I flipped through Jillian's iPod until I found the right song for the mood I was in. Beyoncé's 'Single Ladies' seemed appropriate. I lifted what was left of my beer in the air while I belted out the lyrics and dropped my ass to the floor. It felt like my first night of freedom, and I couldn't wait to get a little crazy.

"What the fuck are you doing?" Jillian walked onto the deck with four beers cradled in her arms. Her face was a mixture of amusement and disapproval. More disapproval than amusement, of course. I had almost forgotten that no one was allowed to have fun when she was around.

"I'm dancing, what does it look like I'm doing?" I grabbed one of the beers out of her hand and began to chug it. This was my night to finally let loose, and I definitely needed a few drinks in me to remember how to do that.

"It looks like someone gave you the herps and you've got an itch you can't scratch."

I gave her a puzzled glance beyond the beer that was fastened to my lips. It occurred to me that inviting her over might have been a mistake. She hadn't changed much since the last time we hung out. She's the kind of girl who puts people down in every way possible just to boost her own self-confidence. [*The Douchebag*] couldn't stand her, and after an incident at a party she held a year earlier I wasn't allowed to see her anymore.

"Slow down! Why are you drinking so fast?" I had finished my beer and was reaching for another.

Because you're only fun to be around if I'm wasted. "I'm just excited to finally go out and be single."

"Alright, well calm down! The bar will still be there when we're done with our drinks."

Normally, my reaction to someone saying shit like that would be extremely sarcastic or far too literal. However, since our friendship hadn't exactly been existent prior to that night, I chose to fake a smile and go inside to finish 'getting ready'. I realized that when you have a friend like that, sometimes it's easier to let them think the things they say are witty or comedic. Everyone within earshot will know your friend is a dumb fuck. It's not necessary to always point it out to them.

WE EVENTUALLY TOOK the thirty-five minute drive into the city and stopped at a club called *La Noire*. The place was packed. I couldn't have imagined a better first night out A.D. (After Douchebag). We could barely squeeze ourselves through the crowd as we made our way towards the bar.

"I'll have two shots of Jameson and a Bud Light!" Jillian threw me a condemning look, but kept her mouth shut. You have to love the loud music in clubs. It's the perfect environment to be in when you just don't give a fuck what the person you're with has to say. And that's exactly the kind of mood I was in that night. For once, I wasn't concerned about anyone's happiness but my own. I did my two shots and dragged her towards the dance floor, beer in hand. No disapproving looks this time.

Through the years I'd known Jillian, this was the one place we always got along. We could always let loose, and allow the music to take control. Our moves were always in sync with one another, and we had the ability to grab everyone's attention when we wanted it. That's how I met Jerimiah.

I first saw him dancing with a few of his friends. They were the kind of guys you see in the club who dance so well that the crowd naturally clears the floor for them, everyone staring and cheering them on. His body moved in perfect tempo with the music, each movement accentuating the muscles in his arms and chest. Sweat was dripping down his face, making it glisten under the club lights. It wasn't long before I had my back to Jillian, becoming another gawker in the crowd. He didn't know it yet, but I'd already decided he would be mine that night.

My whiskey confidence urged me to stare at him until we locked eyes, and I was able to give him my best 'come get it' look. Jillian was giving her attention to some random guy, but it didn't bother me. I wasn't alone for long.

"Do you want to dance?" *Hell fucking yes I do.*

Jillian was too busy trying to chat up the guy she was dancing with to notice me sneak away with Jerimiah. We started dancing next to each other, but it wasn't long before he grabbed my waist and pulled me close to him. His hazel eyes never left my own, staring at me so intensely I couldn't help but blush. I tried to look away, but he wouldn't let me. He took my chin in his hand and brought it towards his face until I had no choice but to give in and lock eyes with him again. We stared at one another as if it were only us and the music. No one else existed.

He pushed my back against the wall, grinding on me with more intensity than I had ever felt with [*The Douchebag*]. I could feel wetness creeping down my thighs as he continued to move with me in every right way imaginable. Our faces were close enough so that the sweat dripping off his forehead landed on my cheeks. I could taste the salt when it finally reached my lips. My hands wandered over his solid chest and arms, increasing the sexual tension that had developed between us. His hands drifted as well, slowly groping the side of my body. My legs grew weak as he slid his hand up the back of my skirt, and slowly dragged it around to the front of my thigh.

Finally, he brought his hand up behind my neck and leaned in. Each second we stared at one another seemed like an hour. I felt like he was able to read my every thought through my eyes. He kissed me softly at first, biting my upper lip. Then we kissed harder, with the passion of reuniting lovers. This went on for a while, but like all moments in life it had to come to an end. He took my number and left the club with his friends.

DAY NINE
PART TWO

IT WAS GETTING LATE, and I was sexually frustrated and wasted. I was left to search the club for Jillian when I realized she had deserted the spot I left her in. Eventually I ended up at the outdoor bar in the back, and sure enough there she was smoking among all of the other future cancer patients of America. Even that shitfaced, the smoke made my eyes water and I was forced to breathe through my mouth.

"There you are! Where the fuck did you go?" She was sitting with a group of girls who didn't seem to be including her in their conversation.

"I was dancing." *And making out. I wonder when I'll hear from him.*

"I was looking for you for like an hour!"

"You were with some guy last I saw you." *Some*

guy who obviously realized how incredibly fun you are to be around, which is why he's… well, not here.

"After this cigarette we're going home."

"Okay." *Shit, I want to fuck him so bad. Is there still a three-day rule? Is that how long he'll wait to call me?*

"Excuse me, can I bum a cigarette?" A tall, slender girl in a tight black dress approached Jillian. She was a pretty mix with mocha skin, and long jet-black hair. Jillian offered her the open cigarette pack. "Thank you sweetie! Are you guys having a good time? I'm Nyani by the way." She sat down and joined our conversation like she had known us for years, which I could tell made Jillian uncomfortable. We introduced ourselves as she lit her cigarette. I didn't think much about her sitting with us, when I'm drunk I'll talk to just about anyone.

"So, do you guys come here a lot? I've never seen you here before."

"No this is my first time here," I answered. Jillian had shifted her body away from us to show me she wasn't interested in contributing to the conversation. "What about you?"

"Yeah, I usually come here a few times a week after I get out of work. It's close by, and I know the bouncer so I don't have to wait in line. It's ladies night Thursday nights though, so I try to make it here early for free drinks!"

I giggled. She said it with such enthusiasm, I couldn't help myself. "What do you do that you get off so late?"

She hesitated and smiled slyly, "I do a little bit of everything." There was something alluring about the way she spoke. I couldn't help but be drawn to her.

"Are you here with anyone else?" Jillian butted in, almost rudely. Nyani probably didn't pick up on it, but that was her way of saying 'go talk to them and leave us alone'.

"No, my friend was here earlier but she had to leave. Do you smoke? I have a blunt in my bag if you want to smoke it with me." Her question was directed to me but Jillian felt the need to respond anyway.

"Um, no. We don't smoke."

"Actually, I wouldn't mind smoking a little." I could feel Jillian's eyes burning holes in the side of my head, but I refused to give her the satisfaction of thinking she could answer for me like that. *Who is she to say I don't smoke?* I mean, at that point I hadn't before. [*The Douchebag*] would never have allowed it. But that night was about finally being myself and doing what *I* wanted to do. Falling into another controlling relationship, friendship or otherwise, would be a step backwards. Also, I wanted to be around Nyani more. I envied her free spirit, and ability to be in a packed club with no one to fall back on. She came off so confident, and her hair and makeup were flawless. The word beautiful wouldn't have been enough to describe her. I thought if I spent more time with her, her energy might rub off on me a bit.

"So lets go! I don't live far, we can smoke at my place." Nyani was already up and heading towards the exit. "Where are you guys parked?"

"In the back," I shouted over the crowd. Nyani led the way through the mob of people as I hurried after her.

"What the fuck are you doing?" Jillian shouted in my ear as she scurried behind me trying to catch up. "I don't want to go to this bitch's house! And since when do you smoke pot?" She said it loud enough so that I wasn't the only one that could hear her, but Nyani was now too far ahead of us to notice the dispute.

"Calm down, I'm just trying to have a good time. You're so uptight sometimes!" I said this with a smirk on my face, patting her on the head. It may have been a bitchy move, but drunk Eva was out to play and I didn't give a fuck if I never heard from Jillian again. Nyani would be my new friend, at least that's what I hoped. She seemed to be the kind of girl who would never tell me what kind of person to be, and I needed that kind of relationship with someone more than anything.

"Eva, I just want to go home! I don't want to waste an hour in her apartment watching you two with the giggles and the munchies." *It's really impossible for this girl to just go with the flow.* I could see Nyani waiting for us by the exit, so I threw her a wave to let her know we were still making our way towards her. I needed to come up with a plan to get Jillian on board before we closed the ten-yard gap between us and the exit.

"How about we smoke in your backseat on the way to her place? She said she lives close, we'll just drop her off. I feel bad, I don't think she has a ride." Chicks are never supposed to leave other chicks stranded. It's an unwritten rule. Not that I thought Nyani would have had a problem finding her way home.

"Fine, whatever. Just don't stink up my car!" I smiled at my success, and approached Nyani in a fit of giddiness.

As we stepped out into the parking lot, Jillian instantly quickened her pace in order to take the lead. "She doesn't want to stay out too late so we can't hang out at your place tonight, but we can smoke in her car if you want." I said trying to make it sound as nice as possible, while also putting the blame of our ruined plans on my neurotic friend.

"Yeah, I have to work early tomorrow," Jillian lied.

"That's fine," Nyani shrugged. "I have to pee so bad! I'll be right back!" She ran a few yards up and I could see the top of her head as she squatted between parked cars. I couldn't help but laugh until tears came to my eyes. *This chick is fucking awesome!*

"This chick is fucking nuts! I can't believe you're making me take her home!" Jillian stormed off to her car, and sat in the driver's seat with what I imagined was a pout on her face.

Instead of giving in to her childish behavior, my attention was drawn to a high-pitched squeal coming from Nyani's direction. My head turned just in time to see her tumble onto a grassy median in hysterical laughter. I got to her as fast as my intoxicated, five-inch-heeled legs would allow me.

"Are you okay?" I asked through drunken giggles. She lay sprawled out on the sidewalk, struggling to roll over like an upside down turtle.

"I can't get up! I'm so wasted!" Her eyes bulged from her face when she said that, and I couldn't help but fold over in hysterics. I reached a hand out in attempt to help her, but her weight just pulled me down to the concrete next to her. Tears came down my face as we both floundered on the ground.

"I better not be laying in your piss!" I shrieked causing us both to continue rolling around in fits of laughter.

Nyani was finally able to get a grasp on where the ground was, and propped herself up and on top of me. She straddled me with one leg on each side, causing her dress to come up far enough for me to know she wasn't wearing any panties.

"I can see your cookah!" I shouted in her face, still in hysteria from our tumble.

"Yes, and it was just waxed this morning!" She took one of my hands and brought it up her skirt, forcing my hand to feel the smoothness of her freshly waxed bikini line. "See?"

"Yes, it's very smooth!" I continued to giggle.

She leaned in so close I lost my laughter. Her lips lingered close to mine, hovering far too long before they finally touched. Our kiss was brief before we tumbled over in drunken hilarity.

After a short struggle of getting into Jillian's car, and briefly giving directions to her place, Nyani lit the end of the blunt and we began passing it back and forth.

"Am I doing this right?" I choked out through the coughing.

She laughed at me and responded saying, "Yeah, just put it on the edge of your lips though so you don't get it wet. Like this." Nyani put her lips lightly on the end of the blunt and inhaled before passing it to me to try. I didn't know what the fuck I was doing, but my mouth started to get dry.

"I need a drink."

"You have cottonmouth," she said giggling.

"I have the rest of an eighteen pack under my seat," Jillian offered. *Nice!* I reached under her seat and pulled out three beers. We all cracked them open, and I made some drunken toast to my first night of freedom. Jillian pulled onto the expressway, heading back towards Long Island. *I guess Nyani doesn't live as close as she said.*

We lit another blunt as I listened to Nyani talk about legalizing weed, and her grudges against the American government. I nodded and pretended I was following what she was saying, but I couldn't keep up. My mind was too far gone.

"Do you know how to do a shottie?" *A what?* "I'll show you, just inhale when I blow smoke in your mouth."

She took a long hit from the blunt and leaned in towards me. As her lips touched mine, I could feel her tongue lightly caressing mine as she blew smoke into my mouth. I inhaled, feeling the burning in my lungs. Every inch of my body was tingling, and my eyes felt heavy but I couldn't stop grinning.

Red and blue lights filled the car. "Shit! Hide your beers!" Jillian threw her open beer into her glove compartment, letting it spill everywhere. We were being pulled over.

"Give us cigarettes! It'll hide the weed smell!" Jillian grabbed one for herself before tossing the pack at Nyani. I put my open beer in a small compartment on the side door, and grabbed a cigarette for myself.

Jillian stopped her car on the side of the road, and we all simultaneously lit up. I tried to keep a straight face, but I couldn't. For some reason the idea of us all getting busted with open beers and who knows how much pot excited me. Not that I wanted to get in trouble, but living a bit more dangerously was definitely appealing to me.

I puffed that nasty cigarette as the cop grilled Jillian. Her ability to act sober when in fact she had just as much to drink as I did came in handy that night. Jillian's taillight was out, and the cop let her off with a warning. As soon as he pulled away, we all let out a sigh of relief. Nyani and I busted out in hysterics over what happened, but Jillian didn't seem to think it was very funny. The rest of the car ride was pretty quiet. I spent most of it sipping on my beer and gazing out the window, high as the stars. The drive could have been three minutes or three hours, I really had no idea.

"This is my house right here," Nyani said pointing to a house on our right. It was set back behind a large gate. The driveway alone looked as long as a football field, and even at such a great distance I could tell the house was enormous.

"Wow, your parents have a beautiful house!" I wished we could go inside.

"Actually, my parents don't own the house. I live here alone." *What? How is that possible?* She threw her arms around me and gently kissed my cheek. "It was so nice meeting you guys! Thank you so much for the ride! Maybe I'll see you on ladies night?"

She didn't wait for my response before she got out of the car and shut the door behind her. "Bye!" I shouted, but I didn't think she heard me. I climbed into the front of the car, watching her open the gate and start walking up the driveway. Jillian didn't wait for me to be seated before quickly pulling away from the curb, hurling my body headfirst into the dashboard. *Bitch.*

"That was fucking ridiculous. Lives right around the block my ass! And how the fuck can she afford a house that looks like that? She can't be much older than us!"

Ugh, this psycho is ruining my high. "I don't know, maybe she inherited it or something." I reached into the back for my purse, and began digging for my ChapStick.

"Yeah, that's bullshit. She's probably dating a drug dealer or something. And what the fuck were you doing in the street with her before? I saw you!"

"Umm, okay. I wasn't trying to hide from you." I checked my phone, and it was almost three o'clock. *Way too early to be going home.*

"Are you gonna, like, hang out with her now?" she demanded. Jillian sounded insecure about our freshly reunited friendship, like what we had was so special and she was afraid of losing it again. *If she acts like this with me, I can't even imagine how clingy and controlling she is with the poor bastards who actually date her.*

"You're being a crazy bitch right now. Why do you care if I hang out with her again or not?" I kept my voice calm, but stern. She could yell at me all she wanted, but I wasn't going to let it get to me and I definitely wasn't going to let her think it was okay to talk to me like that. All she was to me at that point of our friendship was a wing-woman, and a semi sober ride home.

My phone vibrated in my hand, and I saw that I had a new text message.

"HEY ITS JERIMIAH - SORRY WE LEFT SO EARLY MY FRIEND HAS TO BE SOMEWHERE EARLY TOMORROW. HOW WAS YOUR NIGHT?"

I smiled to myself. *I guess he couldn't wait the three days before contacting me.*

"Excuse me, but I think *you're* the crazy bitch! I have every right to know what kind of people you're going to be hanging out with if you and I are going to be friends! I don't want to be around any pothead losers, and if that's the kind of person you want to be then you can forget about this friendship!" *How can someone who says shit like that ever call someone else crazy?*

Instead of responding to her insanity, I texted Jerimiah back.

"Hey! Its ok I'm actually on my way home

now. I had so much fun! How was your night?"

"Who are you texting?"

"Woah, so demanding! Why don't you ask nicely?" My fingers finally wrapped around my ChapStick. I took it out of my purse and slid it over my lips while I waited for Jillian's response. It gave me a small amount of pleasure taking her control away, and I let it show in my smirk. I got another text from Jerimiah.

"IT WAS FUN, WISH I COULD HAVE SPENT MORE TIME WITH YOU THOUGH".

I debated for a good five minutes what my response would be while Jillian and I sat in silence. After typing and deleting what I wanted to say over and over, I finally got up enough courage to send it.

"Well I'll be up for a bit if you wanna come over".

I began to feel the excitement of every butterfly in my stomach fly up my throat and flutter in my mouth despite the Jameson buzz and purple haze high I had going on. The anticipation caused by my bold gesture ran through me like an electric current. I didn't get to enjoy it very long, however, before Jillian broke the silence with her pathetic apology.

"Sorry, I'm just really depressed lately. I haven't had a boyfriend in over six months and I'm just starting to think the right guy just doesn't exist."

Tears were falling down her face. *Oh, boy.* "I just don't understand why every guy I meet is only interested in making me a booty call. Why can't I find a guy who wants to settle down?" I checked my phone, no response from Jerimiah yet. *This is no time for girl talk, honey.*

"You're only twenty-two, you don't need to find your soul mate right now. No guy our age wants to settle down, they're only interested in getting laid." It was the most cliché response I could think of, but I just wanted to shut up her whining. *Looking for a life partner at this age is fucking ludicrous...almost as ludicrous as wasting my teenage years and early twenties on [*The Douchebag*] when I should have been out fucking every hot guy I set eyes on.* I checked my phone again. Still no response.

"You're only saying that because things with [*The Douchebag*] didn't work out. I've been doing the single thing for long enough, and I'm over it. I need to have someone I can take care of. It's just how I am." *Whatever stop talking! Why hasn't Jerimiah texted me back yet?* "I'm just sick of the games guys play."

"Well, I have very little experience with the games guys play since I've only been single for like a week.*" But I have every intention in learning how to play these games. Relationship Eva has officially left the building.* My phone finally vibrated.

"SURE WHERE DO YOU LIVE?"

Five minutes later we were pulling up to my

apartment and I was texting Jerimiah my address.

At some point later that night, I vaguely remember opening the door to Jerimiah, standing before me in the same black v-neck and jeans he had worn to the club. My outfit, on the other hand, had changed from my dress to a silk nightie. It was apple red with a black lace trim that barely covered my bare chest. Somehow through my drunken stupor I had managed to also put on the matching panties, and black heels. I wanted to make sure he understood I hadn't invited him over to chat.

Jerimiah stood in the doorway for a moment looking me up and down while I held open the door, enjoying his lingering eyes. He didn't smile or say anything about my wardrobe change. The only sign that he liked what he saw was in his eyes as he brought them back up to my face. They were boiling over with desire as he held my gaze for what felt like an eternity. I tried to keep a straight face, encouraging my eyes to smile instead. Finally he crossed the threshold and in one quick motion pulled my face towards his, hurling my back against the wall.

His kisses were rough and forceful, teasing my lips with soft bites. They got progressively harder as I reached around the back of his head and pulled his face closer to my own. He scooped me up effortlessly, wrapping my legs around my torso. Our breathing got heavier as his lips migrated to my neck. He leaned his body against mine, pinning me to the wall with my hands above my head.

Letting my legs fall gracefully to the ground, he took my hand in his. He looked around the room. *This is it. He's waiting for me to take him to my bedroom. Too bad I don't have a fucking bed.* I led him towards the couch and playfully pushed him down to the cushions. Jillian's iPod and dock were sitting on the floor where she had left them. *I hope this chick has some reggae.*

He sat back while I danced for him, watching me sway, teasing him with my eyes. I'd like to think I was sexy about it, but it's more than likely I looked like a fool. Either way, he liked it. He grabbed my ass and pulled me underneath him on the couch. The familiar feeling of a man's weight on top of me eased my mind, and I didn't hesitate to let him inside of me. That was my last clear memory of the night.

DAY TEN

THE DAY CAME with a nasty headache and a rotten stomach. I rolled around on the couch for a good hour, groaning and trying to avoid the sunlight that was tearing through the blinds. Constant vibrations coming from my phone finally convinced me to open my eyes and begin the wake up process. I was completely naked, barely covered by the light blanket I kept on the couch ever since it became my bed. Through my blurred vision I could see that my nightie was crumpled in a pile on the floor by the front door. Jillian's iPod dock was knocked over, and her iPod was a few feet away on the floor. The memory of tripping over it started to come to me. *Was Jerimiah here to see that? No, it was after he left... right? Yeah, it must have been. I had walked him out and was making my way back to the couch when it happened.* Relief swept over me. *That's one dumbass thing he fortunately didn't get to see, but what* did *he see? Did I say anything stupid?*

I attempted to replay the end of the night in my

head, with little success. Bits and pieces came to me, but there were so many holes. *I remember dancing for him, and fucking on the couch.* The memory of him bending me over the coffee table and thrusting his cock deep inside me made my whole body shiver. *I remember his lips on my thighs, and him eating me for… twenty minutes? An hour? Who knows. I do know that the sun was rising when I walked him out.* A smile crept on my face and remained there as I lay on the couch reminiscing.

Nothing stuck out in my mind that would qualify as humiliating enough to avoid reaching for my phone, so I plucked it up off the table and peeked at the screen. One new text, four missed calls, two new voicemails, and one new e-mail. I started with the missed calls. All four were random eight hundred numbers. *Fucking bill collectors.*

The text was from Jerimiah.

"HEY CUTIE, I HAD A GREAT TIME LAST NIGHT. I HOPE WE CAN DO IT AGAIN SOON."

I smiled, relieved that my wasted ass didn't somehow screw up the possibility of seeing him again. The voicemails were all from bill collectors, the first for my overdue rent and the second for my student loan. *I'm well aware of the fact that I owe you dicks money, but thanks for the reminder!*

Lastly, I checked my e-mail and was pleased to see that I had gotten a response to the babysitting ad

I applied to. She wanted to meet with me as soon as possible! I e-mailed her back with my availability (*any day, any time*), and got my lazy ass off the couch. It was well past two o'clock, but my body didn't feel at all rested. The smell of empty beer bottles hurled itself up my nostrils as I passed the kitchen on my way to the bathroom. My stomach flipped, but I held back the vomit and jumped in the shower.

After a quick rinse, I was finally getting comfortable enough on the couch to possibly fall back to sleep when my phone vibrated. It was another e-mail from the woman who wanted me to watch her kid, Diane Weisman, and she wanted to meet me. *Today? Are you nuts lady, it's almost five o'clock and I'm hungover as fuck!* I agreed to meet her though, seeing how desperate I was to make some money. I got dressed and threw on some makeup to hide the dark circles. Her next e-mail came with an address, so I sucked it up and began my walk. I was still a bit drunk from the previous night, and before I had the chance to realize what hell the hike to her house was, I was already knocking on her front door.

The smell hit my nose the second the door swung open. My stomach did a double back flip before it finally landed in my mouth. *Gotta swallow that shit Eva!* I felt the vomit burn every inch of my throat as it settled back in my gut... at least, for the time being.

"Hello, Diane right? How are you?" I stuck out my hand for her to shake, and she took it cautiously.

"Eva? Come in," she said as her eyes shifted away from my face for a moment. She examined me behind her designer glasses that one would never think she could afford after taking one look at the shit hole she lived in.

The floor of the foyer had been stripped of any carpet or tiles. Paint chipped off the walls, adding to the thin layer of dust collecting underneath my feet. The smell in the air was sour, and impossible to ignore. It was a familiar scent, but I couldn't put my finger on what it might be. I tried to smile through my disgust as I turned to face her, but without making eye contact she motioned for me to follow her.

Diane led me to a room straight off the foyer that I assumed had been a living room at one point. However, it was now taken over by children's toys and clothes. Everything from Thomas the Tank Engine and Legos, to (hopefully) unused diapers lined the floor and the couch. The coffee table had stacks of children's books covering every square inch. She didn't even acknowledge them as she took a seat on the table. Without waiting for an invitation, I moved enough crap out of the way for me to sit on the very edge of the couch across from her. She was looking down at a tiny notepad, which I could see had my name scribbled at the top and a few notes written underneath.

"So, why don't you tell me a little bit about your experience with children," Diane said while staring intensely at her lap. Her grip around her pen was so tight I could see her knuckles turning white.

"Sure," I said and began talking about the things I remembered being listed as my experience on my embellished resume. "I've worked several summers as a camp counselor, working with young boys between the ages of three and five. I also tutored kids after school when I was a senior, and I studied elementary education in college." The lies came so naturally I almost believed them myself. I didn't feel guilty. My back was against the wall, and I didn't think I had another choice. It was either lie to get a job, or be broke and homeless.

Diane was scribbling furiously on her tiny pad, apparently writing down my every word. *Is this really happening? You could have easily printed out the resume I e-mailed you and saved your hand from early arthritis.* There was a long pause in the interview as I waited impatiently for her to finish writing a short manuscript. I tried to keep my attention on her, but it was easy to find other things in the room to entertain my mind.

"And it said on your resume that you are CPR certified?"

I snapped back to her pathetic questioning and answered simply with a 'yes', yet her scribbling continued onto the next page of her notepad. *What the fuck is she writing? I said one fucking word!* My patience was running low, and my stomach was churning on high.

I spotted a small television out of the corner of my eye. It was one of those fat televisions from the eighties with giant knobs on the front, and a VHS player sitting on top. I remembered my parents having one similar in our kitchen when I was a little girl. It was always fuzzy and you could only watch like four channels. This one, however, gave me the creeps. Not only was it in the wrong decade, but it was facing the wall rather than the couch. Also, it couldn't have been more than a twelve-inch screen, which is far too small for a living room.

"Mom! MOMMM!" Shouts were coming from upstairs. Without excusing herself, Diane left the room to attend to her child. She crossed the foyer and lifted a gate more suitable for a dog than a child that blocked the stairs. I hoped its purpose was to prevent the kid from accessing any of the rooms on the first floor that I'd seen so far. *Instant death-trap.* As she disappeared beyond the dog gate, I couldn't help but want to peek at her notepad. I had to know what she'd been writing.

It was turned over on the coffee table, hanging off the edge of one of the taller piles of books. I scooped it up, while keeping one eye on the stairs. The pages, I was stunned to see, were covered with dark marks where she had repeatedly drawn circles in the same spot until it nearly tore through the paper. She'd reproduced these until the entire page was covered in small black orbs. *What a nut job!* The entire notepad was covered with them excluding four pages which each had a girl's name on it, including my own. Under my name she listed my qualifications, or at least what she thought my qualifications were. There were similar things under the names of the other three girls except there was additional information on the bottom. Under a few of those crazy circle drawings it read in bold lettering, "NO HIRE". Next to that, on each girl's sheet of paper was Diane's reason for not hiring them. 'Too young', 'Too loud', and 'Too fat'. I rolled my eyes, and wondered what my 'NO HIRE' statement would be. *Too short? Too quiet? Smells too much like a bottle of liquor and an ashtray?* I smiled to myself, and tried to place the notepad back exactly as I had found it.

I heard her coming back down the stairs and my heart began to race. *Will she notice I looked at her book?* I unexpectedly felt like I had read the diary of serial killer, and feared that my eyes would give away what I knew. The anxiety awoke my stomach, which had somehow managed to ignore the wretchedness of the air up till then. *Gotta suck it up Eva! Ten more minutes, just swallow it for ten more fucking minutes.*

Diane sat back down, bringing with her an extra waft of the house's stench. "The job is Monday through Saturday morning, from five to twelve, at ten dollars an hour. My son wakes up extremely early, and I like to sleep in. Are you interested? Our current nanny can't get here until noon, so I'd need you to start tomorrow." It was the most she'd said the entire time I was there.

"Umm, yes I'm very interested." *And I need to get the fuck outta here before I ralph all over your face.*

"My husband goes to work early, but I'm a stay at home mom and will be here if you need anything.

I'd prefer not to be woken up though unless there's an emergency. I will leave the back door unlocked for you, and my son Spencer will call for you at the top of the stairs when he wakes up. Spencer's clothes are all down here in the living room for you to help him change, and I'll prepare his breakfast and snack the night before and keep it in the refrigerator. Spencer has a special diet, and can only eat what I prepare. He will tell you when he's hungry, and what activities he would like to do for the day. We do not allow television before noon, so you and Spencer will not be watching television together. There's a park around the block, Spencer knows how to get there. Any questions?"

I had a ton of questions. Like, *why the hell does your three-year-old son need to be on a special diet? What the fuck is that smell? And most importantly, if your only job is to be a stay at home mom, why the hell do you need two nannies? You're hiring me so you can 'sleep in'? Seriously lady, get a real job or take care of your kid.*

"No, I can't think of any questions."

"Ok, then I will see you tomorrow," Diane said as she walked towards the front door.

I guess I'll meet the kid tomorrow then. "Thank you, it was nice meeting you Diane."

The fresh air hit me like an old friend, but I knew it was too late. The smells from my drawn out interview had already pushed me over the edge, and I began to gag. The possibility of Diane watching me from her front door was the only thing that motivated me to keep it down a few extra minutes. I made a right down the first block, sidetracking from what would have been a more direct route. As soon as I was sure I was out of sight, I let it out all over the street.

DAY ELEVEN

IT WAS DAY ONE of work, and I was a fucking zombie. Nothing could have prepared me for how I would feel about being awake and walking fifteen blocks at four-thirty in the morning. My eyes fought to stay open, and my legs could have been dragging cinder blocks.

Wandering through the Weisman's yard and opening the unlocked back door felt nothing less than criminal. As I navigated my way through the darkness, I was greeted by the familiar stench that I had spent the previous night trying to forget. The sour feeling instantly hit my stomach, which fortunately for me was still empty. Even so, it was hard not to gag.

After finding the disastrous room my interview had been held in, I made a beeline for the couch. I cleared the piles of assorted shit off it with one quick hand motion, and collapsed in exhaustion. It seemed like only seconds went by before I passed out. Next thing I knew, I was awoken by my name being shouted from the top of the stairs. *The kid knows my name?*

I got off the couch groggily, and let the kid out of his dog cage. "Good morning, Spencer. I'm Eva, your new nanny." It was the best attempt I could make at perkiness before sunrise.

"I know," the kid whined. "Get me my clothes." I brushed it off as morning crankiness, but after meeting his mother I should have been smart enough to know his attitude would continue all day. And it did.

I practically begged the kid to come to the kitchen for his breakfast, but he made it very clear that he had no interest in getting to know me or eating anything. Things had to happen exactly how he wanted them to and precisely when he wanted them to, which made our day together quite interesting. We started by taking a walk to the park with empty stomachs. The kid wouldn't shut up about trains the whole walk there. Yes, trains. His life's dream was to collect people's tickets. *Way to dream big, kid.*

"Push me on the swing," the kid demanded and I let out a frustrated sigh. *So this is how I'm gonna spend the rest of my summer, being jerked around by a three-year-old brat.* The park he took me to wasn't your typical park with a ton of kids and a huge jungle gym. It had two sets of swings, and across a small grassy field was a slide. Just one. Other than me and the kid, the place was deserted. I pushed Spencer on the 'big kid' swing as he sang some ridiculous song about trains. As I let my mind wander, it naturally settled on thoughts of

Jerimiah.

My scandalous daydreams got me through the first two hours at the park. I almost felt guilty pushing the kid on the swing as I imagined Jerimiah's tongue between my thighs. By the time we got back to the kid's house I had decided I should text him.

"Hey Jerimiah, what are you up to tonight?"

That sounds okay right?

"Lets play trains!" The kid dumped out an entire box of wooden train tracks, and tossed the instruction booklet in my lap. "Make one!" *Fuck my life.*

"Which one do you want to make?" I flipped through the booklet, skipping all the complicated looking tracks with tunnels and bridges. "How about this one?" I asked, showing him a picture of track number eleven. It was just a basic oval.

"No! That one's too easy!" *Exactly.*

"Well, that's the only one I know how to make. If you want to make a different one you'll have to make it yourself." I stared at him, daring him to challenge me. Part of me expected the brat to freak out and start throwing shit at me like a monkey until I did what he wanted.

"Fine!" he shouted and began bulldozing all the crap on the floor with his hands to create space for his train track. I was relieved I would get a break, and popped a squat on the floor. *Ten dollars an hour is not enough to have to deal with this kid.* My phone vibrated and I whipped it out immediately.

"I'M GOING BACK TO LA NOIRE TONIGHT. YOU SHOULD COME."

A smile quickly spread across my face. *Hell yes! Should I go alone or should I invite Jillian? It would be nice to have a wing woman… but she'll be such a cock block and nag me the whole night. It's Thursday night, right? Maybe Nyani will be there.* I decided to go alone.

"Sounds fun, but I don't have a ride. Can you pick me up?"

"What are you doing?" the kid asked. "Stop playing on your phone and pay attention to me!" *Wow, no woman is ever going to make this kid happy.*

"I'm waiting for you to finish building the track, so we can play with the trains." *I should never be allowed to have children.*

"But I need your help!" he shouted as loud as he could, throwing a piece of the track at the wall in frustration. I really wanted to lock the kid in the bathroom until he learned how to behave.

"You aren't going to get what you want in life acting like *that*. Go pick up the piece you just threw, and come sit down like a boy who behaves nicely and maybe I'll help you build the track."

"YOU GO PICK IT UP!" he said and threw another piece before he burst out in laughter. *Yeah, keep laughing you little shit and watch me lock your ass up.*

My phone vibrated again.

"YEAH, NO PROBLEM. I'LL CALL YOU LATER AND LET YOU KNOW WHAT WE'RE DOING."

"Go pick it up nanny!" *Fuck you kid, fuck you.*

I WAS ABLE TO take a nap despite the hours of torture endured by the kid that morning, and woke up with plenty of time to get ready to go out with Jerimiah. My wardrobe was plain, and consisted mostly of shorts and t-shirts. After much debate, I chose to wear the same skirt from Day Nine, with a white tank top. Accompanied with four-inch heels and three-inch round hoops, I eventually felt sexy enough to go out.

By the time he picked me up that night, I was already three beers in. Two of his friends were in the car with him, Lamare and Tyrone. They were the same two guys I had seen him dancing with the night we met. We weren't at the club ten minutes when I saw Nyani. She came over immediately, throwing her arms around me. "Hey sweetie! This is my friend Lacie," she pointed to a pretty redhead who smiled and quietly sipped on her drink. I introduced them to the guys, and before I knew it we were being whisked away to Nyani's reserved table to do shots.

My memory of the next few hours is fuzzy. Between the six of us we went through four bottles of liquor and countless beers. The dance floor spun around us as we all paired off, shouting and laughing over the music. Jerimiah barely left my side, always giving me his full attention, and I fucking loved it.

Around three o'clock, Nyani asked me if I wanted to bring the guys back to her place for an after party. So we all packed ourselves into Jerimiah's car, me up front with him and the girls in the back swapping spit with Tyrone and Lamare. I had my hand on Jerimiah's thigh, rubbing his leg and struggling to stay awake. The streetlights burned my eyes as I stared out the window into the darkness. Other than the radio, and occasional giggling from the back seat, the car was quiet. Jerimiah took my hand and made sure I could find his dick. I could feel how hard it was through his jeans and I couldn't wait to rip his clothes off. He glanced at me every few minutes, flashing a sexy smile before focusing back on the road.

Twenty minutes later, we were sitting in Nyani's living room passing around a bong. Her house was gorgeous, but still modern and youthful. It was the kind of house that might have given off the museum vibe if anyone other than Nyani had lived in it.

"How do you do this?" I whispered to Jerimiah as the bong being passed around rapidly approached me.

"I have no idea," he laughed. "I've never smoked before."

"Really?" I looked at him surprised.

"What, you think cuz I'm Puerto Rican I smoke weed?"

"I... uh... I didn't mean..."

He smiled and kissed me on the cheek. "I'm just messin' with you."

The bong was handed to Jerimiah, but he waved it off leaving me to figure it out by myself. I think I did it right. If not, everyone else was too fucked up to notice. After we passed it around a few times, we all leaned back on the couch and glared at the television cockeyed and giggling.

Nyani stood up, breaking my trance. "I'll be right back."

She left the room leaving Lacie sitting between Tyrone and Lamare on one couch, and Jerimiah and I on the other. Lacie was barely conscious. She had her head tilted back, and her arms limp by her sides. Her eyelids barely fluttered when Tyrone started kissing her neck, but he continued nonetheless. He nudged her cheek with his nose hard enough to get her to part her lips, and let him kiss her.

Out of nowhere, Lamare reached over and pulled the top of Lacie's dress down, revealing her pink bra.

He slipped his hand under the lace, pinching her nipples while moving his mouth over her shoulder.

"Dude! What the fuck are you doing?" Tyrone asked angrily pushing his friend's hand away.

They exchanged harsh whispers, before Lacie finally quieted them with a nod of approval.

"Whatever man," Tyrone said with aggravation. "I get her pussy, and don't fucking look at me." He pulled her up by her stomach, giving her ass some leverage and pushed her dress up on her back. Tyrone didn't hesitate to spread her legs and start undressing.

Lamare was holding Lacie by the hair, helping her with the motions. "Just open your mouth a little wider, yeah, there you go gorgeous."

Is this really happening? I can't watch this. "Help me find a bathroom?"

I followed Jerimiah up a set of stairs. "I'll go look for a room we can chill in," he said with a wink and disappeared down the hall. Shivers were sent down my spine in anticipation.

When I left the bathroom only minutes later, Jerimiah was nowhere in sight.

"Hey cutie!" It was Nyani. She was still wearing the same dress, which made me wonder where she had vanished to for so long. I had assumed she was changing into something more comfortable.

"Hey! Where have you been hiding?"

"Come, I'll show you!" She grabbed my hand and started pulling me towards one of the rooms.

"Well, Jerimiah's waiting for me…" I started.

"Let him wait! This will only take a second."

Before I knew it, we were sitting on her bed. There was a television, too large for the table it rested on, against the wall closest to the door. On the screen, a busty woman was being held down and pleasured by several people.

"Smoking always gets me so horny!"

I chuckled, confused. "So you came up here to watch porn? Instead of hooking up with Jerimiah's friend?"

"Well, I'm not really in the mood for cock tonight. I was hoping…for something different." She paused. "See how that girl is squirming?" she asked, motioning towards the screen. I looked and nodded innocently. "I want that girl to be you." *She's joking right?* "Don't worry," she assured me. "Just lay back, and I'll do all the work."

I let her push my shoulders down towards her mattress. My heart pounded as I lay there, bewildered by her words. Nyani hovered over me, desire in her eyes. She took her hand and brought it slowly down my neck and across my chest, slipping her fingers under the top of my tank top, and tugging it lightly until my bra was exposed. She slipped the straps off my shoulders, and rolled it off my chest.

"I'm going to kiss you now," she leaned in and whispered in my ear. "Just relax." I could feel her breath on my cheek, then her lips on my own. Our tongues touched lightly before she moved her mouth to my neck, and reached around my back to find the zipper to my skirt. My mind was barely conscious of what was happening, but her touch felt good against my skin and I couldn't help giving myself over to her. Just as she finished sliding my top off, Jerimiah walked in.

"Woah," he said startled at first. He stood in the doorway with a goofy grin on his face, waiting for us to send him away.

"Why don't you lock the door, and have a seat?" Nyani motioned towards the bed. "I just want to show Eva something, and then she's all yours."

Jerimiah did as she said, dumbstruck. *Show me something? What the hell is she showing me?* She started kissing my neck again. "Do you like when I kiss you there?"

"Yes," I muttered. My heart was hammering in my chest, but I didn't want her to stop.

She moved her lips over my bra, and every nerve in my body started to tingle.

"What about here?" she asked.

"Yes," I muttered again. Nyani reached around my back, and unhooked my bra. She threw it at Jerimiah, who was beaming ear to ear as he watched.

"Do you like when I kiss you here?" she asked running her tongue gently over my hard nipple.

"Mhmm," was all I could manage to get out. I looked over at Jerimiah and saw that he had his cock out, and was stroking it slowly.

Nyani glided her lips across my stomach, her eyes locked on mine as she brought her mouth towards the warmth between my legs. She kissed my inner thigh, while allowing her hand to brush over my panties.

Fifteen minutes later, after all the moaning died down, Nyani got up and grabbed her robe. "I'll let you two be alone now," she said and walked out of the room.

DAY TWELVE

JILLIAN SAT ACROSS from me rambling about her newest fling, which she had successfully morphed into a serious relationship in her head. I had to admire her ability to create an ideal life. Even if she was the only one who could see its perfection, who was anyone to say it wasn't real?

I didn't mind the fact that she had stopped by unannounced, only because she brought with her an enormous jug of wine, which was quickly disappearing as I helped myself to a third glass. My life may not have measured near perfection, in my mind or otherwise, but I thought another glass of wine might get me there. It wasn't too late into the night, but considering the time my day now began I reminded myself I only had six hours left of the night available for sleep.

The second day at my new job was even worse than the first, probably due to the fact that I was experiencing a massive hangover. Getting out of bed wasn't as bad as I thought it would be, since I never made it home in time to actually sleep. I barely had a chance to throw on jeans and try to look a bit less wasted before running out the door. Not that it mattered to that brat kid what I looked like, but just in case Diane decided to get her lazy ass out of bed I wanted to look... decent.

Jerimiah was nice enough to drop me off, so I didn't have to deal with stumbling the fifteen blocks to work. I was barely two minutes late, but when I walked in the door I could already hear the kid shouting my name from behind the dog gate at the top of the stairs. The only safety precaution I noticed during my employment with these people was that ridiculous gate. It was like they didn't notice their foyer looked like a construction site and their living room looked like a bomb went off in a toy store. No one ever apologized for the mess or mentioned that they were remodeling or doing repairs. Not that I felt like it was necessary, but normal people would show some kind of embarrassment if a stranger entered their house when it looked like that.

The first two hours went by quickly. I was still pretty drunk, and I had a lot of great memories of the previous night to keep my mind occupied. It wasn't long before the hangover started to kick in though, and every minute with the spoiled brat felt like an eternity. He whined and cried until he got his way, and it was obvious that his parents gave him whatever he wanted just to get him to shut up. I quickly adopted this strategy. *Whatever, he's not my kid!* If anyone was going to fuck this kid up for life it would be his circle drawing, can't get out of bed to hang out with her kid, 'mother'. And after Day Twelve I could add insane dietitian to her list of motherly qualities. Since Spencer had decided to skip eating on my first day with him, it wasn't until day two that I discovered his breakfast consisted of two hardboiled eggs and a strange blended liquid concoction. For snack he was allowed half an avocado, and these disgusting nutritional crackers. No wonder the kid didn't like to eat. It definitely explained where some of the strange smells came from.

Nanny number two didn't show up until after one o'clock. No apology for keeping me waiting for over an hour, just a pathetic smile in my direction as she blew past me to give the kid a bubbly greeting. The only recognition I got was the extra ten bucks she handed me out of her pay envelope Diane left for us daily on the heap of shit on the couch. I would have given her a twenty to have shown up on time that day. Counting down the minutes until you can leave and then… nothing. It's the worst possible feeling. Especially when you have a stomach full of beer and vodka sloshing around like it's a fucking wave pool. I tried to get the kid to go upstairs to wake up Diane when the nanny was a no-show after twenty minutes, but he seemed shocked that I would even suggest it. "No, we can never wake up Mommy," he said.

On the way home I stopped at the bank in attempt to feel accomplished, since I knew I would be sleeping the rest of the day away. I made a deposit, which brought my bank account to a total of $145. It had been at negative $5. *Who knows how the fuck that happened… a bad check maybe.*

I walked in the door, collapsed on the couch and passed out almost instantly. It wasn't until Jillian slammed the palm of her hand on my door around nine o'clock that I came out of my coma. She banged on my door like she accidentally left a ticking time bomb under my damn couch cushion. Any longer and she would have been smashing windows to get my attention.

"What the fuck, were you sleeping?" she asked when I opened the door looking groggy as hell. I really wanted to slam the door in her face and crawl back under my blanket on the couch. "Get wine glasses and meet me on the deck!"

I did as she said, but only because I was starving and the jug of wine she had in her hand looked inviting. That had been one hour, two glasses of wine, and a peanut butter and jelly sandwich ago. She didn't shut up about some guy she met only two days before the entire fucking time, leaving little room for conversation. The first half hour or so wasn't so bad because I was half asleep and had my sandwich to keep me occupied. As I began to actually listen to the things she was saying I decided she was being incredibly optimistic about a guy she just met. She had barely spent a few hours with him and she was already planning future dates, and holidays together. They had texted nonstop since they met, so that means they're meant to be right?

"What if he sucks in bed?" I abruptly interrupted.

"What?" she asked confused.

"Well, you're planning a future with a guy you barely know. What if you get him in bed and it's awful?"

"What are you talking about? That's impossible!"

"No, I'm pretty sure bad sex is possible," I said laughing. She appeared to be getting angry, but I couldn't help myself. I was overtired and trying to get her to shut up.

"When you're in love the sex is always good!" *In love?*

I thought back to the only reference I had of being 'in love' and immediately disagreed with her. Sleeping with Jerimiah proved to me that the only reason I ever thought [*The Douchebag*] knew how to fuck me was because I didn't have much to compare it to. All the love in the world wouldn't make me want to be stuck with his tiny cock, and inability to hold off his orgasm the rest of my life.

"What if his dick is so small, you don't even notice when it's inside of you?" *Oh, the things I do for entertainment.*

"Slim chance! I'm sure he has a normal sized…*penis.*"

I snorted with laughter at the sound of her stumbling over the word 'penis', nearly choking on the wine I had in my mouth. After struggling to get it all down and wiping off what had dripped onto my chin, I continued to coerce her. "Well I guess you're right. I guess all that wouldn't matter as long as you have a good vibrator. That's how I got through my relationship with [*The Douchebag*]!"

"You have a *vibrator*?" Her shock didn't surprise me, but I acted as if it did.

"Uh, yeah. I have three! Why, you don't?" Jillian shook her head timidly. I was just past tipsy and in the mood to show off some of the skills I had learned the previous night. "Come inside, I'll show you."

She followed me to my bedroom-without-a-bed, drink in hand. I opened the tiny drawer to my bed stand, revealing my collection of sex toys, condoms, lube and batteries. The first toy I took out was a small vibrator that could slide right on to my fingertip. "This one was perfect during sex. [*The Douchebag*] didn't find it intimidating since it's so small, and I was able to get off before he finished occasionally," I said showing it to her.

"It's so tiny!" Her eyes bugged out of her sockets a bit, and I could tell she was pretty drunk. *I wonder just how drunk she'd have to be to really relax…*

I flipped on the tiny switch on the toy and slid my vibrating finger down her neck and across her chest. "It may be small, but it gets the job done! [*The Douchebag*] may have thought he was doing most of the work, but it was all this little guy."

"What else do you have?" she asked cautiously. I could tell my touches made her a bit uncomfortable, but she had curiosity lingering behind her eyes. It was only a matter of time before she'd be willing to let go of some of that innocence and open her mind. *Isn't that what Nyani had done for me last night? It would only be fair to pay it forward.*

I took out my vibrating nipple clamps next. They had been a gag gift that I had never actually used, but I could never convince myself to get rid of them. "These go right on your nipples, like this." I pulled the straps of my tank top off my shoulders, and rolled the shirt down exposing my bare chest. The cold air greeted my nipples, making them stiff and perky. After turning the toy on, I clipped it to my right nipple letting the vibrations direct a tingling sensation throughout my body. "See?"

She just stared at me in disbelief, but I wanted to keep going. I wanted to push her boundaries. The pulsations on my chest were sending signals to every inch of my body. They were all saying I needed something big and hard between my legs. "You should try it," I said as I began unbuttoning her blouse. "It kind of tickles," I added with playful encouragement.

Her bra was boring and uptight, just like her. It was a sort of plain white thing, with no lace and no pushup, which she desperately needed. But the wetness between my thighs had taken over, and I didn't hesitate to yank out her tiny tits. She moaned in surprise as I clipped the other half of my toy to her nipple, forcing us to maintain a close distance. I could smell the wine on her breath, and it pleased me that she was enjoying herself rather than asking me to stop.

"The next one I have is a little bigger," I warned and reached into the draw to pull out 'The Rabbit' and its nine inches of glory. "This one's my favorite."

"How do you, uh, use it?" Jillian asked slightly blushing. *I thought you'd never ask.*

Without saying a word, I took the clamp off my chest and clipped it on to her other nipple. I stood up, lifting my tank top over my head in the process. Then, I slid my shorts and panties off and fell to my knees, completely naked in front of her.

"First, you have to make sure I'm wet enough. Why don't you check that for me." My hand pulled hers slowly down my stomach, encouraging her to also drop to her knees. "Now, put your fingers inside of me and make sure my juices are pouring out of me." She reached between my legs needing little persuasion, and nodded her head to let me know I was good to go. *Yeah, no shit I'm soaked. I can't believe I'm getting you to do this right now!*

I took the rabbit and slid all nine inches inside of me, groaning as the ears vibrated against my clit. Jillian watched in amazement, and I began to wonder if this poor girl had ever had an orgasm before. "I need you to play with these, since you're using my nipple toy." I put her hand on my tits, and she squeezed my nipples like a pro. While sliding the world's greatest invention in and out with my left hand, I took the opportunity to use the first toy I showed her which was still on the pointer finger of my right hand.

Jillian's business attire was perfect for me to slide my hand right up her skirt. First letting it vibrate on her thigh, I couldn't wait long before reaching for her warmth. She immediately pulled my hand away, but didn't stop her nipple play with the other. I wanted her to want it. My lips fell to her neck, gently kissing every crevice while slyly bringing my hand back up her leg. I kissed her lips, and this time she didn't object when I brought the vibrator to her panties. Her wetness had soaked them, making it easy to push them aside exposing her pussy. I glided the vibrator against her clit and stuck my other finger inside of her, soaking it in her juices.

She moaned into my mouth as our lips never parted, and I bit her top lip to quiet her. I fucked myself harder with my toy, until I could feel my fluids dripping on my hand. "Wait! Eva, stop!" Jillian suddenly started to lean away from me, so I let go of my toy and pulled her closer. Her moans grew heavier, and her pussy tightened around my fingers. *I know you're close, let me finish you!* She stopped pushing me away and gave in to the pleasure. Her moans grew high pitched, and she stopped kissing me letting her mouth fall to my neck. I grabbed my toy again, thrusting harder and harder inside of myself until I joined her long agonizing cries of pleasure.

Jillian left pretty quickly after that. I had a feeling she wouldn't be stopping by unannounced again anytime soon.

DAY THIRTEEN

I SLEPT THROUGH EVERYTHING. Through my alarm… through babysitting… through the bratty kid's demands. The first five seconds after I opened my eyes and realized the sun was already up, I panicked. I sat up abruptly, tossing the blanket off me and quickly searching the coffee table for my phone. It was too late. Too late to make it to the Weisman's, and too late to make rent this month. I had done the calculations in my head the night before as I lay in the darkness waiting for sleep to take over my body. There was no way I was going to make enough money to cover the rent with this nanny gig. It was already the twenty-first. *How am I going to make $1,700 in ten days? Even if I can figure out a way to make that much money I'll still be a month behind in rent.* I had no idea what I was going to do, but I wasn't going to stress about it just yet. I rolled over and closed my eyes. *Maybe a great idea will come to me in my sleep.*

I woke up around two o'clock, refreshed and with an idea. *Call Nyani.* When I reached for my phone, I saw that I had two new voicemails and a text message. The text was from Jerimiah:

"HEY CUTIE WHAT ARE YOU UP TO TONIGHT?"

I ignored it for the moment, and listened to my voicemail.

The first one was from my landlord. "Good morning, Miss Palmer. This is [*Asshole Landlord*]. I'm just reminding you that if you do not pay your rent by five o'clock on the 31st, next Sunday, you will be asked to leave the apartment. Anything left in the apartment will be thrown in the garbage, and locks will be changed. *Click*." *That still gives me ten days to figure shit out, asshole. A phone call was not necessary.*

The next voicemail was from my 'employer'. "Hello, Eva? This is Diane Weisman, uhh, Spencer's mom. It looks like I forgot to unlock the back door for you this morning. It's unlocked now though. Do you think you can come back and work until the other nanny gets here? I'll pay you for the full seven hours. Okay… bye." *Fucking psycho! I would have been so pissed if I actually got up this morning and walked all the way there to find the door locked. Ha! Keep your money bitch!* I sat there for a moment imagining what Diane's morning must have been like. It pumped my insides with absolute joy as I pictured the expression on her face when she realized she would actually have to get out of bed and take care of her son.

I scrolled through the numbers in my phone,

looking for Nyani's. She had stored her number when we were in *La Noire* the other night. I found it saved as 'Nyani's The Shit' and hit dial.

"Hello?" she answered.

"Hey Nyani, it's Eva!" I said trying too hard not to sound like I just woke up.

"Oh, hey Eva! What's up? I was hoping you would call." She sounded like she was chewing on food.

"Oh, nothing. I just wanted to see what you were up to today. I'm kind of stressed out and need someone to vent to." It wasn't a complete lie.

"Oh, no! I hope everything's okay Eva! I'm actually in Paris right now, but I'll be home in a few days if you want to meet up for lunch?"

"You're in Paris?" I couldn't hide the shock in my voice, which caused her to giggle on the other side of the line.

"Yeah, one of my clients took me here yesterday. We're only staying for a few nights though, so it would be no problem meeting up with you this week." *Clients?*

"Okay, sounds good. Just give me a call whenever you're back in town."

"See you soon, Eva!"

"Bye," but she had already hung up.

Curiosity overwhelmed me. I wanted to know what she did for a living, and who her clients were. More so, I wanted in. I wanted to be glamorous like her and live a comfortable lifestyle. There was something intriguing about her life, and I couldn't shake the feeling that she would know how to make all of my money problems disappear. *And if she can't? What's Plan B Eva?* There was no plan B. I had no other options.

"HEY, CUTIE? DID you get robbed or something?" Jerimiah was walking towards me in nothing but his boxers. I had invited him over for a movie and sex. Now that one was done, we were about to start the other. I asked him to bring the movie since the only one I owned was shattered into pieces, and figured I'd just pop it in my laptop. It never crossed my mind that he'd actually want to watch it.

"No, unless you robbed me," I said teasing him.

He laughed, "You know, if you don't stop with the Puerto Rican jokes I might have to tickle you to death." Jerimiah sat next to me on the couch and playfully began to poke my stomach. I giggled before I pushed his hands away. "No, really, were you robbed? The bathroom seems so empty, and I looked in your room and there's no bed." *I didn't realize letting you find the bathroom on your own was giving you permission to snoop.*

"No, I wasn't robbed," I faked an awkward smile. *To lie or tell the truth?* "I, uhh… well, it's a long story," I mumbled.

"Well, I'm definitely not watching *Scarface* on your tiny-ass laptop so I have all night to listen." *Damn, I've always wanted to see* Scarface. *The truth it is then.*

"I used to live here with my boyfriend. When he decided he was done with me, he took a bunch of shit with him," I looked at him to try and catch his reaction. "That's the short version."

"Why don't you tell me the longer version?" His eyes were so genuinely interested that I couldn't help but do what he asked. So I told him everything about [*The Douchebag*], starting from the beginning of our relationship. I told him how amazing I thought he was, and until the day he left I thought we'd spend the rest of our lives together. Of course I included how happy I was that it didn't turn out that way, and his particular involvement in my realization of what I had been missing out on. I admitted that I had been sleeping on the couch, and I didn't own a television or have the money to buy one. It turns out, I really did need to vent and I even told Jerimiah about my rent that was due and the little shit I babysat for. He laughed when I was funny, and kissed my forehead when he thought I needed it. In actuality, the story didn't take as long to tell as I thought it would and Jerimiah was the perfect listener. When I was done, he didn't bash [*The Douchebag*] or tell me I deserved so much better. He didn't offer to loan me money or a place to stay. Nothing he said next was predictable.

"You are definitely one of a kind Eva. I'm so glad I met you, and that you feel comfortable enough to open up to me." I assumed by the way he kissed me afterwards that my being 'one of a kind' was a good thing, so I took it as a compliment.

"So, I've always wanted to see *Scarface*, and the screen on my laptop isn't *that* small…" I gave him my best puppy dog eyes, hoping he'd change his mind.

"Fine," he said pretending to sigh. "But next time you want to watch a movie with me, we'll have to go to my place. I like to watch Al Pacino do his thing on the big screen!" We both laughed at his serious demeanor as he got up to get the DVD from the coffee table, which we had moved towards the door during foreplay. "By the way, how do you know those two girls we hung out with at the club the other night?"

"Who? Nyani and Lacie?" I asked.

"Yeah, I guess."

"I don't really know them, I met Nyani at *La Noire* the same night I met you. And that was the first time I met Lacie. Why?" I asked curiously.

"Just wondering," he said as he popped the DVD into my laptop.

"No, tell me." I could tell he was hiding

something.

"Well, that girl Lacie," he paused as he fiddled around with my laptop, trying to get the movie to play. "You know she's a hooker right?"

"What?" I asked laughing. "What do you mean a hooker?" He turned to look at me, and I was giving him my 'I know you're lying' look.

"You know, a hooker. A prostitute. A hoe." We were both examining one another, searching for a clue that the other was lying. "When my boy was tryin' to talk to her in the club, she told him he'd have to pay if he wanted to get with her."

"No, way!" I just couldn't believe him, and I laughed to show that I thought he was joking. "You're making that up."

"No, I'm serious. She made him pay a hundred and fifty bucks before we got to the house. Then when my other boy wanted to join, she raised the price another fifty and didn't tell 'em until after." I was shocked, but it made sense. Lacie was alert enough to at least attempt to push them off of her on the couch, but she didn't. Instead, she let them both go at her at the same time. Only a paid professional would allow that.

"Is Nyani a hooker too?" *Please say no…*

"I don't know, she didn't say anything to my boy about paying to hook up." The movie started and he got up to turn off the lights. "I wouldn't be surprised though, those kinda girls travel in packs. At least *we* got her for free!" he said eyeing me playfully. The lights were off, and he gave me a quick kiss before joining me on the couch.

Shit. I need Nyani to be my way out, but not like this! There has to be some kind of explanation for all of it. Maybe she didn't know Lacie was a hooker; Maybe she's not a hooker and thought it would be fun to see how much they would pay to fuck her. Her 'clients'…. would a hooker call the people she fucks her clients? I don't think so. And would a man ever take a hooker on a three-day trip to Paris? No, fucking way. That doesn't make sense.

Jerimiah interrupted my worried thoughts by whispering in my ear, "I don't suppose you have any snacks, right?" I nudged him with my elbow, and giggled at his joke. We spent the rest of the night in each other's arms watching Al Pacino make enough money selling coke for me to seriously consider the profession. *Whatever Nyani can offer me, I'll have to suck it up and accept it. Legal or not… hooking or not… it's already looking better than any of my other options.*

DAY FOURTEEN

I WOKE UP IN Jerimiah's arms far too early that morning considering my new work schedule was now non-existent. However, since *his* existed, he ran out in a hurry leaving behind his *Scarface* DVD. It was nice waking up next to him, even if it *was* seven in the morning. *I could definitely get used to this.*

Taking advantage of my early rise, I checked every form of communication that could possibly have a job opportunity stored in it. Cell phone first, then the landline, and finally my e-mail. To my surprise I had received a response from one of the stores I applied to on Day Eight. It was a small jewelry booth that I had never bothered to glance at twice prior to my days of desperation, when I was able to go to the mall and actually shop. The e-mail asked if I could come to the store to meet with him *(the manager? Owner?)* at around one o'clock. It was very short and to the point. No details were given as to why I was going there, but of course I agreed and assumed it was for an interview.

The walk wasn't exactly brief, but I didn't have to

wake up before the sun rose or deal with the shitty kid. It was a potential job, and I would have walked my desperate ass triple the distance if I had to. I arrived ten minutes early for my interview, slightly sticky from the summer air. I had frequented the mall with [*The Douchebag*] during our good days, so I had a general idea of where the booth was.

A short, stocky man greeted me with an accent from who knows where. He appeared to be in his mid-thirties, and described himself as the owner of the 'kiosk'. Everything about him was foreign except his ridiculously common American name, something like Dan or John. Obviously fake. He spent five minutes showing me how to use the register, and how to throw a giant tarp over the booth when the mall closed. The job was only part time, but it paid cash plus commission. I assumed it was off the books, and quickly figured out that I could easily make more money than I did at my babysitting gig.

"You've been wit' jewelry, yes?" he asked in an indistinct accent.

"Yes," I said with a reassuring smile. *I mean, I've worn jewelry before.*

For whatever reason, he believed my white lie and asked me to start immediately. *Hell yes.* He left me there alone saying I could come back the same time the next day, and gave me his cell phone number in case I had any questions. And that was it. No interview. It seemed he didn't have any other options, and I officially had a job.

So I sat at the 'kiosk' and waited. After I got bored with doing that, I decided to use my free time to get familiar with the jewelry. There was maybe a hundred pieces, including the backup I found in a small draw. It was all extremely overpriced for what it was – junk. The cheapest item I found was a pair of earrings for eighty dollars. *At least my commission check will be high!*

Hours went by without a single person stopping at the booth, and I quickly gave up on the idea that I would make a decent amount of money at this job. I calculated that without any sales I would make a little under ninety dollars. *Not bad for sitting here and doing nothing. Still not enough to make rent though.*

"Excuse me," an elderly woman said approaching the kiosk. *Yes! Finally, a customer!* "Where is the ladies room?" she asked and I groaned.

"I think it's up here on the right," I said pointing her in the direction I remembered the bathroom being in. She walked away without saying thank you, so I gave the stink eye to the back of the bitch's head.

It was another hour before I had my first real customer. She scared the hell out of me, snapping me out of my daze with her snooty 'hello'.

Ignoring the attitude behind her greeting I responded with, "Hello, how are you?" It was with fake sincerity, but I doubt she could tell.

"Can I get some help?" Her attitude was

undeniable as she stared me down with her best 'I'm better than you' glare. She was middle-aged, and obviously a housewife. One of those wealthy stay at home moms who spend their days doing nothing important, like shopping or getting their nails done until the children are home from school or daycare. *Nice.*

"Of course, did you see something you like?" This time I let my sarcasm shine through.

"How much is this?" she asked pointing to a necklace on the shelf. I picked it up and saw that the tag read $99.99, but I quickly ripped it off and crumpled it in the palm of my hand as I continued to pretend searching for the price.

"Hmm, that's strange. There doesn't seem to be a price tag. I'm pretty sure all of the necklaces are $300 though."

She looked at me in disbelief. "That's far too much money." *No shit dumbass.*

"Why don't you try it on, and I'll call my boss to see if I can do something about the price." I handed her the necklace, and left her to admire it around her scrawny neck. The only benefit to her wearing something so chunky and hideous was that it hid her disgustingly loose neck skin. It reminded me of what an eighty-year-old woman's vagina might look like.

The crumpled price tag found its way into the garbage as I grabbed my cell to call 'my boss'. I actually called my apartment, and hummed the theme song to The Brady Bunch. When it was done, I hung up and told her the good news.

"My boss didn't pick up, but I'll give it to you for $200 as long as you promise it'll be our little secret," I said to her with a sly smile. That comment was exactly what was needed to finalize the sale. Nothing would be worse in her over-privileged suburban universe than if she came back the following day, and had to pay a hundred dollars more for the same necklace.

"Are you sure? I wouldn't want to get you in trouble," she said not even glancing in my direction. I knew I had it in the bag, and assured her it wouldn't be a problem.

"He'll never know," I said with confidence. Two minutes later, she walked away with a worthless piece of junk around her vagina neck and I had a hundred dollars in the register and another hundred in my pocket. *Now it's time for dinner.*

The boss with the common American name never said anything about leaving the booth to go get food or use the bathroom. I didn't think he expected me to sit there for eight and half hours without having to take a piss. So I asked the elderly woman at the perfume kiosk to keep an eye on the jewelry and took a much-needed break.

I was standing in line at the pizzeria when it happened. If only I had waited a few more minutes, or had decided to get McDonalds instead. He was sitting off to my left in a booth with the girl I recognized from his Facebook pictures as his new girlfriend. My heart dropped into my stomach as I watched them kissing and laughing, cozied up on the same side of the table. It made me sick.

[*The Douchebag*] looked away from his new love long enough to catch my gaze. My face must have been a mixture of disgust and devastation. I didn't look away though, that would only indicate defeat. Instead I continued to glare at him, watching him squirm in discomfort. Our stare down caught the attention of his new girlfriend, who looked my way and finally noticed my presence. I wondered if she knew who I was. I knew she had to know *of* me, considering she helped him plot the epic downfall of my life, but did she know what I looked like? Did she know it was her love's first love that was staring her down in that pizzeria? Who knows. If she didn't know at that moment, she found out soon enough. I broke the connection with my favorite 'fuck you' smile, and a roll of the eyes.

There were no words exchanged, and I made sure to walk past them again with zero acknowledgement when I left with my pizza. I hoped I appeared to be calm and together. The last thing I wanted was for him to know he broke me when he left. On the inside, I was crushed. It took everything I had not to let a single tear fall from my eyes. When I got back to the kiosk, I buried my woes in my slice of pizza wishing I had gotten a second slice and maybe some pasta. I spent the remaining two hours of my shift pretending to look busy, and hoping [*The*

Douchebag] and his hoe didn't walk by. They didn't.

My walk home was spent drowning my sorrows with a six-pack of the cheapest shit they had at the twenty-four hour convenience store I stopped at. I didn't cry though… I got drunk, but there were no tears.

DAY FIFTEEN

IT WAS DAY TWO at the mall, and I was almost excited to get out of the apartment. I woke up slightly groggy, but thankfully without a hangover. On the second day of my career as a jewelry sales associate I decided I would be more prepared. Instead of spending $4.50 on a slice of pizza and a soda, I stuck a peanut butter and jelly sandwich and a bottle of water in my bag. I then spent the $4.50 on a large coffee and a trashy magazine that I picked up on my way to the mall. *Today I will be prepared for the long hours of boredom.*

Perhaps I shouldn't have been surprised to see that upon arrival, everything was gone from the kiosk. Not a single piece of jewelry was out, the lights were off, and all that remained of the register was a thin wire. I just stood there with my mouth open wide, coffee in one hand and oversized purse in the other.

"Excuse me? Eva?" the woman from the perfume kiosk approached me. I nodded. She handed me a white envelope telling me that the man with the common American name left it for me. She explained to me that he decided to close his business since recent sales were so bad. I was disappointed, but it seemed to fit in with the direction my life was headed. Even if I had worked every day until my rent was due, it still wouldn't have been enough money. It was time to move on, start packing, and figure out a place to stay for a while. I needed to accept the reality of my situation.

DAY SEVENTEEN

I WOKE UP TO Nyani's call around noon, offering a groggy response to her offer to pick me up for lunch. After rolling around for twenty more minutes, I forced myself off the couch and into the 'bedroom' to put myself together.

"Hey girl!" Nyani said as I slid into the passenger seat of her car. I don't know cars very well, but this one had leather seats and an expensive new car smell. The exterior was a shiny charcoal grey. No scratches, no bird shit, no mud. I assumed it was a recent gift from one of her 'clients', and I quickly decided I wanted one just like it.

"Hey!" I said back, imitating her enthusiasm and kissing her cheek. I had decided on a royal blue sundress for our lunch, simple and elegant. At least that's what I thought until I saw what Nyani was wearing. She had on a head-to-toe designer ensemble that made me want to scurry back inside to change. Not that I owned anything nearly as sophisticated, but my royal blue sundress was looking more and more like a royal blue garbage bag.

We stopped at a restaurant on the water that I had never heard of and began with drinks outside. I was shockingly insecure sitting there with her, gulping down my mimosa with hopes of gaining some liquid courage. *How can I ask this girl to help me? I've barely known her a week.* The sun was blaring, and I squinted to see Nyani's face as she caught me up on her life. She mostly chatted about her trip to Paris, leaving no shopping trip or nightclub out of her story.

"Oh, you just reminded me!" She reached into her purse and pulled out a small box. "I bought these for you!" The top of the box read Dior, and I knew immediately that they were sunglasses. I opened it, and let my jaw drop. "Do you like them?"

"Oh, Nyani. You didn't have to... I love them!" And I truly did love them. I had never owned anything designer before, and just holding those sunglasses in my hand brought back my confidence. "But I can't accept these, they must have been so expensive!" I tried handing them back to her, but she casually brushed my hand away.

"Nonsense! I bought them for you! Plus I'd have to go all the way back to Paris to return them. Put them on," she demanded. I did as she asked and immediately felt like a new person. My dress wasn't a garbage bag anymore, and I no longer felt like a pencil in a crayon box sitting next to Nyani.

"Thank you." I wondered how much they cost. *Maybe if this lunch doesn't go well I can sell them for cash. I better not scratch them.*

"So, how's that brat you nanny for doing? What was his name again?"

"Spencer?" I asked, not recalling telling Nyani about him.

"Yeah, that's it. How's the little shit doing?"

"Well," I paused in order to choose my words carefully, "I actually decided it wasn't worth my time to stay at that job." *Yeah, that sounds so much better than 'I couldn't get my ass outta bed'… or off the couch…*

"That's a shame," she blurted sarcastically. "You weren't going to be able to make your rent with that job anyway, right?"

"Uhh, no. Not even close. Did I tell you that?" I asked, cautiously taking a sip of my mimosa.

Nyani laughed. "You don't remember? We talked about it for like an hour the other night." I looked at her and shrugged. "Wow, you were so fucked up!" We both laughed. "I offered you a job at the hotel I work in. In the city."

I still had no idea what she was talking about but I shrugged it off, relieved that there was a job offer on the table. "I vaguely remember that. What kind of job is it again?" My head was spinning with images of girls lined up in cum-stained lingerie, wiping the coke off their noses as men paid for them at a cash register before dragging them up to a hotel room. Perhaps that image was a bit exaggerated, but expecting the worst could only make whatever job Nyani offered me sound like a dream.

"It's a high-end escort service." *Damn, Jerimiah was right.* I doubt I hid my disappointment well. "Wealthy businessmen from all over the world pay beautiful women to be their long-term or short-term escort. With our long-term arrangements the men pay for their escort by providing them with an apartment, a car, and the occasional trip to Paris or Cancun. In return, the women are there for them if they need a date to a business event, or just want company on their nights off. Basically, they're paying for the girlfriend experience. I think you would be great at that."

She went on for the next half hour telling me amazing stories about trips all over the world, and about all the fantastic cars and clothes she had owned complimentary of the men from this club she ran. Of course I sat there and ate it all up. Her life sounded ideal, and it sounded so easy for me to have it all too. She was literally handing me everything I could ever want, and I didn't see anything strange about that. Three cocktails and an offer to live in the hotel free of charge later, she asked me if I was interested in the 'job'.

"What's the catch?" I asked, practically slurring my words at that point.

"Well, there are some rules. Nothing too crazy. As a member of the club you should keep the details of your real life separate. It helps keep up the appearance of being their idea of a perfect woman. Then of course, no kissing on the lips, no hard drugs, and no fucking anyone outside of the club for money. Unless you have a serious drug problem I don't know about, I think you'll be fine," she laughed. Her tone was casual and reassuring. "I was unsure about it at first myself, but I'm so happy I went in this direction. We'll start you off slow, and give you some time to feel it out. If it's something you enjoy, you'll sign our contract and become a member. If not, you got a free place to crash for a while. There's really no downside."

So I said yes. I said yes to a job as a high-end escort because I didn't feel like I had any other options. In my head, Nyani was saving me from living on the streets and I was lucky to be offered such an amazing opportunity. Lucky… lucky to be offered a job as a whore.

DAY TWENTY
PART ONE

MY NEW ROOMMATE'S name was Tanya. She introduced herself with a bubbly smile and a mouth full of braces. It could have been her mousy voice, or the fact that she barely hit five feet tall, but I wouldn't have guessed she was any older than seventeen. And even that was being generous.

I didn't look at the tiny space I was moving into as the prison cell it was. Instead, I saw it as a temporary arrangement. I thought it would only be a matter of time before one of my own 'clients' got me a bigger place. In the meantime, I needed a place to crash, and if it meant living in a stuffy hotel room with an underage Filipino prostitute for a little while, then I was going to suck it up and do it. It was a small price to pay for everything I expected to get in return.

"So, the last girl who lived here snored. Do you snore?" Tanya asked me, as serious as a cop asking a reckless driver if they've had anything to drink that night.

"Umm, I don't think so," I replied uncertainly. Her tone only solidified my assumption about her age.

"I guess we'll see tonight. The last girl kept me up half the night, and I *need* my sleep."

I smiled awkwardly, and began to unpack my suitcase. *An entire lifetime behind me, and everything I own fits in a single suitcase… how pathetic.* None of that mattered though. I had made it to New York City, and it was time to start living the dream. My mind exploded with all of the possibilities. To me this job meant stability and independence. It meant finally answering my phone without the fear of a bill collector being on the other end, and having enough money to buy a new pair of jeans or to see a movie. I opened the dresser on my side of the room and noticed it was already stuffed with clothes.

"Sorry. I didn't realize this was your dresser," I mumbled and swiftly closed it.

"It's not!" she exclaimed excitedly. "Nyani dropped off a few things for you!" *This chick is way too perky for me.*

"Oh, nice." I opened the draw again and pulled out several items. It was an array of lingerie. Pink, black, red, white… garter belts, teddies, thigh highs, corsets… all with tags still intact. My stomach dropped at the thought of wearing them.

"Oh, those are so cute! Did Nyani tell you we call

ourselves 'The Lingerie Girls'? Sounds classy, right? Those are yours too," Tanya pointed to a clothing rack against the wall by my bed. Cocktail dresses, skirts, and accessories hung from the bar, again all with tags on them. Shoes lined the wall, all in my size. *Jackpot!*

As I sifted through the clothes on the rack I was consumed with excitement. Each dress was skankier than the last, and I loved it. Everything Nyani bought me was designer. Michael Kors dresses, Marc Jacobs purse, lingerie from Victoria's Secret, and a pair of Manolo Blahniks. What she'd spent on me was probably worth three months rent, including all utilities. I immediately ripped one of the dresses off the hanger and threw off my clothes. As I tried on dress after dress and ogled at myself in the mirror, a massive smile became permanently fixed to my face. [The Douchebag] *never would have let me wear anything like this!*

A rush of confidence ran through my veins as I flew through the dresses on the rack, tossing them recklessly on the bed when I was done with them. *I want to dress sexy... I want men to look at me with desire... I want to be noticed... I want to be loved by men and hated by women.*

"You act like you've never worn a dress before," Tanya said as she watched me admire myself.

"Yeah," I laughed, "my ex was a bit controlling." When I looked over at her, I noticed she was putting on makeup. "Can you show me how to do that?"

Two hours later, I left the hotel room looking sexy as hell and headed to the hotel bar, *Slayers*. Tanya was nice enough to give me the hooker makeover; smoky eyes, red lips, and 'come fuck me' hair. She even helped me pick out the right lingerie to wear under the dress I chose.

I was on an adrenaline high. Everything was new and exciting. New city, new friends, new wardrobe, new confidence, new occupation. There was no one to hold me back this time. It was a new me, and a fresh start.

DAY TWENTY
PART TWO

"I DON'T KNOW about this, Nyani. I'm having second thoughts." *Slayers* was packed with men in suits and ties, leading conversations with their money instead of their charm. Some were obviously from out of town displaying a little western flavor, but none were conservative about how loaded they were, flashing their perfect white smiles and diamond-accented watches. There were only a few women in the room, making the ratio maybe one woman for every seven or eight men. The competition was stiff… for the men at least.

As Nyani and I walked towards the back of the bar, a dozen eyes followed us. I could tell they were curious about me, the 'new girl'. Some looked at me like a rare cuisine they couldn't wait to taste. Others saw me as a threat to the secrecy of their club. No one dared to approach us though.

"You'll be fine sweetie," Nyani assured me when we finally reached the back wall. A large red door towered before us. "I have the perfect guy for you!

He's new to the club, and probably just as nervous as you are. You'll like him, I promise!"

"And if I don't?" I asked cautiously.

Nyani took my face in her hands and directed it to the front of the bar. Women were starting to leave hand in hand with men, leaving a trail of disappointment behind them. She leaned over and whispered in my ear, "Look at all the men you have to choose from."

Glancing around the room, I tried to look beyond the arrogant gestures and guarded personas, and truly see all of the lonely faces and broken hearts. I imagined them as men too dedicated to their work to find love, or stuck with wives who appreciated their credit cards more than they appreciated them. In a way, I felt sorry for them.

Before I knew it, I was being whisked away behind the massive red door to a small hidden lounge separate from the rest of the bar. It was dimly lit and completely empty other than a man sitting alone in the back left corner. My heart thudded in his presence.

On the table in front of the stranger was an array of liquor bottles, mixers and chasers. Nyani held my hand as she led me towards the mysterious man, probably to ensure I wouldn't run away. My stomach was in knots, and my nerves had taken over, almost making me forget how to breathe.

About half-way across the lounge I could start to make out his face. He was much younger than I had imagined he'd be, and quite attractive. When he looked at me, I didn't feel like a piece of meat like I had walking into the bar. Instead, he looked at me with what seemed to be admiration and respect. We locked eyes and his smile beamed in my direction, like a schoolboy getting exactly what he wanted on Christmas morning. I blushed and looked away quickly, but I couldn't help imitating his childlike grin. He stood up to greet us, keeping his eyes on me. I was already hooked.

"Hello, Mr. Edison. This is your date Miss Hannah."

Hannah? I looked a Nyani curiously before politely shaking Mr. Edison's hand.

"That's not my real name either," he said to me playfully. I smiled, and quickly understood that fake names were part of the game. He offered me a seat, and Nyani managed to disappear without either of us noticing.

"I wasn't sure what you like to drink, so I got a little bit of everything," he said, motioning towards the table. "Would you like me to make you something?"

"Yes, please. Umm, cranberry vodka is fine. Thank you."

My anxiety was in control of my body, and it was

encouraging me to drink the cranberry vodka rather quickly. My date smiled curiously.

"Nervous?" he asked.

"A little," I practically whispered.

"Me too," he admitted. "Nyani told me you're new at this, is that correct?" I nodded. "Well, I've never done anything like this either if it makes you more comfortable."

It did. "Why are you doing this now then? I mean, this isn't exactly something you see advertised on a billboard," I noted sarcastically. The drink began to kick in, allowing my true personality to show through a bit.

He chuckled. "Well, I travel a lot for my job and I've been working on a project here in New York for the past month or so. Some men I bumped into in the lobby clued me in on these, umm, 'events', and I decided to check it out last week. I guess I was acting a bit shy though, because Nyani picked me out of the crowd within the first ten minutes I was here and told me all about you. And now here we are." He ended with an awkward smile that just melted my heart.

"What did Nyani tell you about me?" I couldn't help myself. *Last week? I didn't even know about this club a week ago. What made Nyani so sure I'd agree to this?*

"Only nice things, of course, like how sweet and pretty you are, and a bit shy which I find endearing.

What really got me interested was that you are a first timer, just like me. It made me feel more comfortable knowing I wouldn't be the only insanely nervous person sitting here, creating awkward conversation. She asked me to come back tonight to meet you, and I assure you I have yet to be disappointed. I'm sure you already know that though. My eyes never lie," he winked.

I smiled politely, but on the inside my brain was still chewing on the fact that Nyani had started advertising my services before I had actually agreed to anything. Sitting there with Mr. Edison was starting to feel less like my choice, and more like Nyani's intention. *What would have happened if I hadn't accepted her offer?* It was a brief moment of panic. Perhaps my instincts had set off an alarm, but I could think of nothing to confirm the idea that she had manipulated me to get me there. *I chose this path. This was just as much my idea as it was hers. She probably had no one specific in mind when she spoke to him, and could have easily passed off one of those other girls as a new employee named 'Hannah'.* So I brushed it off, and returned to the conversation.

"So, Mr. Edison, what do you do that allows you to live such a comfortable lifestyle?"

"Hmm… I'm not sure if I should tell you…"

"Oh, yeah? Why's that?" I asked playfully. It was becoming easier to flirt with him after the initial awkwardness had passed. His enticing grey eyes didn't hurt either.

"I think it may be against the rules," he said with a smirk.

"Oh, so you have rules too?"

"Yup," he put up his hand and began listing them on his fingers. "No kissing on the lips, no details, pay for everything, and no cash exchanges with you. Only Nyani."

"Pay for *everything*?" I couldn't hide my shock.

"Well, not everything," he laughed. "Basically I would pay for your lifestyle instead of leaving cash on the bed stand for your, umm, services." My cheeks turned pink, and I smiled shyly at the mention of my 'services'. "You really are new at this, huh? You're adorable when you blush." I giggled, but chose not to respond to his comment.

"So, what are you looking for? A girlfriend type?" I asked.

"Yes," he said without hesitation. "I find myself bored too often when I'm in New York on business. There's no one out here that I know on a personal level, and I find going out with my colleagues extremely tiresome at times. It would be nice to find a companion to share some memories with. I'm very insecure around women, and this club forces women to like me," he added with a smirk. "It just simplifies everything."

"Well, according to the rules given to *me*, I don't

have to like you. I can just choose someone else." I waved my hand around the room to emphasize my cocky statement.

"Oh, yeah?" He nudged me with his shoulder playfully as I giggled. "So, do you like me enough yet to accompany me to my suite upstairs? Or would you rather go choose someone else?" He mimicked my hand motion to add humor to his heavy question.

I'm pretty sure I let out a small gasp, and allowed my eyes get wide. My heart raced faster with each moment he waited in anticipation, sending my mind in every direction. *Is he testing me? To see if I'm a good fuck before he makes me his 'girlfriend'? Testing the milk before he buys the cow? Being his girlfriend would be amazing though. The bill collectors would finally stop calling me, and I could probably earn enough money to go back to school. But am I ready to be this person? To be Hannah? Hannah the call girl… Hannah the hooker… the prostitute… the whore. Am I ready to be all of these things? Even if it's just part time, is this a world I want to be part of? Or am I just taking the easy way out…*

"Hannah? Are you okay?"

I was snapped out of my trance and found all the answers I needed there on Mr. Edison's concerned face.

"Yes, I'm sorry." I blushed and looked down into my lap. "I'm just nervous."

Mr. Edison took my chin into his hand and lifted

my head towards his own. He looked me square in the eye before saying, "I'm not going to pressure you or force you to do anything. I promise. If at any time you feel uncomfortable, just walk out. I won't stop you. I'll be very sad because I'm really starting to like you, but I won't stop you. We can order room service and just hang out." He dropped his hand. "There's just too much pressure here in this lounge. I feel like I can't be myself."

My body instantly relaxed, and I was finally able to exhale. His words sounded sincere, and it made me think I could do this. I could be an escort.

I agreed to go to his room, so he had our drinks sent up along with an array of finger foods from the room service menu. Seeing him take charge like that made my knees weak, and my stomach flutter. We held hands and giggled, taking our time going up to his suite. By the time we got upstairs, all of my butterflies seemed to have flown away.

THE PHRASE *HOLY SHIT* came to mind when I walked into Mr. Edison's suite. At least twice the size of my old apartment, I felt like I had stepped out of my life and into a Julia Roberts movie (you know the one I'm talking about). When we walked in the door, we stood in a small, softly-lit foyer. To the right was a full kitchen and dining room, complete with a stove and all.

"I never go in there," he noted during the tour.

Straight through the foyer was the living room. The decor was mostly modern, the type of furniture you only see in showroom windows on Fifth Avenue. Everything was white and black, with small hints of red here and there. A flat screen TV took up most of the left wall, while the furniture all sat on the right.

"It all looks too nice to sit on, huh?" I nodded in agreement, but could not shake the amazement from my eyes. "Yeah, that's why I told them to get these!" Mr. Edison plopped down on one of the two beanbag chairs that hung out in front of the television. They were both black, matching the color scheme of the room. "There's no way I'm paying $9,000 to replace that hideous white couch after I spill soy sauce or something on it. Plus I had one of these things in college, so it brings back memories."

I laughed and plopped down on the beanbag next to him. One would never expect that the kind of person who would stay in that insanely gorgeous suite would also be the kind of person to order in Chinese food, and prefer to sit on a bag full of Styrofoam beads. We stared into each other's eyes for a quick moment before he hopped up, grabbing my hand on the way.

"Let me show you the rest!" His excitement won me over, and we were off to one of the bedrooms.

The first one he showed me was the 'guest room'. I couldn't imagine why he would need a suite with an extra bedroom, but I went along with it. The room was just as modern as the living room, but with a different color scheme. Everything was covered in red, yellow and blue polka dots. I felt like I had walked in on the world's largest game of twister. The bed was so perfectly flat on top, it made me think it would be hard as a rock if I actually sat on it. Everything in the room looked completely untouched. Not untouched that day, but untouched since the day it was delivered and put together so perfectly. Mr. Edison admitted to only having been in the room once before, when he checked in. The bathroom had two rooms separated by a beautiful golden-brown oak door. The first room held a long table and couch in front of a vanity mirror, and the second held the toilet and a stand up shower. Fit for a queen, or at the very least a princess.

Next, he took me to the master bedroom. My first impression was that it was a typical bachelor room. The lighting was quite different from the other rooms. It was dim with soft pink hues climbing up the walls, radiating from lamps on either side of the bed. The bedspread was black with a maroon trim, complete with matching pillows. Unlike the bed in the polka dot room, this bed looked worn in and comfortable. In the corner of the room was a stripper pole, raised on a small platform.

"I designed this room myself!" he claimed proudly. "Minus the stripper pole, that was the request of a previous guest."

"Yeah, right!" I said teasingly.

"I swear!" he nearly shouted. "You're more than

welcome to hop on it anytime you want though," he replied with a wink.

I giggled. "I'd have to take some pole dancing classes before I embarrass myself on that thing!"

"That can be arranged," he whispered into my ear and kissed my cheek. He took my hand and started walking towards the back corner of his room. "We can skip my bathroom, I want to show you one more thing."

Behind a long black curtain were sliding glass doors. He flipped a switch and twinkling lights appeared behind the glass. It was a balcony, nearly as long as the suite. I had remembered seeing a second entrance to the balcony in the living room.

"This is my favorite part," he said as we stepped outside. To our far left were two lounge chairs, perfect for lazing out in the sun during the day. Next to that was a small metal table accompanied by four chairs. I immediately began fantasizing about eating breakfast there with Mr. Edison, gazing out at the city skyline after long nights of making love; playing footsie under the table, and throwing hungry glances at each other. I was fucking delusional.

To our right was a hot tub, fit for four but perfect for two. *Mr. Edison and I could spend our nights here drinking wine after dinner, making our own waves of sorts.* It was incredible how my brain worked so quickly to create a relationship between Mr. Edison and myself. Our entire future was mapped out in my head before our first meeting had ended. Jillian would have been proud.

The entire balcony was enclosed by thick grey glass, decorated with lights that reminded me of the ones on my holiday trees growing up. Mr. Edison walked over and tapped on it and winked at me saying, "We can see out, but no one can see in." The sexual tension had been slowly building during his tour, so I was relieved when the doorbell rang.

"That must be the food!" Two full carts of food and drinks came through the door. "Again I wasn't sure what you liked, so I got a little bit of everything."

We laughed together at the abundance of food before us. The sight was almost ridiculous, but I found his concern for my happiness adorable. His ability to put me at ease amazed me. He left me momentarily in the living room to gaze at the room service carts. There was everything from full meals like chicken Parmesan and turkey legs, to finger foods like French fries and mozzarella sticks. I was tempted to dig in, but Mr. Edison reappeared wearing gym shorts and a white t-shirt. In his hand were another set of clothes.

"Here," he said handing them to me. "I don't expect you to pig out with me while wearing that tight little dress." He blew me a kiss and pointed me in the direction of the guest room. Giggling, I followed his directions. Speaking was obviously not my forte that evening.

The clothes he gave me smelled of cedar wood and laundry detergent. I hurriedly stripped off my dress and put them on. It was just an old college t-shirt and grey sweatpants, but they managed to make me more self-assured than I had felt all night. Taking off the hooker dress made being in Mr. Edison's room less like a job.

I came out of the room to find him mixing more drinks for us. "Wow. You look adorable," he said with that child-like grin.

Blushing, I thanked him. "I think these pants are a bit big on me though," I said lifting up my shirt playfully to show him that the pants had fallen off my waist. By doing this I was also revealing some of the lingerie Nyani had given me. "Maybe I'll just wear the t-shirt." I slid the pants off over my heels, which weren't visible until then. I stood there staring him down with an uncontrollable craving. Probably ridiculous to try to seduce a man who was paying to fuck me, but it's what I did. I wanted to give it my all that first night, to ensure he would come back for more. He'd pay my bills and rent me an apartment, and we'd live happily ever after as business associates until he got bored of me.

Mr. Edison's jaw dropped as I stood before him in my black thigh high stockings, and four-inch stilettos. The t-shirt he gave me barely covered my ass, allowing my garter belt to peek out. I wanted him, and I wanted him before we stuffed our faces with all that food and my bloated stomach took away my confidence.

"Take off the shirt." It was stern and out of character, but I immediately did as I was told. He didn't look anywhere but my face as he walked toward me at full speed. The intensity in his eyes held me there, frozen in place. He reached for the back of my head and pulled me towards him, forcing his lips to meet mine. My mind screamed at him to stop, but every other part of my body wanted it, and wanted it bad. He stroked my cheek, letting his tongue explore my own. I could feel his kisses everywhere, and my knees began to shake violently. It was becoming hard to stand. He moved his mouth to my neck, finally allowing me to speak.

"Isn't this against the rules, Mr. Edison?" I said it half teasing, half concerned with going against Nyani and her rules.

He looked at me with a devious grin, momentarily prying his lips away from my body long enough to say, "Rules are meant to be broken, right?"

We both smiled in agreement, and the worried thoughts quickly vanished from my mind. In one swift motion he scooped me up, forced my legs around his waist and carried me to his bedroom. Once there, he allowed my legs to drop to the carpet and spun my body around. His hands gliding gently across my back sent chills down my spine.

"How about a massage?" he asked, rubbing my shoulders and gently guiding me towards the bed.

Laying on my stomach, I allowed him to press

113

his palms deep into my back, my entire body shuddering in excitement. I moaned softly in between the childlike giggles his rough hands brought on. Mr. Edison changed his touch to light caresses, while also warming me with the weight of his now bare chest. My fingers gripped the comforter, and my cries grew louder as I fell into a world of indescribable agony and craving for his every stroke. His lips teased my skin, and my yearning sent pain to my favored insides.

The warm breath of a man I barely knew was sending me over the edge as his tender nibbles worked my thighs. I didn't want his teasing to end, and I battled my thirst for his cock. His teeth found my panties, and I felt them slide to my knees. I had no choice but to surrender my body to him.

Without warning, I was flipped onto my back and blinded by pleasure. Mr. Edison had his fingers and tongue in all the right places, using his dominant arm to keep my legs spread and pinned to the mattress. They trembled harder and I almost immediately began to cry out God's name. I grabbed his arm, digging my nails into his skin as I was overcome with blinding ecstasy. My limbs continued to quiver after my body had reached its dramatic climax. Mr. Edison hastily stripped down to nothing, exposing the goods.

"Your cum face is so fucking hot! You're a dirty little girl, aren't you? I bet you want this dick raw," he said as he gradually slid himself inside of me. I squealed as my insides were slowly stretched out. "Oh, you like that don't you?"

I could only stare at him, wide eyed as I nodded my head. My thighs vibrated around his hips as he teased me with his dick.

"You filthy girl, you're getting my cock soaking wet!" He threw my arms up over my head, restraining them with a single hand. "Tell me what you want," he whispered . "I need you to talk dirty to me."

Fuck, what do I say... "I want you, to fuck me!" *So lame.* As Eva, I'd never been one to talk dirty or even be sexy on purpose. In that moment, I felt overwhelming amounts of pressure to be this sex-hungry vixen for Mr. Edison, and immediately adopted that as one of 'Hannah's' characteristics. It was much easier to flip a switch and become Hannah than it would have been to change who Eva was. Who I was.

"Hmm, like this?" he asked continuing to tease me with slow thrusts.

"No, harder," I demanded lustfully. And that's what he did.

I could tell immediately he liked it rough. There was no fear when he brought his hand to my throat, choking me just as hard as he was fucking me. My face grew hot and my eyes felt as if they were about to pop right out of my head. I tried to push his hand away from my neck, but he kept a firm grip. My vision was slowly going from blurred to black, but still I didn't panic. Surprisingly, I enjoyed the combination of pain and pleasure.

It started in my toes, and worked its way up my thighs. Before I knew it, every inch of my body exploded over and over. There was little time to enjoy the experience though before Mr. Edison dragged me by my feet to the edge of the bed.

"Stand up." I obeyed his orders and stood next to him, swaying on my unstable legs as I struggled to catch my breath. "I want to eat you again, I'm hungry," he teased.

"Okay," I said uncertainly. He blocked me when I tried to crawl back in bed, shaking his head. My cum-happy brain couldn't think of how that would be possible if we were both standing. "Umm, how…"

"Make me get on my knees, girl!" he smirked at my inexperience. *Oh, shit. Duh! Stop acting like Eva…*

I pulled him by his hair towards my face and pressed my lips against his before pushing him down by his shoulders. He fought it for a moment, but he finally gave in and fell to his knees. *Yeah, you're mine now.* I used my body to pin him against the bed, and fucked his face. He moaned in protest, so I leaned on him harder forcing his mouth to please me. Wetness dripped down my trembling legs. I tried grabbing him by the hair to keep steady, but I couldn't stand any longer. My knees buckled and I fell to a squatting position, landing right on his cock. His face, covered in my cum, was shocked by my bold decision to ride him. I opened my mouth, letting the juices dripping off his chin find my tongue before licking it off his lips. He moaned in approval as I threw my pelvis towards his over and over.

Unexpectedly taking back the dominant role, Mr. Edison threw me on my back. He pounded me on the floor as his face twisted in a form of tortured pleasure, cumming harder than I ever could have imagined. I couldn't wipe the grin off my face as he collapsed on top of me panting. *Oh... My.... God...*

We eventually made it back to the bed where we lay in each other's arms, stuffing our faces and going over every detail of what had happened in the prior forty-five minutes. I told him how amazing his massage felt, and he told me how hot it was when I licked my own cum off his face. Then we talked about everything from favorite television shows to our crazy families. Three hours later, we decided I should probably head back to my room and after a long kiss goodnight, we parted ways.

DAY TWENTY-TWO

MR. EDISON WAS on Long Island taking care of 'business stuff' for a few days, so I knew it would be a while before I saw him again. It was pretty depressing hanging out in a dimly lit hotel room all day, alone with my thoughts and nothing to do but stare at the television. Tanya hadn't been back to the room nor slept in her bed the last two nights. While it was nice to have the room to myself, I was desperate to find something to occupy my day.

Jerimiah worked in the city occasionally, so we arranged to meet up for an early lunch. He said he wanted to talk to me about something. *Something? That doesn't sound good.* I despise the phrase 'we need to talk' or anything similar that implies someone has something specific to talk to me about but makes me wait an extended period of time to hear it. It always sends my thoughts to the worst possible scenario, leaving me anxiously waiting for the moment they deliver their news. Before text messaging and e-mail, it was easy to tell what kind of 'talk' it would be. Something as simple as a person's tone of voice would eliminate all concern. Things are different now.

I can't remember the last time someone actually called me to chat. Of course what they have to say is never as bad as whatever my mind concocts, but I liked to be prepared for the worst.

I decided to stick to a simple outfit for the meeting, something Eva would normally wear. As much as I loved my new wardrobe, none of it was appropriate for grabbing a quick lunch with a fuck buddy. Shorts and a tank top seemed suitable for the occasion, and I decided to dress it up with Hannah's hooker makeup. I liked it. It made me feel sexy. Plus, I needed practice putting it on myself.

Jerimiah was waiting for me pretty far downtown, so I had to take a subway and walk a bit. I stuck a few bucks in my pocket before I headed out, leftover from my short lived career as a jewelry saleswoman-slash-swindler. Honestly I expected Jerimiah to pay for my meal, but to be caught without any cash would be pretty embarrassing. I mean, I'm all for women's rights and what-not, but I was broke as hell and really fucking hungry.

As the hot air of the subway station hit my face, my mind had finally uncovered the worst of the worst possible scenarios. *He just wants to be 'friends'. He's no longer interested in me and I'll never hear from him again. It's over.* I sat on the train and let my mind wander even further down the rabbit hole. *Or maybe he wants to hang out more, as my boyfriend? Which is worse? Him not wanting me anymore, or him wanting more commitment? Can I have a boyfriend if I decide to get into this new profession? Wait, no, no, no, no!* It hit me. *He must know! Someone must have told him I'm the new whore in Nyani's social club! Probably that stupid slut who banged both of his friends. Maybe she left behind her vagina's business card, and one of his friends decided to call her up for round two. Somehow my name got brought up, and the cunt spilled the beans about me hanging around the hotel these past few days.*

I'd reached my stop. I had to put my mind on pause, and focus my energy on forcing my legs to carry my body out of the subway car and back up to the city streets. However, as soon as I got my sense of direction back, the thoughts continued. *What the fuck am I gonna say to him if he knows? Should I just deny it? Tell him Nyani is just helping me out with a place to stay and he's crazy for thinking I would become a whore just to get by?* The truth was, I liked Jerimiah. Not enough to jump into things right away and change my relationship status on Facebook, but enough to want to get to know him better. Maybe even enough to dabble with the idea of becoming something more serious in the future, when my life was less of a mess. I knew if he found out I was even considering this long-term escort nonsense it would be over faster than it began, and I wasn't ready to lose him yet. *So I'll deny it. Might be hard to do that with all the whore makeup on your face, Eva.* I kissed my wrist, blotting the lipstick I wore with the hope of it appearing slightly less red and slightly less like I recently changed my profession.

"Hey!" I said waving towards Jerimiah who had already been seated outside at the small cafe.

"Wow, you look…different," he pointed out standing up to give me a kiss on the cheek. *Different?*

"In a good way I hope," I said having a seat across from him.

"Course! You look sexy as hell girl. You should've seen how many guys were breakin' their neck tryin' to get a look at you as you were walkin' down the street," he said with a smirk. He almost looked sad.

"Jealous?" I questioned with a cocky undertone, but he didn't laugh at my joke. He barely acknowledged I spoke. *Shit, he definitely knows.* "Jerimiah? What's wrong?"

"Nah, we'll talk about it after we eat. I don't wanna ruin lunch," he said lifting his menu. "Order anything you want, it's on me. I suggest an alcoholic beverage. Or two."

I smiled back uneasily, but he was too busy reading the menu to notice. The vibe he put off told me that he didn't know anything about my potential new career, it was something else. I ordered two mojitos and scrambled eggs. Technically it was my breakfast since I hadn't eaten anything yet that day, so ordering off the brunch menu felt appropriate. It was hard to concentrate on the small talk we kept going throughout the meal when I knew something bigger was coming. I participated in the bullshit though, telling him all about my move to the big city. I may have fibbed a bit, telling him Nyani let me move in with her temporarily until I got on my feet. Which was almost true, I just forgot to mention the part about living in a hotel and possibly becoming an escort. I also left Mr. Edison out of my life update.

Jerimiah spoke about work, and joked about whether or not I ever asked Nyani about her friend being a legit prostitute. *Okay, he definitely doesn't know. Shit, what does he have to talk to me about then?* I told him I never asked, which was the truth. Then it was finally time. Time for him to tell me what I'd been patiently waiting to hear throughout the entire meal. Our empty plates had been cleared, he had to go back to work soon, and I only had a few sips of my second mojito left. *This is it. Embrace yourself.*

"So, there's something specific I wanna talk to you about."

I could tell he was uneasy, and maybe even a little scared about how I would respond. My heart abruptly plummeted into my stomach, and a small sadness found its way behind my eyes. It became apparent to me that whatever it was that he needed to say was going to be the end of us now, and the end of the possibility of us in the future. But I couldn't let him see my grief. I began to mentally prepare my reaction before he had the chance to say anything. In front of him, I would be calm and understanding. Perhaps even suggest a friendship. Any tears that might want to fall would have to be saved for later. Whether I liked it or not, he was my closest friend at that time in my life. He was the only one I was able to open up to, and my heart knew I was about to lose that bond.

"I don't know how to say this," he muttered towards the table.

"Just say it." My tone was cold. I was quickly losing patience, and the anticipation at that point was killing me.

"I don't know how you're gonna react," he said cautiously. "I know we've only known each other a short time, but I feel like we've grown so close. And I wish we could continue to get closer, but..." he paused. I waited a few seconds for the rest of his sentence but nothing came.

"It's okay, just tell me," I urged.

"I'm married."

What? Those were not at all the words I expected to hear him say. That had *not* been any of the scenarios I ran through my head, and I suddenly felt extremely unprepared.

"I'm married, and I have two kids." Jerimiah finally looked up at me when he said this, trying to get a feel on my reaction.

I just sat there, wide-eyed and in shock. *Is this a fucking joke?* My plan to remain calm, and have an understanding reaction went to shit. Everything he said after that flew right through me. My head was spinning, and I couldn't formulate any words. Zero.

"Are you okay? You look like you're about to cry," he said reaching for my hand across the table. I snapped out of my trance, pulling my hand away from his as I broke out in hysterical laughter. *This is literally unbelievable.* "I'm really sorry I didn't tell you sooner, Eva. I never expected to have such strong feelings for you, and my wife and I have been separated for a while. I just feel like I owe it to her and our children to try and work things out."

I laughed harder, and stood up. There were still no tears, and still no words. Just amusement as I walked away from him. He may have called after me, but I didn't recognize the name. Eva had checked out.

Hannah, on the other hand, stopped around the corner and used a window reflection to reapply her red lipstick. Then she walked the thirty-or-so blocks back to her hotel room, enjoying every second look, grin, and whistle men sent her way. Her smile was intoxicating and contagious. It wasn't until she got back to her empty hotel room and hopped in the shower that Eva came rushing back, forcing her to collapse into a ball and finally allow the tears to fall from her eyes.

DAY TWENTY-THREE

TANYA REAPPEARED that day, if you'd consider just before sunrise and last night's dress 'that day'. The clock read exactly 5:37 when she came stampeding into our room, screeching into her cellphone with zero consideration for her sleep deprived roommate. The sudden uproar threw me out of my slumber, sending my heart into a panic as I reached for my phone to check the time.

I listened for a moment to the clearly one-sided conversation Tanya was having, growing impatient as I waited for her to hang up or take the conversation elsewhere. She didn't. *Maybe she doesn't see me?* So, I got out of bed and walked to the bathroom. I was sure that when I got out she'd be off the phone and apologize for rudely waking me up. Once again I was wrong. Instead she was screaming and cursing, saying things like 'You said you loved me you fucking liar!' and 'How could you do this to me?'. She was obviously having a fight with a guy, but it was nothing that couldn't be resolved in the hallway… where I wasn't trying to sleep.

"Umm, Tanya?" The bitch scowled at me like I was fucking insane to interrupt her while she was on the phone. But I continued nonetheless. "I'm trying to sleep, maybe you can finish your conversation somewhere else?" Instead of acting like a normal human being and leaving the room, she rolled her eyes at me and continued to yell. I just stood there glaring at her for a moment. *Is this chick for real?* But what could I do? The last thing I wanted to do was start a war with the girl I'd be stuck rooming with for an indefinite amount of time. At least, I *thought* I'd be stuck rooming with her for a while.

Instead of ripping the phone out of her hand and smashing it against the wall like I wanted, I crawled back into bed with the impractical expectation that her conversation would soon end. It didn't. The best I got was her relocating the discussion into the bathroom for twenty minutes causing her squealing to be slightly muffled by the closed door.

Tanya finally left at ten after seven, not failing to make as much noise as possible on her way out. It seemed like whoever she was having a dispute with had asked her to meet him somewhere. *Thank God.* I was exhausted, but my anger wouldn't allow me to fall asleep just yet. The bitch left the bathroom light on, which blinded my restless eyes when I was finally able to lay in silence. I figured I'd take a quick piss since I had to get up to turn off the light anyway.

My eyes began to adjust as I squatted over the toilet, and I noticed it first on the floor. Thick strands of long black hair were everywhere. When I glanced up at the sink I noticed a clip-on weave laying there, soaking wet. A bottle of shampoo and conditioner sat next to it, and I quickly came to the assumption that she'd been trying to wash it. *I hope someone poured a drink on her dumbass head. An apple martini or daiquiri. Something sticky.* The imagery made me grin.

Mid-piss, I got a brilliant idea. At least it was brilliant to someone who had been rudely woken up and kept awake half the night by juvenile quarreling. I needed to retaliate in order to let go of the anger and fall back to sleep. So, without flushing the toilet I got up and grabbed the nasty weave off the counter. Holding it between my fingers, I dipped the horsehair into my piss water until I felt it was sufficiently soaked.

Sick as that was, it wasn't enough to satisfy my anger. I took one of those plastic cups they always keep near the sink in hotel rooms, and filled it up with some piss water. It still held my body's warmth. I proceeded to pour the diluted pee into both her bottle of shampoo and conditioner, with a satisfied grin on my face. After shaking it up a bit and turning off the lights, I was finally content enough to attempt sleep. I made a mental note to lock the door from the inside before I went to bed from now on. Little did I know, Tanya would never come across my disgusting pranks. As far as I know, she never made it back to the room after that morning.

LATER THAT AFTERNOON, I decided to hang out by the hotel pool. I was relieved when I woke up and saw that Tanya hadn't come back yet. I couldn't wait to see her walking around in that weave, completely clueless as to where that funky smell was coming from.

Over the years of living so close to the town beach with [*The Douchebag*], I had collected a number of bathing suits. Most of them made it to the city when I relocated, so I threw on the newest one, a cover up, some flip-flops and left the confines of my prison cell.

In every hotel I had stayed in up to that point of my life, the pool was always on the same level as the lobby. You would walk into the main lobby and basically follow the signs. Perhaps I was a bit sheltered, but if not for the elevator button labeled POOL/SPA I doubt I would have ever found the pool on the roof. I was glad I did though. It was the most luxurious place I had ever been. Palm trees and twinkling lights surrounded the pool area giving it a tropical vibe. The bar looked like a tiki hut, complete with bartenders in grass skirts and drinks in coconut shaped glasses. Neon lights radiated from the four hot tubs, one in each corner of the roof. The pool itself had a waterfall backdrop, and a pool bar. Thinking back, it was probably all a bit tacky but at the time I thought it was fucking spectacular.

Before I even had the chance to take it all in, I heard Nyani shouting my name from one of the lounge chairs. Well, Hannah's name. I waved back and headed towards the empty seat beside her.

"Hey!" I said enthusiastically as I began to put my things down.

"Towel miss?" a young man in a grass skirt asked me, towel in hand.

"Oh, umm, yes please," I said taking it from him. "Thank you."

"So, Hannah, how are you enjoying your stay?" Nyani asked as I stripped down to my bathing suit. "Nice sunglasses by the way," she smirked. "They really do look good on you."

I was wearing the Dior sunglasses she had given me. "Thanks," I responded. "And also thank you for all the clothes and lingerie you left for me in my room! I love it all!"

"You deserve it," she said sipping on her drink. "You need a cocktail!" With a wave of her hand she got the attention of a waiter who brought me some kind of fruity concoction in one of those coconut cups.

"Thank you," I said to the waiter before taking my first sip. It was the kind of drink that made you pucker your lips from all of the sugar and question whether there was actually any alcohol in it.

"So, how was your night with Mr. Edison?" I guess we were skipping the small talk and going straight to the dirty stuff.

"It was great, I think we really connected. Did he say anything about me?" I asked curiously.

"Of course he did," she said pulling out a cigarette. My heart stopped, and I waited impatiently for her to light up before she continued her response. "I think you have a good shot at being his escort." I grinned at the idea. "That is, if that's what you want?"

"Yes, that's definitely what I want." I had made that decision the second Jerimiah told me he was married. He was the only reason I would have been unsure, but since he was now out of my life for good, I had no reason to hesitate. I thought I had nothing to lose.

"Well, here's your pay for the other night." She reached into her bag and pulled out a white envelope. I couldn't help but notice how thick it felt as she handed it to me. Everything in me wanted to peek inside, but I buried the urge and tucked it under my bathing suit cover up on the floor.

"Thank you, Nyani. I really appreciate everything you've done for me."

"It's $1,000. I know you're curious."

"What? Why so much?" I nearly shouted. My shock caused her to laugh.

"Since you are not yet in a contract with him, and

he's not paying for your accommodations in the city, he had to pay the hourly rate. And I don't take a cut out of a girl's first time. It's a small taste of what you'll get when you officially become a member of the club."

I had nothing to say. To hold that amount of money, in cash, was extraordinary to me at the time. All the bullshit she was saying about contracts went in one ear and out the other. *Where can I put it all? I need to hide it from that crazy bitch Tanya. I guess I'll have to put it in the bank, or maybe there's a safe in the room...*

"So, tell me about the sex! Was it good?" Nyani asked, interrupting my train of thought.

I immediately blushed. "It was better than good," I bragged. She looked at me waiting for details, so I continued. "He ordered a ton of food, and gave me comfy clothes to change into. So I came out in just a t-shirt and heels, showing off some of the lingerie you got me. To get him in the mood, ya know?"

"Scandalous!" she exclaimed. "Tell me more!"

"Well when he saw me he just couldn't control himself, and picked me up and threw me on his bed." I quickly became aware that a play by play might not be the greatest idea. *Can I tell her he went down on me and made me cum like crazy? I know kissing is against the rules, is getting me off against the rules too?* "We went at it for like an hour!" I decided to skip everything and sum it up. *It's really none of her business anyway... or is it?*

"Sounds hot!" she said.

I could tell she was waiting for more, so I quickly changed the subject before I got myself in trouble with my own damn mouth. "So, what's the deal with this Tanya chick that I'm rooming with?"

"Ugh," she moaned and puffed on her cigarette. "I know, she can be difficult at times. Why, what did she do?"

I explained to her what happened that morning, leaving out of course the incident with her weave and hair products mysteriously getting covered in my piss. Nyani didn't seem very surprised to hear how inconsiderately Tanya had behaved.

"Don't worry, she won't be around much longer." Nyani's response was a statement, not a hypothesis or a theory. I didn't question her confidence though, and I didn't doubt that I wouldn't have to deal with Tanya anymore. There was something about the way Nyani spoke that made me think I should change the subject again, but my curiosity wouldn't allow that.

"Who was the last girl that roomed with her?" I asked cautiously.

"Her name was Dawn, why?" Nyani looked at me, trying to read my face.

"No reason," I shrugged and focused my attention back on my drink. "Tanya just mentioned a few things about her, so I was curious."

"Oh, she's still in the club. One of her clients got her an apartment uptown."

"Oh, nice." *So the fairy tale does come true.*

"Well, I have some business to attend to," Nyani said standing up as she smothered her cigarette on the ground. "Enjoy the rest of your day. We'll have to get all the girls together for drinks so you can meet them! I'll let you know!"

She was gone before I could respond. I spent the rest of the day laying by the pool, soaking in the sun and saturating my liver with alcohol bought on Nyani's tab. It's amazing how time flies when one is wasted. Tanya didn't show up that night, at least not before two in the morning. I felt that was a reasonable time to assume she wasn't sleeping in our room, and locked the door from the inside. If she tried getting into the room any time after that, I didn't hear her.

DAY TWENTY-FOUR

"HEY BEAUTIFUL, HOW ARE YOU?"

It was the text message I woke up to from Mr. Edison. Having been agitated awake the previous morning, I welcomed his text with a smile on my face. *Let him wait a few minutes for my response though, I don't want to seem too eager.*

I rolled over and peeked at Tanya's empty bed, relieved to see that she hadn't managed to bypass the locked door. The sound of her mousey Sweet Valley High ranting two mornings in a row would have absolutely forced me to choke a bitch. After rolling around in bed for a few minutes contemplating what my response to Mr. Edison's text would be, I started wishing he was there in bed with me. Not in a 'fuck me I'm horny' kind of way, but in a 'let me rest my head on your shoulder' way. I was lonely.

I hadn't yet acknowledged how much I had relied on Jerimiah to give me the comfort and attention I was left without quite abruptly after [*The Douchebag*] left, and it hit me hard that morning. I would no longer get those texts asking me how my day was going. I wouldn't have him to turn to when I needed a night out or better yet, a night in. Jerimiah was a great substitute boyfriend. He helped me forget for a little while that I was missing all the little things. Things I took advantage of when I was with [*The Douchebag*]. A small tear fell from my eye as I realized how alone I truly was.

No, fuck this shit. This is absolutely not how I'm spending the day. I jumped out of bed, and threw open draw after draw tossing my belongings out of the way. *Where the fuck is it?* There was nothing but clothes and hooker makeup. *Where are the things from my old life?* I got on my hands and knees and reached under my bed until my hand found what I was looking for. *My suitcase. It has to be in there.* And it was. The letter, that is. So I sat on the floor, and read it over and over until all the hate sank back in. I needed the hate to block out the loneliness and I needed my confidence back before I could text Mr. Edison. I couldn't afford to be broken in this new life I had found. Literally. I was being paid to be sexy and alluring, not an emotional wreck.

After putting the letter safely back in its place, I reached for my phone. Whether I was feeling shitty or on top of the world, I couldn't keep Mr. Edison waiting much longer. I mean, it was my job to be there for him at any time. As Hannah.

"Hey cutie, I'm great! Just laying in bed thinking about you ;-) How are you?"

At first I just sat in bed staring at my phone, waiting for his response. Ridiculous, I know. After a few minutes went by and there was still no answer, I brought the phone with me into the bathroom and eyed it impatiently as I washed my face and brushed my teeth. Finally I got the response that I needed to permanently turn my day around.

"I'D BE BETTER IF I COULD SEE YOUR GORGEOUS FACE."

I giggled and blushed. It was almost like his compliments confirmed that I had him hooked. Like he had already decided to hire me. I already had the layout of the apartment he'd get me mapped out in my head.

Since it was another gorgeous summer day in New York, I put on a bathing suit with the intention of eventually making my way up to the pool to work on my tan. I tossed my hair around a bit, threw on some blush, and whipped out my camera phone. It wasn't a scandalous photo; it was exactly what he wanted. A picture of my face, with the hint of some cleavage. But before I could find my flip-flops, I got a picture back of his adorable face in a sexy suit and tie. Under it, it said:

"IS THAT A BATHING SUIT YOU'RE WEARING? THAT'S SO HOT, I WANT TO SEE MORE!"

I spent the next ten minutes taking full body shots in the mirror of my hotel bathroom, deleting at least thirty of them. I'd created the idea in my head that I had to be perfect for him. Flawless. And I didn't send him a single picture that didn't appear that way. All PG of course. Well, maybe PG-13.

"DO YOU HAVE A LAPTOP? I WANT TO VIDEO CHAT WITH YOU."

I had never video chatted with anyone before, but what the hell. There's a first time for everything. *The sun will still be there when we're done.* A large part of me felt like I *had* to do everything he asked me to. If I wanted to be a part of the club, I had to be at Mr. Edison's beck and call. I had to fulfill his every need. If I didn't, I understood that there were plenty of other girls in line behind me who would. Without the offer to be his long-term escort in writing, I feared I would once again be homeless…jobless…and alone. I couldn't let that happen. So, after a few minutes of texting back and forth on exactly how to set up this video chat, I was finally able to see his adorable smile on my computer screen.

"Hey," he said red faced and beaming. The background showed that he was in some kind of office, a private office I assumed.

"Hey," I said with a quick wave. His coyness gave me a sense of empowerment, making my job that much easier. "You look so *sexy* at work, behind that desk and all dressed up."

He blushed and looked down for a second. "Yeah, I'm not getting much work done though.

Someone is distracting me."

He gave me this suggestive look accusing me of being that 'someone'. It made me laugh. "I have a feeling your mind was distracted before you even got my pictures!"

"Yeah, I guess I did wake up craving you but those pictures just, uhhhh!" he made these animal noises while simultaneously shaking his computer screen. "Now I'm stuck at work with this crazy hard on," he added after the screen steadied itself.

"Oh, yeah?" I teased. "Show me." I knew what direction our video chat was headed, and I just wanted to help him get there. Plus, I needed to get to the pool in time for peak tanning time at noon. There was no time to dick around.

He paused before responding, giving his office a quick glance. "Okay, hold on." I heard some shuffling in the background, and the room grew dim. I assumed he was closing the blinds. *Paranoid much?* "Okay, I'm back. I think my hard on went away though. Maybe you can help me with that?"

Eva was mentally rolling her eyes, but Hannah giggled and put her hair behind her ear in an act of interest. "What did you have in mind baby?"

"Hmm…perhaps a dance?" he asked almost innocently. Before I responded I could hear music coming from his end. It was the stereotypical tune you'd expect to pop up when you type 'porn music' into a search engine.

I threw my head onto the bed, and out of view of the camera trying to hold back my laughter. It was hard to keep my composure with Eva's sarcastic remarks consuming my mind.

"So *this* is what you like?" I asked playfully as I tried to find a higher surface for my laptop to rest on that would allow him see my full body when I danced for him.

"Well I'd have to see you dance first before I can tell you if I like it or not." He was smug, but his smile was so charming it barely showed.

I started slowly, trying to get a feel for the beat. It wasn't exactly the kind of music I could really sway to, but I could tell by the look on his face he was enjoying it. *I wonder if this counts as a date? If I brought this up to Nyani, would he have to pay for it?* I made a mental note to casually mention it to her, see if some money popped up.

"Do you like this, Mr. Edison?" I asked leaning in towards the camera. My tits were nearly coming out of my bathing suit top. "Is your cock big and hard yet baby?"

"Almost," he smirked. *Ugh, almost? Fucking hurry up.*

"Hmm, I might have to step it up a little then." I put my laptop on the floor, and got on my knees in front of it. 'Pour Some Sugar On Me' was the first song to catch my eye as I scrolled through my iTunes, so I turned it up loud enough to drown out his silly porn music. I let the music take me over, whipping my hair in front of the screen and running my hands over my curves.

"Oh... my... god," I heard him mutter. His eyes were fixed to my body, fascinated by my movement. I wanted to take it to the next level quickly so I could lie by the pool. My hands found the strings to my bathing suit top, and I flung it to the floor allowing my tits bounce freely to the pulse of my strip tease.

I momentarily paused my dance to bring his attention back up to my eyes. My finger founds its way up to my mouth, covering it in saliva before slowly dragging it down my chin...my chest...my stomach. As my finger slid under my bathing suit bottom, I let out a soft moan before engulfing it in my wetness. I played only for a second before my finger gradually found its way back to my mouth so I could taste myself.

"Are you playing with yourself, Mr. Edison?" I could see quick hand motions going on, but nothing I wanted to see was yet on the screen. He nodded yes, with a sheepish smile. "You naughty boy! But I can't see anything," I said in my best baby voice adding the notorious female puppy face.

He slid his chair back, allowing me to see his cock in his hand. "Much better. Now tell me where you want to put that thing," I demanded as I spun my body around and got on my hands and knees in doggy style position. I could see on the screen through my legs that he had a perfect view of my ass. Once again my hands found the strings to my bathing suit, and I let the bottom piece fall to the floor. I was completely naked. "Do you want to put it in here?" I asked as I reached around putting my finger inside of myself. "Mmhhmm, look how wet you made me!"

"Oh... my... God. Yes, I want to put it in there!" he nearly whispered.

I assumed Mr. Edison's soft voice was due to the fact that he was at work and he didn't want anyone to overhear. My goal quickly became to make him cum so hard, and loud that everyone in his office building heard his tortured moans. "What about in here?" I asked pulling my cum-soaked fingers out of my twat and forcing them into my tight asshole. "Do you want to put it in here, Mr. Edison?" I was nearly shouting.

"Yes! Yes! Yes!" was all it seemed he could say for a moment. "Do you have any toys?"

My eyes lit up as I spun around to face him. "I'll be right back," I said with a sly smile on my face. Unlike my letter, I knew exactly where I kept those. I found my favorite, the rabbit, floating around in my lingerie draw. "How's this?" I asked waving it around excitedly.

"Perfect. Now show me how you use that thing gorgeous."

And show him I *did*! I turned on the vibrator and sat on that rubber cock, riding it until tears of pleasure fell from my eyes. He finally finished with a silent moan, forcing me to orgasm loudly all by myself. *Damn, I failed.* I was legit bummed that he didn't make any noise for me. *Who the fuck wants to orgasm quietly? How boring.*

"You're so fucking adorable," he said smiling at me as he cleaned the jizz off his hand with a tissue.

I was curled up in a ball on my side giggling like I always do after a good fucking. "So are you," I said. "When do I get to see you?"

"I'll be back in the city tomorrow night," he said. "I'm staying in my usual room. Meet me for drinks at the bar at eight o'clock?"

I nodded excitedly. "I can't wait!"

We waved goodbye, and ended our video chat. Twenty minutes later I was walking up to the rooftop pool with a goofy grin on my face, and leftover wetness between my thighs.

DAY TWENTY-SIX

IT DIDN'T TAKE me long to become completely infatuated with Mr. Edison. That's exactly what his intentions were though, and I'm certain that's why throughout our companionship I found his face between my thighs every time we went to bed together. Each orgasm brought us closer and made me more willing to let my freak side out. While I was busy focusing on all the financial support coming my way, I was unknowingly falling right into his trap. I was a fucking idiot.

"I have a surprise for you," Mr. Edison whispered into my ear.

When he got back from his 'business trip', we met for drinks and eventually made it back to his room. I hadn't left since. After breakfast that morning, we spent hours in bed together laughing and fucking. Eventually we'd grow tired and close our eyes for a bit, however it wasn't long before we'd go at it again. He had the Energizer Bunny of cocks.

"Get dressed. I want to take you somewhere."

My eyes fluttered open, and I rolled over groggily while trying not to moan in protest. I wanted to stay in bed a little while longer, but I got dressed with a smile to appease him. The only thing I had with me to wear was the skanky dress I wore out the previous night when we met at the bar. It wasn't exactly a daytime outfit, and surely I looked out of place walking around like that in the middle of the day. Mr. Edison, however, was kind enough to wear a suit which helped give off the illusion that I had intended to put on such an outfit to walk the city streets in.

He held my hand as we left the hotel together for the first time. The sun felt warm against my skin, and I closed my eyes to soak it in for a moment. I took a deep breath, searching for the aroma of summer air through the piss and shit odor of the city streets. It wasn't something I thought I could ever get used to. I missed the smell of the beach... the smell of my old apartment. But one glance in my direction from Mr. Wonderful, and those feelings quickly disappeared. He was good at that. Always clearing my head of any thoughts that might have sent me running home to Long Island. Making me feel like being there with him was exactly where I was supposed to be.

"Where are we going?" I asked inquisitively. I wasn't in the least bit suspicious, even though I should have been considering the circumstances. How well did I really know Mr. Edison? I'd known him for six days at that point. Six fucking days was all it took to hook me.

"If I told you that, it would ruin the surprise now

wouldn't it?" he smirked. I smiled back, and took in the scenery as we continued our stroll. Since moving to the city, I'd rarely enjoyed my days outside roaming the streets anymore. When I lived on Long Island, it was often a day trip I took by myself, clearing my head and doing some shopping. Now, with the city so close, I chose to remain cooped up in Mr. Edison's luxury suite ordering room service and multiple orgasms. And when I wasn't with him, I was bumming around in my room or drinking by the pool. I made a mental note to take some time to get away from the hotel and walk around the city a bit the next time Mr. Edison went away for 'business'.

"Here we are!" We stopped at a brick building only a few blocks away from the hotel. It was an apartment building.

"You didn't…" I said looking up in awe.

"I'm not sure, let's go see!" He grabbed my arm, pulling me past the doorman standing at the entrance to the building. I was overcome with anticipation as soon as we entered the lobby. It was one of those fancy lobbies with exotic wallpaper covering the walls behind a striking statue, which spout water into a fountain, and gave off the illusion that you were no longer in New York.

Mr. Edison excitedly pulled me across the room towards the elevators as I rushed to look around, trying to take in its every detail. He got the okay nod and proper greeting from security before we started going up… and up. "The top floor is always the best." My mouth was dropped open in amazement, and my eyes were stretched. *This is what I've been waiting for; what will make it all worth it. Now I get my own place.*

"Here we are," he said. There was only one door when we stepped out of the elevator. "You have the whole floor to yourself!" he exclaimed excitedly as he played with the keys in the lock. "Surprise, Eva!"

The door to my new home swung open and I lost my breath. It was massive! I immediately ran around like a child on a playground, looking in every room and closet. There was a living room, and a dining room, and a kitchen, and *furniture*! It was a fucking house! Just as I entered the master bedroom, it hit me.

"Do you like it?" he asked wrapping his arms around my waist when he finally caught up to me.

"You called me Eva." He seemed taken by surprise, and drew back his arms. *How the hell does he know my real name?*

After some silence he responded. "Yes, well, that's your name isn't it?"

"Yes," I spoke cautiously. "But how did you know that?" He reacted as if I was accusing him of something, and maybe I should have been.

"I thought we weren't going to follow Nyani's rules, and do this how *we* wanted?" he acted hurt, like I wasn't on his side anymore. I just observed him in silence, waiting for him to say something to make sense of it all. And he did. "Your name was on some papers in your hotel room. I noticed them when I snuck away last night to pack your things and move them here. I wanted to surprise you." He walked over to the bedroom closet and opened the door. "See?" Inside the insanely large walk-in closet were all of my dresses hanging to the left (Hannah's clothes), and my shirts and pants to the right (Eva's clothes). The back wall was covered with a shoe rack meant to hold thirty pairs, but held my only three plus the few given to me by Nyani. It looked pathetically empty for such a beautiful closet.

Mr. Edison walked back over towards me and grabbed my hands. "I want this to be real, Eva. I know how we met isn't exactly ideal, but I have real feelings for you. Can I please call you Eva?"

I felt like an asshole for even questioning him. Nyani made rules for a reason, but at that moment I couldn't see the logic behind them. I was drawn to the idea of breaking the rules with him. Its danger appealed to me, and my mind was so convinced that Mr. Edison was real that I ignored my instincts. *What's it to her if he kisses me on the lips, and calls me by my real name? At the end of the day, she still gets paid and we get to be ourselves. Everyone ends up happy.* Now I know the 'rules' were made with the intention of being broken. It was all part of getting me to trust Mr. Edison and bringing us closer. And *shit,* it worked.

"Okay, you can call me Eva," I said finally, "but then I get to call you by your real name as well."

He smiled, and kissed me. "It's Hunter," he said before kissing me again. "My name is Hunter."

DAY TWENTY-SEVEN

THE FOLLOWING DAY came with even more surprises. Hunter had disappeared on Day Twenty-Six to allow me to get settled into my new place almost immediately after he showed me my new closet. We didn't get the chance to christen it, and my vagina was thankful for the break. He had some 'business thing' to do, but promised me he'd be back the following afternoon. So when my doorbell rang on Day Twenty-Seven, I made sure I was dressed in a way to properly demonstrate my gratitude for the new roof over my head. And by proper, I mean I was wearing a black lace teddy, complete with garter hooks and thigh highs.

I could tell he liked what he saw the second I opened the door. Without saying a word, he scooped me up and hauled me into the bedroom. *My* bedroom… with an actual bed in it! His eyes burned into my own with pure, animalistic desire. I buried my giggles and attempted to look back at him with matching intensity. Our lips rushed towards each other, and for a while we just lay in bed kissing. My body ached for him, but he kept everything PG as he

149

teased me with each caress. It brought me back to high school, back to my senior year when I first started dating [*The Douchebag*]. We would just kiss for hours. Innocence is something of the past, something I know I will never get back. Who would want it back? Along with innocence comes naivety, crushed dreams, and broken hearts, but it was nice to be reminded of the moments before the heartbreak, the moments when everything was new and exciting. This moment, as quickly as it came and went, is one of the few moments I enjoy looking back on when I think about Mr. Edison. When I let myself think about him.

"You're so beautiful," he said between soft kisses. "I can't believe I'm laying here with someone as gorgeous as you. And your body, it's just amazing! You probably hate my jelly belly. I'm sure it's torture for someone as pretty as you to have to spend so much time in bed with someone like me."

"You really have no idea how good looking you are, do you?" I stared into his eyes searching for sincerity. He shook his head no. "Well, you definitely don't have a jelly belly," I said as I poked his stomach with my finger. "In fact, I think you're sexy as hell. And as far as you torturing me, the only thing I find torturous is laying here kissing you while my pussy is aching for you to play with it." He beamed as we continued to gaze at one another.

Backing out was no longer an option. I was in too deep. He had become more than just a client to me, more than a financial crutch, and there was nothing I could do but kiss his lips and hope for the best.

"So," he said pulling back from our lip lock, "I have something for you." He pulled a folded up piece of paper out of his pocket and handed it to me. It was a magazine ad for Head and Shoulders shampoo.

"Umm, I don't understand. Do I have dandruff or something?"

"The other side," he said with a chuckle as he helped me flip it over. It was an advertisement for a car. "I was going to wait until it got here, but the guy at the dealership said it would take a few weeks because I wanted it in a specific color and I just couldn't wait to tell you!"

"You bought me a car?" I asked almost shyly.

"In that exact color," he said, nodding towards the glossy photo. It was the kind of car that only young women or middle-aged men could pull off driving around in. Knowing very little about cars, the only thing I could say about it was that it was a beautiful cherry red and I fucking loved it. I squealed and threw my arms around him.

"This is amazing Hunter! Thank you!"

"Oh, uhh, you're welcome." He smiled in a way that made me feel like my reaction was too much for him and I quickly withdrew my arms. "As soon as the car arrives, I promise, I'll drop everything and we'll take her for a ride!"

Her? No way in hell any car I own is going to be a her! I couldn't wipe the grin off my face as I imagined myself behind the wheel of my first vehicle. It would be the ultimate freedom. With a car, I could go anywhere and see anyone. I closed my eyes and imagined the wind blowing through my hair as the car's engine vibrated around me. *Yeah, a car that sounds and vibrates like this could never be a female. Only a cock can make my legs shake this hard...*

"Does that sound good?" Hunter interrupted my fantasy.

"Umm, hell yeah!" I shouted enthusiastically. "I, um, I actually don't know how to drive though," I added without looking in his direction.

"Wait, what?" he said as he sat straight up in bed. "How do you not know how to drive?"

I shrugged. "I don't know, I just never learned. Wasn't that in Nyani's profile on me? I think it's listed somewhere after 'barely five foot tall' but before 'no college degree'." I laughed at my joke alone.

"You don't have a college degree either?" He sounded disappointed. Perhaps this is when his image of me as 'Hannah' began to fall apart, and I started to become a real person to him. He began to see me as more than just a wet hole.

"No, I took a few classes but I never graduated."

"Well, we'll have to change that. Then your

profile for your next lover can say 'drives well… for a chick' and 'graduated with honors'." I smiled and let him kiss my cheek. "So, when I was moving your stuff I noticed a few, umm, toys mixed in with your panties."

"You knew I had toys, silly. Don't you remember our video chat?" I put on a sad face and pretended to be hurt by his memory loss.

"No, I knew you had *a* toy, not *toys*. There was no plural when we talked about it," he poked my belly laughing as he teased me with his words. "What do you think about whipping one out and letting me play with you a little?" he smirked as his cheeks turned a crimson red.

"I think that's a fabulous idea." We got to christen every room in my new apartment that afternoon… and night.

DAY TWENTY-NINE

NYANI WANTED ME to meet some of the other girls that night, so we gathered behind the red door, a door I would eventually become accustomed to seeing in my nightmares. As I walked into the lounge, I immediately noticed six new faces occupying the furthest corner. Even though I was ten minutes early, the girls each glared at me impatiently and had already downed most of their drinks. Maybe I got the time confused. Nyani stood up first, throwing out her arms as she greeted me.

"I'd like to introduce you guys to Hannah! She's a potential member of the club, and hopefully we'll be seeing much more of her around the hotel."

Each girl stood up and introduced themselves to me with a hug and a kiss on the cheek. It was all very simulated, almost rehearsed. I wanted to escape from the threatening stares that peeked out from behind their phony smiles, but my legs were glued to the spot where I received greetings of forced enthusiasm.

"So, Hannah, tell us about yourself!" the wide-eyed girl who took a seat on the couch across from me nearly shouted. Her name was something like Missy, and her thick Mississippi accent went well with her southern belle look. I was almost envious of her perfect smile and thick blonde hair. It was the kind of blonde you can only get if you're born with it or had enough money for a nice weave. Definitely not something you can get from a visit to the salon.

I wasn't quite sure how to answer Missy's question since I'd been introduced as Hannah, and not Eva. *Should I just make something up?*

Nyani picked up on my hesitance and added, "We aren't your clients, Hannah. You can tell us anything." I heard one of the girls snicker, and threw her a curious look. *You mean we can tell each other anything but our real names. Why would I want these sluts to know anything about me anyway?*

They all glared at me, irritably waiting for me to speak. I squirmed in my seat with an awkward smile on my face, feeling put on the spot as I desperately searched my mind for something to say. I took a sip of my drink to ease my anxiety, and nearly shuddered as the overwhelming amount of vodka hit the back of my throat. *Ugh.*

"Umm, well, I grew up on Long Island and moved in with this guy a few years ago. He basically screwed me financially, leaving me with a ton of bills and that's how I ended up here."

I'd decided to go with a vague version of the

truth. As I took another sip of my poisonous drink, I leaned back to indicate that I was done speaking. Perhaps it was intuition or just plain luck, but I'd decided these women couldn't be trusted with any identifying details of my life. My vision of having all these new friends to hang out with quickly deteriorated. *Who would want to be friends with a bunch of whores anyway?*

"Yes, well we all have our reasons for being here." The sarcastic tone shouldn't have surprised me, and I looked to my left to see that it had come from a pale redhead. Not a natural ginger, but the kind of red that only comes from cheap bottled hair dye found in supermarkets. I couldn't remember her name, but I definitely remember thinking something along the lines of *bitch* or *cunt* after her comment. The redhead sat back, slouching on the couch with her arms crossed. It was obvious she didn't want to be there, and had no interest in meeting me. *So, then why come? Don't do me any favors.*

Thankfully the charming Missy broke the tension that had begun to escalate throughout the few moments of silence with a ridiculous confession. "I know how awful that can be darlin'!" Her eyes had grown so far past the doe-eyed look that I became legitimately concerned they would pop right out of her head and roll onto one of the platters of finger food on the table. "My ex-boyfriend was such a crazy fool! He actually threw all my things out into a pile in our yard, and set 'em on fire! Can you believe that! I had to wear the same dress for two weeks!" She seemed more upset that her clothes were ruined than about losing her boyfriend.

"Well that's what you get for lettin' one of them barn boys stick his dick in yo' mouth, sneakin' around behind yo man's back," one of the girls on the couch to my right said. I recognized her thick Brooklyn accent immediately, and remembered her name was Carmen.

"Damn, girl! I can't believe you just said that!" Honey, the busty woman sitting next to Carmen exclaimed as they both burst out in obnoxious laughter. Honey shared the same complexion as Carmen, but was almost three times her size. She pulled it off well though. *Gotta love a big girl with a big attitude.* The two of them continued to crack up about it while Missy pouted, keeping her eyes down at her drink.

"Jesus, Carmen! Why do you always have to talk to her like that?" A petite Asian girl with hair down to her ass and an unnatural orange glow had her arms around the southern belle, who was now fighting tears.

"She really needs to grow some backbone! I'm so sick of her cryin' all the damn time." The girl next to the skinny redhead had finally decided to contribute to the conversation. I recognized her immediately as Nyani's 'friend' Lacie who Jerimiah accused of being a prostitute. *She must have skipped the hugs and kisses line.*

"Nah! I like when her weak ass cries! It's hilarious!" Carmen said looking right at Missy when she spoke. This really broke her down. I could hear the sobs as she stood up and hurried out of the room.

"Real hilarious, Carmen!" the petite Asian said as she aggressively rose from her seat. "Why don't we talk about how your Daddy put his bitty cock in your five year old mouth? Cuz that really cracks *me* up!"

"You bitch!" Before I knew it, drinks were being thrown and girls were snatching at each other's throats. There was a clear divide among them, as punches were thrown and hair extensions went flying. I sat there amused, watching what I imagined would make a great premise for a reality show. My amusement quickly faded, however, when I glanced over at Nyani. Her initial reaction to the fight can only be described as the calm before the storm. She strongly suggested I go freshen up, and meet her back in the lounge in ten minutes. There was no eye contact along with her suggestion, and no response on my end. Her words were like ice, and I wouldn't have dared to disobey.

I found the bathroom on the other side of the red door quickly, and immediately started dabbing at my dress with a paper towel. While *I* was able to avoid any harm caused by the brawl, my dress was not so lucky. Unfortunately it had fallen victim to the many cocktail bombs that were thrown. *At least I didn't pay for the thing.* Sniffles could be heard from one of the stalls, and I realized I wasn't alone. The bar was deserted when I walked in earlier, so I had a feeling it was one of the girls.

"Umm, hello?" I peeked under the stalls searching for a pair of feet. *Surprise, surprise. It's Missy or whatever her name is.* I recognized the bottom of her dress, which swept the bathroom floor and covered her shoes. "It's Ev- Uh, Hannah. Are you okay?" I asked as I tapped lightly on her stall door.

"No I'm not okay! Those stupid sluts are right! I deserve this life!" She sobbed harder with each word, causing me to regret having said anything to her at all. *Too late now.*

"What do you mean 'this life'?"

"Exactly!" she shouted. "You're so right Hannah!" *Huh?* "This isn't a life, this is PRISON!" I hadn't meant to sound sarcastic, I truly wanted to know what kind of life she could have in this club that in my opinion was nothing less than spectacular. I thought over my next words very carefully. Somewhere in the back of my mind, I knew this conversation was against the 'rules'.

"How *exactly* is your life a prison?" My heart was racing as I pressed my ear up against the door. I didn't want to miss a single word through her blubbering.

"Are you mad? Isn't it obvious?" I imagined her eyes bulging out of her head so far that blood vessels began to burst in protest. "I'm a fucking hooker! I have sex with disgusting old men for money, and I don't even get to keep it! It all goes to *her*!"

"I don't understand. You must get a cut of the money, right? And if you don't like having sex with so many men, why don't you become a long-term escort?" The sobs from the other side of the door turned into laughter so suddenly it startled me away from stall.

"You stupid bitch!" Her cackles grew louder. "And I thought I was naive!" she shouted at me just as I headed out the door. *What the fuck was that?*

Back behind that red door, Nyani was helping the hotel staff clean up the mess from the fight. She immediately stopped when she saw me walk in. The other girls were nowhere in sight.

"Sorry about that Hannah. You know how girls get sometimes." Nyani handed me a drink and offered me a seat in an area of the lounge unaffected by the dispute. "I have some exciting news for you," she announced as she sat down across from me. "Mr. Edison spoke to me earlier this afternoon, and said he's been having an amazing time getting to know you. He would like to make you his escort during his stay in New York. How do you feel about that?"

I was ecstatic, but I tried not to let it show in my face. This was it. The final step in getting everything I thought I wanted. After receiving an apartment and the car, I expected this to happen. However, the conversation in the bathroom was off the charts on the psycho-meter, and it had me second-guessing my decision to join the club. "Well, what exactly would that require of me?"

Nyani smiled. "I'm glad you're being smart about this." She reached under her chair and picked up a red folder. Inside were what appeared to be legal documents. "I like to put it all in writing, just to make the actual moment someone joins our club legitimate. On paper our company is a dating service. You won't find anything in here about sex being required, it's more of an understanding." She handed me a stack of papers a half an inch thick. "It's a bunch of nonsense really. I've just found that girls are more likely to stay out of trouble and follow the club rules when they've signed something. The short version is that while Mr. Edison is in town, you are to escort him to any business or social event he invites you to. You are also required to spend one on one time with him at his request, and be easy to reach by phone or any other means of communication. In return he must supply you with a place to live, and pay for all expenses such as meals, travel, and clothes."

I took a sip of the drink she made me. Again, the vodka burned the back of my throat. *So strong!* "How long is the contract valid?"

"I wouldn't call it a contract exactly. You're a member until you don't want to be one anymore. The signed documents are more for if you were to break the rules and we had to ask you to leave the club. If Mr. Edison wants to end the relationship with you, then there are plenty of other men dying to be part of our club. Short-term escorting will also be accessible to you, but only when Mr. Edison is out of town. While he's in town, you must only be available to him."

Everything sounded so good, but there had to be a catch. "When do you need these papers back? I'd like to take my time and read them over." I was forcing myself to sound as adult as possible, like I actually knew what the fuck I was talking about and that the vodka haze her drinks put me in weren't preventing me from hearing a few key statements.

"You can have as much time as you'd like, Hannah! I believe Mr. Edison could be of some assistance. I'm sure he deals with a ton of legal documents at work." I nodded in agreement like I had any fucking clue what he did for a living and finished off my disgusting drink. "However, girl to girl, can I tell you something in confidence?"

That fluttering feeling came to my chest again. "Sure," I mumbled unexcited to hear what she had to say.

"Well, when I spoke to Mr. Edison this morning, he requested that I send a different girl to his room later tonight if you seemed unsure about joining the club. He's eager to commit to this with you, but only if you're just as interested in him as he is in you. It's something about not knowing how to approach women, and wanting the feelings to be legit. I don't know. I think he's just being insecure, but he *is* the client. My job is to make sure he's happy, so I'm going to have to start offering this position to the other girls. You know, just in case." She paused and chugged the rest of her drink. "We can always find you another club member though if you need more time to look over the papers."

The thought of *my* Hunter with another girl made me enraged with jealousy. It quickly occurred to me that this was an opportunity with a rapidly approaching expiration date. If I wanted it I had to grab it, or someone else would. And I did *not* want to be anyone else's escort. "Okay, I'll look this over with Mr. Edison right now and make a decision within the hour."

MR. EDISON OPENED his door in nothing but his boxers. They were a solid black, and hugged his waist nicely. It continued to baffle me why someone so attractive would ever need to use an escort service, and the obvious answer to that always seemed to escape my mind just before I could grasp it. Perhaps it was all the vodka or just my stupidity, but I accepted Nyani's explanation. It even made me more secure about the kind of relationship Hunter and I were developing. Like he thought of Nyani's club as an actual dating service, and I could one day be his actual girlfriend.

I showed him the contract, and he immediately got down to business with me. The first few pages were a description of the club, mostly bullshit about it being strictly for men who are looking for 'dates'. I assumed this is how she was able to arrange meetings in a hotel. *She must pay off a shit ton of people to be able to do this so publicly… but she also must be making a shit ton of money.* The next few pages went over the 'rules', including a dress code and appropriate level of class, which I was quick to comment on my opinion that some of the girls could use a refresher course in that area. Perhaps it was my way of informing him that it wouldn't be so easy to find my replacement, while also putting down my competition. He didn't even acknowledge my comment though.

Right around page seven of bullshit, I could no longer stand the nibbling on my ear and kisses on my neck that Hunter had begun torturing me with around page two. I let what I was reading escape my mind momentarily as I straddled him, giving in to his persistent teasing. If only I had made it to page twelve I would have known what I was really agreeing to. Then again, Mr. Edison was there to ensure that didn't happen. Our impulsive flirtations quickly turned animalistic as he threw me onto the inadequately sized kitchen table.

"Great first time use of this room," he joked after a few minutes of gentle fucking on a table my own ass could barely fit on, let alone both of ours. "Let's continue in the hot tub." The thought of letting another girl take my place was overwhelming, and I had a feeling my hour was at its end.

"I just have to run these papers down to Nyani. I'll meet you in there in ten minutes?"

"So, you're going to sign them? Does that mean you're my girlfriend now?" In his excitement, his dick fell out of me letting our cum drip to the floor.

"I'm not your girlfriend, I'm your escort!" I teased.

"No, I'm going to call you my girlfriend." I never thought it was possible for every part of one's body to individually smile until that moment. "Get me a pen, I'll sign it too."

DAY THIRTY

I WOKE UP TO my doorbell ringing. It was late enough in the morning to be embarrassed to still be in bed, but Hunter had told me he would be working all day. Without him to keep me company, I had nothing better to do. So when the doorbell rang again, I quickly threw on a pair of jeans and brushed back my hair before answering it.

"Miss. Eva?" the young man at the door asked. He was holding a white box in his arms, and held it out to me when I nodded.

"Thank you," I said as I let the door close. *Wait, should I have tipped him? Shit… oh well, too late now.*

I opened the box and pulled out an envelope that lay on top. My name was scribbled on the outside of it. The note inside read 'Put this on, be ready in an hour.' It was from Hunter.

Inside the box were black spandex booty shorts, and a red workout top. *What the hell…is he sending me to the gym?* Hidden underneath the clothes were an

166

interesting looking pair of shoes, decked out with silver straps and six-inch clear plastic heels. *Okay, definitely not going to the gym.* The excitement of not knowing had my stomach in knots, and I quickly started running around the apartment with a silly grin on my face. After trying on the outfit, I decided to throw on a sensible pair of sneakers and bring the heels in my shoulder bag. It just didn't seem like appropriate attire to wear, well, anywhere. *Ha, a hooker worried about her outfit being inappropriate!* It made me laugh. *No reason for everyone to know what I do for a living though.*

Exactly an hour later, almost to the minute, my phone rang. It was the doorman downstairs at the front desk.

"Yes, hello?"

"Good afternoon, miss. Your car is here." *My car?*

"Okay, thank you."

It was a black sedan. The driver stood outside and opened the door for me, greeting me with a nod of his head. I didn't ask him where we were going. The suspense added to the thrill of my adventure, and the driver didn't seem like much of a talker anyway. We got there in about twenty minutes. I probably could have walked there faster, but walking would have understandably ruined the illusion of being whisked away to an unknown destination.

"Here you are, miss." The car had pulled over in the right lane, blocking all traffic behind it. I looked around scanning for a location that jumped out at me, but I was still clueless as to where I was meant to go.

"I'm sorry, but where exactly is my destination?" Horns blared behind us from impatient vehicles.

"Right here, miss. Number 306. The dance studio upstairs," he said pointing towards a nearby building. "I'll be back in two hours to pick you up."

Dance studio? My heart raced as I spotted the door that read 306, and cautiously headed up the stairs. *I've never taken a dance class in my life. What the hell is Hunter up to?*

"Hello, are you Eva?" the girl behind the front desk asked before I finished walking through the door. *Awkward conversation consisting of me having no idea why I'm here, officially avoided.*

"Yes," I said feeling slightly less apprehensive.

"We've been expecting you. Right this way."

She led me down a lengthy narrow hallway with glass windows offering a peek into each dance studio. Music and laughter could be heard from every direction. I peeked curiously through each window, watching young girls in tutus learning ballet. Another room held a group of older women who were doing some kind of aerobics or jazzercise. A third room held a smaller group of teenagers practicing a hip hop routine as the instructor clapped fiercely to the beat, shouting demands at them. My heart thudded with anticipation.

"Right in here Eva," the receptionist said pointing me towards one of the last doors.

I smiled as I thanked her politely and walked in the room. To my amazement, it was filled with over a dozen stripper poles.

"Hey Eva!" I was greeted by a tall, skinny blonde. She was pretty in an 'I've obviously had plastic surgery' kind of way. That included, but was not limited to, a nice set of huge fake tits that threw off the entire proportion of her body. "My name is Ginger, welcome to your first pole dancing class!" *Well, that explains the skanky stripper heels in my bag.*

"Hello," I muttered looking around the room in disbelief. It wasn't exactly the kind of activity I'd hoped for, but technically I did ask for it.

"So, your boyfriend set this up for you as a surprise right?" she asked. My stomach did a flip at the sound of someone else calling him my 'boyfriend'.

"Yes," I said blushing. "He did."

"Well, I know this is your first time so we'll start off slow! I'll be teaching you privately for the first hour, and then you'll be joining a class the second hour if you feel comfortable."

Feel comfortable? No, I don't fucking feel comfortable! I better get paid extra for this. "I have heels with me," I said nodding towards Ginger's feet. She was wearing shoes very similar to my own. I had a feeling they were Hunter's inspiration for my 'gift'. "Should I put them on?" I asked.

"Absolutely!" she nearly shouted as she skipped through a few songs on an iPod.

We began with a 'warm up', which wasn't exactly easy to do in six-inch heels. Ginger did it gracefully though, of course. I was surprised she was able to balance herself in those shoes with the weight of all that silicone on her chest. Maybe I was just in a shitty mood because my surprise ended up being something more for Hunter's perverted pleasure instead of something thoughtful or generous, but I kept imagining Ginger falling on her face and all the Botox and lip-plumper oozing out of her skin. It cheered me up a bit. That is, until we started working with the poles.

"Just wrap your leg around there, yeah just like that, and hold on to the pole up here." We started off with something 'easy' called the Fireman's Spin but I didn't think anything was easy in those goddamn shoes. My only dance experience was in the clubs, and even *that* I doubted I could do in heels so high. "Now make sure you have a good grip, and pull up your other leg as you swing your body to your left."

I did what she said, but I was intimidated by the choreography and it definitely showed. There is a certain level of confidence one needs to get up on a pole like strippers do, and I just didn't have it that afternoon. Perhaps it was the amount of pressure I felt surrounded my 'gift'. *He most certainly will want to see what I've learned and lucky for me, he has his very own private strip club in his bedroom. This is more of a gift for him than it is for me. My ass another hotel guest requested that pole for the room! Fucking sicko probably installed it with his own two hands.*

Halfway through my private lesson, my mind was still spinning with rage towards Hunter. I guess I thought his surprise was going to be more... genuine. Or at the very least something designed more for me instead of a class on how to be a better sex toy for him. His presentation, I must say, was flawless. Everything from the doorman bringing me the clothes to the personal driver, kept my blood pumping. But it raised my expectations far too high for what was presented. The class was a forced reminder of who I was now. A prostitute. And whether I liked it or not, this was what my client was asking of me.

So I sucked it up and got over it, using my fury to focus on the pole dancing instead. I should have realized then what a fine line there was between the reality of my relationship with Mr. Edison and the fantasy relationship I had been mislead into with Hunter. But I didn't. I almost acted as if Mr. Edison was just someone I had to deal with every now and then if I wanted to be with Hunter. Anyway, I kicked ass the rest of the private lesson.

"Wow, Eva! I'm so impressed!" Ginger beamed at me. "You had a rough start, but you're picking everything up so quickly! You won't have a problem at all keeping up with the girls in the next class."

As the girls started pouring into the room, I knew she would be right. I was by far the youngest woman in the class. They weren't at all the dozen plastic Barbie dolls I had expected to walk in. The majority of the class looked like the average New York City version of a stay at home mom.

I decided to use a pole in the back, so I could 'observe' if I happened to get lost in the routine. As soon as the class started, my confidence went through the roof. It was definitely a beginner class, and I laughed at the thought of Hunter and Ginger planning this out together. Ginger might have said something like 'I have two classes with spots open' and Hunter would say something like 'in which class would her spastic dance moves blend in?' I giggled out loud at the thought, finally releasing most of my anger towards him.

I ended up having a good time in the class, but it was still practice for the big show Mr. Edison would surely expect. Just the thought of dancing for him made my heart race, and my palms sweat. I closed my eyes during the car ride back to my apartment, trying to control my breathing and let go of the anxiety. *It's better than taking care of that bratty kid.*

DAY THIRTY-ONE

IT WAS THE ONLY night Hunter ever took me out, and we were headed to some 'business thing'. He never told me what it was for, but then again I never really asked. I spent the entire day trying to figure out what to wear, and eventually decided nothing I owned would be suitable. The dresses Nyani gave me were just too trashy, and the clothes I brought with me from my previous life were so incredibly childish. I must have texted him a dozen times asking him what he was wearing, what he thought the other women attending would be wearing, asking what *I* should wear. He finally picked up on my irritation, and told me he'd take care of it.

However, as it got closer to the time he was picking me up and I still had no dress, I became increasingly impatient. *How am I supposed to pick out shoes or do my hair when I have no idea what I'll be wearing?* And the longer I sat there waiting, the more frustrated I became. Perhaps some of my emotions were leftover from the previous day. I assumed I would be required to perform my new pole dancing routine for him later that night. For the first time my little

arrangement with Mr. Edison felt like a job, and I
didn't like it.

Eventually, I got fed up and just started getting
ready without the dress. I blasted house music to clear
my mind of anything related to the predictably awful
evening ahead of me, and tried to focus on stupid shit
like shades of lipstick. For some reason, it got into my
head that this dinner had to go perfectly. I mean,
nothing is more important than the first time a guy
introduces his new girlfriend to his friends and
colleagues right? And that's exactly who I thought I
was… his new girlfriend. The fear of accidentally
slipping, and revealing who I *really* was barely
occurred to me. It became more and more imperative
that I got his friends to not only like me, but to love
me.

The doorbell rang, and my dress was at the door.
"Thank you," I said, quickly grabbing it and closing
the door. Hunter had mentioned to me that he took
care of the tip when he sent things up with my
apartment doormen, so I didn't awkwardly hesitate
before shutting the door this time around.

The dress was radiant. It was a mermaid green
backless gown that fell graciously to my ankles, and
hugged my body to accentuate the right curves. My
auburn hair and pale skin stood out against the green
fabric. I was glad I had chosen a sexy up-do, which
went nicely with my exposed back. It was the perfect
dress for me. I would have never found anything like
it amongst the things in my wardrobe. As I stared at
myself in the mirror, I could finally let go of some of

the stress. The dress gave me a sense of security, like my true identity was suddenly hidden beneath it. *Now I just need to figure out what shoes to wear.*

Twenty minutes later, the doorbell rang again. It was Hunter. *I'm glad I didn't wait for the dress to get here before I started getting ready. Why the hell would he think twenty minutes would be enough time?*

"Wow, Eva! You look…" he paused, looking at me with his mouth open. "I'm speechless." I smiled, blushing at his compliment. His words swept away any annoyances I had with him in an instant. "These are for you." He handed me a bouquet of red roses as he stepped in from the hallway. He looked sexy as hell in what appeared to be an extremely expensive suit, but I kept that compliment to myself.

"Thank you," I said pushing my nose into the soft pedals of one of the roses. "I'll put these in water before we leave."

My heart stuttered as we held hands walking through the halls of my apartment building together. He gently kissed my head in the elevator and playfully squeezed my hand as we entered the lobby. Without asking, he knew my nerves were reaching their peak and his silent gestures were meant to comfort me. I put on a forced smile to hide the anxiety behind my eyes as I stepped into a black limo. It was more than I could have ever imagined, and as happy as I was I could only focus on the added pressure of the evening.

"Would you like a drink?" he asked me as he reached for the liquor in the mini bar.

"Yes, please." *Anything to dull my nerves and make this night go smoothly.* I needed his friends to love me. I needed to be hilarious and unforgettable, which was never my role in the past.

"We need to come up with a story," he said handing me what tasted like a rum and coke.

"A story?"

"Yeah, like how we met and stuff," he said sipping his own drink. "I don't think my colleagues would approve of me paying for a girlfriend because I'm too shy to find a real one." He laughed too hard at his comment while I smiled politely behind the glass I had decided to glue to my lips.

Real one? So I'm not a real girlfriend? His words hit me hard. It wasn't that I didn't know what my role was. The gorgeous living space he created for me made me well aware of that. But hearing it out loud like that abruptly burst the bubble I had created in my mind to make it easier to accept my career as an escort. I preferred to pretend he was my *real* boyfriend, and that he wasn't paying for me through a service. It helped me sleep at night.

"I was thinking we could say we were set up on a blind date. That sounds believable, right Eva?" he asked. I smiled and nodded my head as he blabbed on and on about the details. Each sentence was putting another crack into my own crafted story of Eva and Hunter, and my frustrations with him were rushing back.

"May I have another?" I blurted out, interrupting his awful interpretation of the Eva and Hunter show. He took my glass, looking startled by my sudden rude outburst, but made me a new drink without another word. "I think I'll just let you tell the story of how we met if anyone asks."

"That's probably best," he said handing me my preferred poison. It was consumed before we arrived at our destination three minutes later.

IT WASN'T AT ALL the kind of business affair I'd expected. There were no miserable teenage servers walking around with trays of finger food, or the distinct crowd of ass-kissers surrounding who you'd assume was the head honcho at the office. We entered the building and found ourselves in a small lounge, which did not appear to have been reserved specifically for the event. I immediately felt overdressed. Most of the women I noticed were wearing short cocktail dresses, and appeared to be starting their nights at the lounge with some food before they hit up the clubs and the after parties.

"This way," Hunter shouted over the obnoxious music as he took my hand and led me through the bar. To say we turned heads would be an understatement. Girls looked me up and down like I was their arch nemesis who fucked their high school sweetheart. If I could read their minds I'm sure I would have heard things like 'who does this bitch think she is?' and 'what prom did this chick come from?' I wanted to run away. This wasn't me. *But I'm not me. What the fuck am I doing? I'm Hannah!* And that was all I needed to get my swag back. Maybe Eva would have run and hid in the bathroom, but Hannah was going to smile at all these sluts staring her down and make sure they knew what kind of girl she was. I pushed back my shoulders, and held my head high. The look on my face could only be described as arrogant, and while my lips smiled politely, my eyes translated to 'I dare you to test me'. *This is going to be a fun night.* The stares turned to glances, and as we reached the VIP area I stopped noticing who was looking at me.

Hunter waved at a few people sitting in the small arca roped off for this 'special event' before leaning in to give the bouncer standing at the entrance his name. He glanced up at me, and checked a list he was holding before letting us through.

Like I already said, it wasn't at all what I expected. Three other couples sat around a table, laughing obnoxiously and drinking heavily. My first thought was that our cocktails on the ride over wouldn't at all be enough to put us at their level of intoxication. My second was that his colleagues were far too old to be behaving like drunken college students after a rough week of finals. Hunter went around shaking the hands of the men, and kissing the hands of the women. *Suave.* He introduced me as Eva, and they all stood up to shake my hand as well. *A party of six? What the hell kind of party is that?*

To my relief, each woman was wearing a gown that reached their ankles and had their hair pinned up in a similar fashion to my own. Each man introduced himself saying his name first before introducing his 'wife'. Even if I remembered their names, it wouldn't be important. They were all fake. The whole night was a charade. I just didn't know it yet.

The evening's conversation was juvenile, and pointless. Everyone appeared to be in their mid-forties other than Hunter and myself, yet the topics of conversation were those you could easily find in a high school cafeteria. Perhaps it was their level of intoxication, or perhaps my own personal standards. I was attending a business dinner with people twenty years my senior, and I guess I assumed they would discuss topics of importance like worldly issues or the stock market. Instead, however, I was listening to them rave about the evening's Yankee game, the latest Xbox system, and some actress' tits that I'd never heard of in some movie I hadn't seen. The story of Hunter and Eva was questioned at some point, and like I said I would, I gave Hunter the floor. It was brief, and quickly dismissed after our tall tale was told. There was no business talk, or even gossip about anyone they worked with. That should have been a red flag, a sign, an omen… fucking something.

I kept a glass at my lips throughout the entire evening. Bored by their conversation, I contributed as little as possible. I was no longer fixed on impressing these people. The other women also kept their lips locked, unless they were laughing loudly along with the men's conversation or asking for a lighter for their long, slim cigarettes. There wasn't enough alcohol in the bar to make these people entertaining, but that didn't stop me from trying. Eventually I had to take a piss, so I tried to excuse myself quietly.

"I'll be right back," I whispered in Hunter's ear and stood up.

"Are you looking for the bathroom? It's across from the bar," he said pointing back towards the way we came in.

I smiled and nodded in acknowledgement, but before I could sneak away one of the wives chimed in. "I'll show you! I have to go too!" Then before I knew it there was a short song of 'me too!' and I was being escorted to the bathroom by three stumbling hyenas in gowns and stilettos. *Ugh, fuck. The ridiculous unwritten rule of being a female is to never pee alone. It must have been decided during the time of the Dirty Dozen Bathroom Bandits! Escaped from a psych ward, it was a tragic time when a woman couldn't go into a bathroom without being cornered by the bandits for tampons and translucent powder! They're still on the loose, and now we must travel in packs!* I smirked at my insane form of sarcastic entertainment. Maybe I *had* had a few too many.

The second we got into the ladies room, they started feeding my brain with lies. All three of them were blonde and plastic-surgery looking. They could have been ordered out of a catalog, they were so damn perfect. The only flaw in their appearance were the bloodshot, droopy eyes.

"You know, Hunter really likes you!" Wife One said. She seemed to be the oldest one of the group, so she had a 'captain of the varsity squad' charm to her voice.

"Yeah! He doesn't shut up about you!" Wife Two pointed out.

"Really?" I asked skeptically.

"Yes really!" Wife Three, who was obviously the rookie of the group, added as she walked into an empty stall.

"I wouldn't be surprised if he drops the L-word soon," Wife One said before applying her lipstick in the mirror.

The L-word? Love? She got me thinking as I scurried into a stall and squatted over the toilet. *Is it too soon to tell each other that?* My fears had nothing to do with him paying me, or the fact that none of this was real. Those thoughts never even crossed my mind, because in my head I had made it real. Hunter of course had his part in helping that happen, but I was stupid enough to force anything that might conflict with the perfect relationship I had created to the garbage pail of my brain. My hesitation came from my new fear of commitment (thank you [*The Douchebag*]), and my concern that if we rushed into something we weren't ready for I would lose

181

everything… again. The apartment, the money, the clothes. The comfort, and confidence that I wouldn't be screwed over again. In my head, 'I love you' was just one step closer to the end. Why would he continue to pay for me after all the lust and love turns into a predictable and possibly boring relationship? Very few people would pay for the comfort of a relationship. He's paying me for the feelings of lust and surprise brought on by my company. *If I don't start doing the unexpected, he'll get bored and be done with me.* It was a drunk thought, but a thought nonetheless.

As I walked out of the stall, I saw the three wives huddled by the sink. I glanced over while I washed my hands and saw that they were doing lines of coke. At least that's what I thought it was.

"Save some for Eva!" Wife One demanded while Wife Three was hunched over, not appearing to have inhaled more than her share.

"Oh, no thanks guys." I waved my hand at them, signaling to continue without me. *I can't believe I thought I had to impress these people.*

It wasn't long after our bathroom trip that we said our goodbyes and parted ways. I couldn't imagine either Hunter *or* Mr. Edison working alongside those people, but I never questioned it. The fact that Mr. Edison was presented to me as an educated person of the upper-class with a high paying job, and that his 'colleagues' were behaving like retail employees of over a decade without even a G.E.D. struck me as odd, but not impossible.

The limo ride back to his hotel was more relaxed than the ride there. Not only did I have a few drinks in me, but also the pressure to get in good with his friends was long gone. Memories of the awful conversation, disgusting meal, and the three coked-out wives were quickly forgotten. The only thing that stuck in my mind from the evening was the conversation I had with the women in the bathroom regarding the L-word. Everything else was stored deep in my brain, somewhere far away from the Hunter and Eva bubble.

The crazy thing is, I knew what I was doing. I was fully aware of the fact that the relationship I had created was all in my head, but I didn't think I could go through with living the escort lifestyle if I didn't keep my mind safe. And that's what that bubble did. It kept all the other shit from poisoning my brain. I didn't think through the consequences though.

"Did you have a good time?" Hunter asked as he put his arm around me, pulling my head towards his shoulder. I nuzzled into his neck and let my eyelids drop.

"I always have a good time with you sweetie." His hand found my own and I rubbed his palm with my thumb. It was a perfect moment of silence and cheesy sideways glances. And as we walked into the hotel hand in hand, we were both grinning ear to ear. We were deep inside my imaginative bubble, and I was giddy with ignorance and intoxication. I couldn't have picked a better moment to run into [*The Douchebag*] if I'd planned it.

He was walking through the lobby shoulder to shoulder with that bitch he thought he could replace me with. They both looked like hell, which only added to my satisfaction. By the way they were dressed, I could only assume they'd spent the day in the city and were too tired to drive home. I was sure Mommy and Daddy were picking up the hotel tab.

I kept the smile inspired by Hunter's kisses on my face when I met eyes with first [*The Douchebag*] and then his whore. We glided past them in our black-tie attire with a sense of entitlement and grace. It could have been all in my head but I was sure his eyes were filled with resentment, as hers were bursting with envy. And as quickly as it came, the moment was gone. But it was all I needed to satisfy the requirements of my 'Yippee ki yay' moment.

My mind was racing with all the thoughts I hoped were running through their heads as Hunter and I stepped into the elevator. I imagined her catching him drooling over me, and punching him in the stomach as the sick realization that she could never fill my shoes finally hit her. Even through the blinding pain from her blow, thoughts of wanting me back find their way to the front of his mind. They'd argue about it all night, and [*The Douchebag*] would make the slut sleep on the floor. That's just the kind of guy he is. Then she'd lie awake all night, realizing what kind of person she got herself involved with and kick him out the next day. It wouldn't be long before he tried to come crawling back to me. I imagined his face as he stepped into our deserted apartment…

"Earth to Eva…" Hunter was waving his hand in front of my face, smiling at my sudden trip to Mars.

"Oh!" I muttered as I started to come back.

"Are you okay?"

"Yeah," I reassured him with a smile. "I guess I'm just tired." I looked around and realized we were in his bedroom.

"So, why don't you show me what you learned at your dance class yesterday?"

Ugh, I guess it's now or never.

DAY THIRTY-THREE
PART ONE

NYANI HAD ASKED ME to meet her in the lounge that night to 'catch up'. So an hour before I was meeting Hunter in his suite, I walked through that giant red door once again. To my surprise, Nyani wasn't alone. She was sitting with a man I didn't recognize, smoking a cigarette.

"Hannah! Come have a drink with us!"

She waved me over excitedly and began mixing my usual drink, four parts vodka and one part cranberry. Perhaps if she had a cock I would have realized that she was trying to keep me at a certain level of intoxication to ensure I wouldn't be too difficult to handle. But she didn't. So I didn't. I accepted my drink with a smile as I took a seat.

"Hannah, this is Mr. McPartland. He's a potential client."

I stuck out my hand for Mr. McPartland to

shake. Instead he caressed it while saying, "Pleased to meet you."

He was rugged looking, and much older than the men I was used to seeing in the club. I could tell he didn't make his money by just sitting behind some desk. His hand felt rough and callused against my own and with his potbelly threatening to pop the buttons off his shirt, I doubted they were from hours spent at the gym lifting weights.

Nyani excused Mr. McPartland, saying they would continue their conversation later. I nodded politely as he left the room, uneasy about the way he glanced back at me.

"Recent widower," she explained. "He's only in town for a few weeks. What's new chick?" She swung her chair around to face me.

"Everything!" I exclaimed. "Hunter got me an apartment a few blocks over, and I met a few of his colleagues the other night. He's even been talking about helping me pay to go back to school and teaching me to drive! Things couldn't be better."

"Hunter?" she questioned but didn't wait for a response. "Well, that's wonderful. I knew you and *Mr. Edison* would get along." She smirked, pleased with herself. "He's heading back home in the morning, right?"

"Yeah, only for a week though," I said between sips of my toxic drink.

"Perfect, we'll find a few people to occupy your time this week while he's gone then. We have to get you making money for this club!" She smiled cunningly before she continued. "What about Mr. McPartland? He might be a bit dated, but there's a lot of passion left in the old bastard. You should have heard the stories he was telling me before you got here!"

I didn't understand. "I don't want to work with anyone else. I'm just going to work with Hunt-uh, Mr. Edison, as a long-term escort." My words were barely audible. I knew in my heart that Nyani was about to fuck my world up.

"My dear Hannah!" She smirked before taking a long sip from her drink. I just glared at her, confused and unexpectedly anxious. "You must *pay* to be in this club! Nothing in life is free, my dear. I mean, you didn't think you'd get all this stuff without working for it did you?" She gestured towards my dress. I was horrified as the pieces began to fall together in my head. Nyani continued to explain. "It clearly states in your agreement that you are to work for *me* every night your main guy is out of town, as a way of paying off your membership to the club. Mr. Edison understands that you are only required to commit to him while he's in town, since he signed the same agreement. As he is leaving in the morning, you wouldn't be breaking your contract with him when you work for me tomorrow night."

My heart was racing and I suddenly felt sick to my stomach. *What the fuck did I get myself into?* "How much is my debt to the club? Maybe Hunter would be willing to…"

Nyani interrupted me with laughter. "No, no my dear! Your debt isn't for *money*, it's for your time! As long as I'm making you happy by arranging for men to take care of you financially, you must make me happy as well. And to make me happy, Hannah, you must make my customers happy. See, I don't make much money off these long-term escorting deals so I need my girls to do both in order to earn a profit and keep things running. If you want out, you're more than welcome to walk away. Like I said when I gave you the contract, you can walk away whenever you want. But you'd be walking away from everything, including Mr. Edison and that fancy new apartment he got for you. You'd also be obligated to pay me back for all of the clothes, and for each night you stayed in the hotel. I only provided you with those things at no cost because you were considered an investment. If you choose to leave, that changes. You really should have read the agreement."

I was stunned. She must have laughed her ass off at how easy it was to lure me into her damn club. "I don't think I could do that to Hunter," I muttered staring down at my glass. "He's done so much for me… I'd feel so guilty..."

"Oh, please! Do you think he feels guilty when he goes back to Ohio or Missouri or wherever the fuck he's from and makes love to his wife? Do you think he feels guilty bangin' her head against the headboard as he's fucking her from behind after he just fucked you the same way that morning? I don't think so!"

"Married?" My voice was small. I couldn't look Nyani in the eyes. Not only was I ashamed to have been so easily manipulated by her, but I was feeling betrayed by Hunter as well. It felt like I was sitting in front of Jerimiah again, hearing the same goddamn story. Except this time I wasn't so in control of my emotions. My eyes began to swell with tears. I wanted so badly to run to Hunter and beg him to tell me it wasn't true, but I was paralyzed with shock.

"Of course he's married Hannah! This isn't the Millionaire Matchmaker Club, this is *my* fucking club! You walk around calling him Hunter, looking at him with your big puppy dog eyes acting like you're *in love*! It's pathetic! You're in desperate need of a reality check. That apartment he got you is *paid for by the week*! That car he's getting you is *a rental*! Both will disappear as quickly as they appeared! *He* will disappear as quickly as he appeared!"

The tears were pouring down my face now. I sat there in disbelief, unable to speak or move. Nyani threw a napkin at me. "Wipe your face. You don't want to look like hell for your appointment with Mr. Edison." She stood up, taking the last puff from her cigarette. "And that's all it is, Hannah, an appointment with a client. We have rules for a reason. Don't break them again. I'll see you tomorrow at four o'clock."

She left me in shambles. I was crying so hard my

shoulders were nearly vibrating. *It can't be true! She must be lying! Hunter would never do this to me…*

I used the napkin Nyani threw at me and the mirror behind the bar to wipe away the dark makeup streaming down my face. It wasn't going to look perfect again, but I didn't give a fuck anymore. *Hunter will fix this… He'll make this all go away.* I snuck out the back exit of the club, with the intention of avoiding as many people as possible.

A pair of sunglasses would be nice right about now. Instead, I kept my head and eyes on the ground as I walked through the lobby towards the elevators. I could still feel the glares of the employees behind the front desk. They must have known the kind of club Nyani was running, and they certainly knew that I was one of them. I wondered how many girls came out of the lounge and walked by them with tear stained faces. The embarrassment was overwhelming, and I desperately wanted to hide.

Somehow I managed to ride the elevator up to Hunter's suite without running into a single person. He opened the door, bewildered by my appearance, but quickly moved aside as I stormed into his room.

"What happened?" I took one look at him and the tears started up again. *There's no way he could look at me with concern if he was so willing to just let other men have their way with me. I know he cares about me, I'm not imagining this!*

"Tell me it's not true, Hunter! Please, tell me it's

not true," I managed to stutter through my sobs.

His arms were around me, soothing me with warm embrace. "Shhh, it'll be okay Eva. It'll be okay," he whispered into my ear.

It was a small amount of comfort from someone I was quickly losing faith in, but it did the trick. My sobbing got under control, and I was finally able to spit my words out more clearly, "Tell me it's not true, Hunter!"

He let go of me and looked me dead in the eyes. "Tell you what's not true Eva? What are you talking about?"

"Tell me you didn't know that Nyani was going to pawn my pussy off to other clients! Tell me you're not married! Tell me the apartment you got me isn't paid for by the week and that car isn't a fucking rental! Tell me Nyani made it all up! Tell me I'm not disposable!"

He stood before me speechless, but his eyes gave away the answer I was dreading. I fell to my knees in sobs as the reality of my situation sank in. My imaginary bubble of Hunter and Eva had burst beyond repair. I felt like a fool. A fool for not seeing through Nyani's lies, a fool for signing an agreement without reading it all the way through, a fool for falling in love with a client, and most of all, a fool for creating a world where he loved me back.

"I'm so sorry, Eva." His hand was on my

heaving shoulder. "I was just trying to follow Nyani's rules, ya know? No details..."

"Fucking liar!" I glared angrily up at him through my tears. "*You* were the one who said 'rules are meant to be broken'! You told me every other detail about your life, and left your wife out on purpose! I thought you were different from the other men in the club, but you're not! You're even more disgusting because you made me believe you actually cared about me!"

"Care about you? Eva, I *pay* for you!" His tone was cruel and out of character. "You're a hooker for God's sake!"

It stung worse than I thought simple words ever could. "That's all I am to you? A hooker? You never cared about me? Not even a little?" I was practically begging him to admit his feelings for me

"I don't care about anyone! Especially not some *whore* I'm paying for!"

The expression on his face was fierce and heartless. I took a moment to just look at him, finally able to see the real person I signed my body away for. There was a hint of regret in his eyes. Whether it was for the things he'd just said to me, or for meeting me at all, I didn't know. It didn't matter anymore. I definitely regretted meeting him. I regretted choosing him instead of any of the other men in the bar that night. They would have treated me like a whore, and I never would have broken the rules. Then I never would have got things so twisted. But that wasn't part of Nyani's plan. I would never have been allowed to pick someone else. She only said that to let me *think* I was in control of the situation, but in reality, I was her goddamn puppet from the day we met.

I managed to stop crying, and picked myself up off the floor. Hunter calling me a whore didn't make me feel like one. I knew I wasn't…but I also knew I'd have to learn how to be one sooner than I liked.

As I headed for the door, Hunter grabbed my arm to stop me. "Please, Eva. Please don't go," he whispered. I ignored him and kept walking. Every emotion had been drained from me. My stare was blank and unreadable. "You can't leave until I get what I paid for!" he shouted after me, but I was already in the doorway. I heard glass smashing against the wall behind me, but I paid it no mind.

Nyani was right. I shouldn't have broken the rules.

Before I could make it into the hallway, I felt his hands on the back of my neck. Next thing I knew, I was on my back and Hunter was closing the door to his suite. I laid there, disoriented and confused until he grabbed me by my hair and started dragging me across the carpet.

"You should have listened to me, you stupid slut. I'm gonna get this done whether you like it or not."

I screamed and flailed my arms and legs in a desperate attempt to grab onto anything that would anchor my body. *No! This isn't happening!*

"Please, Hunter! Stop! You're hurting me!" I felt hair slowly breaking away from my scalp. He ignored my protests, but I was finally able to get my grip on the white couch he joked about spilling soy sauce on the first night we met. That's what was going through my mind as he jerked my head around, trying to force me to loose my grip. Finally, his grasp loosened and I was able to get a long enough break from the pain to scream for help as loud as I could.

"Shut the fuck up, you bitch!" He brought his boot down on my face and everything went black.

WHEN I WOKE UP, I first felt the softness of the bed comforter against my cheek. The stripper pole was a blurry image when my eyes finally fluttered open. I tried to move, but my arms were tied behind my back and to my ankles. *Fucking bastard.* I couldn't even roll over. Wet tears had caused my hair to stick to my chin. I screamed, but thick tape muted my voice. My dress had been removed, leaving me in the lingerie I had picked out just for Hunter only a few hours earlier. *Hope you like it you sick fuck.*

"Well, look who's finally awake." Mr. Edison came into my field of view, wearing only his boxers. There was no way to tell how long I'd been unconscious, vulnerable to his twisted pleasures. "So, we can either do this the hard way or the easy way." He grabbed my chin and spoke barely an inch away from my face. "You can give in to what I'm about to do to you, or you can fight it. Either way, it's gonna happen. And, if you fight it I guarantee Nyani will hear about it. I'm sure you'll end up in the same place as all the other whores who try to walk away from this club." He backed away from my face, and slid his hand over my back. I yelped as he used all of his strength to smack my ass cheek.

"So, what do you say Eva? Are you gonna be a good girl?" I nodded my head, and he smacked my ass again. "What? I can't *hear you*!" The pain shot up my back, and a single tear fell from my eye. I nodded my head harder and screamed 'yes!' as loud as I could through the duct tape.

"Good little slut." He sat on the bed behind me, running his hand over my thigh. "I'm gonna do the dirtiest things to you!" There was a sick excitement in his voice that made me cringe. I closed my eyes. *Take me somewhere else, take me away from this hotel room.*

The torment started immediately. He smacked me across the face and grabbed me by the throat before he started with his finger in my ass, rougher than usual but bearable. I was almost relieved. "Do you like that you little whore? Do you like my finger in your tight asshole?" I moaned in protest as he stretched me out with another finger. "Hmm, I don't think my fingers are big enough to please a slut like you. Good thing I have a few toys."

My heart raced as I felt the bed shift and listened to his feet shuffling out of the room behind me. I wanted so badly to be unconscious again, to be dead even. He was back, and grabbed my hair to pull me towards his face. "Are you ready for this baby?" he asked licking the side of my face and throwing me back towards the bed.

The first object he tried to shove inside of me didn't fit. While I was thankful, he got angry and smacked me on the side of the head. I saw black spots as he hit me again and again. Tears streamed down my face, but I wanted him to keep hitting me. I wanted him to knock me out. The next object he had fit, and I cried and moaned as he roughly shoved it inside me. I tried *so hard* to clear my mind and block out what he was doing to me, but I just couldn't.

He snatched my throat, tightening his grip and cutting off my air. I gasped and squirmed but there was nothing I could do. My face grew hot, and my eyes felt like they were going to explode. *This is it, this is how I'm going to die.* The blackness fogged my vision and my body felt relaxed and went limp. Surprisingly, he released his grip and the air rushed back into my lungs.

"I'm not gonna let you off that easy bitch."

The abuse continued for what felt like an eternity. The sound of my muffled cries, my choked out gargles, him smacking my ass and the side of my face still haunt my subconscious mind. By the time the tape was ripped from my lips, I could no longer muster up the energy to scream for help. My lips felt chapped, and sticky from the tape. I could feel blood dripping out of my bruised ass, and could only be thankful he hadn't touched my other hole. 'I wouldn't want to ruin your money maker, I know a slut like you needs that intact.'

I was dragged by the hair to the edge of the bed, far enough so my head hung off the side. Mr. Edison stood above me, and removed his boxers. My hope of it being over was destroyed.

"Open your mouth slut and suck my fucking cock." He ripped my head up, forced my lips apart with his dick and fucked my mouth, gagging me in the process. I struggled to move away from him, but he just pushed himself further down my throat. Warm vomit came up my throat, and drooled down my chin. My teeth became my only weapon.

"Oh, I love when you bite my cock. Bite it harder!" *You sick fuck!* He smacked me in the face and repeated himself. "Bite it harder!" I did. I was disgusted that he got some kind of sick pleasure out of it, but I enjoyed biting as hard as I could on the most sensitive part of his body. It was the closest I could get to revenge, and I *absolutely* tried to make his dick bleed. He smacked me again, and I was finally relieved of the gagging as he slid out of my mouth. He released his load on my face, and let out an agonizing moan.

I was horrified, but it was finally over. My night from hell was over. He released my arms from my ankles, and every muscle in my legs cried for relaxation. My arms were released, and I immediately curled up in a ball trying to wipe my face off with my hands.

"Let's get you cleaned up," he said lifting me off the bed and carrying me on his shoulder into the bathroom. He dumped me on the floor of the shower, still wearing my bra and panties. I didn't dare to move. The water was ice cold and awoke every nerve in my body, but I welcomed it. Mr. Edison threw a bar of soap at me and walked out.

I sat there hugging my knees, shivering as I tried to hold back sobs. The water flowed red with blood. I let it hit my face, hoping to wash away the memories of what had just happened. The pain was unimaginable. I barely managed to clean myself off before the water was turned off, and my dress and shoes were thrown by my feet. It's all a blur, but I don't think he said much as I left his room. I didn't bother to put on my heels as I headed up to the roof.

The bar was closed, but a few late stragglers were still hanging out. I don't know why I went up there, I didn't want a drink and I definitely didn't want to talk to anyone. I just wanted a moment alone to clear my head. That's not how it worked out though. I barely got a minute of peace before a stranger interrupted my thoughts.

DAY THIRTY-THREE
PART TWO

HE SAID HIS NAME was Martin. I didn't even glance in his direction when he plopped into the lounge chair next to mine, greeting me with some cheesy comment about my disheveled appearance. I flat-out ignored him. Everything about my demeanor was screaming 'fuck off', but he kept speaking nonetheless.

I kept my eyes up at the night sky as he blabbed on and on about his shitty life. The city lights made the sky appear nearly as bright as day. I was longing to be back home on Long Island, just long enough to get a glimpse of a star or two. Or anything that would give me that spark of hope I needed to jumpstart my motivation and get through this bullshit. My mind was spinning with ideas of escape, but I was frozen to that chair. Whether it was shock or fear, I couldn't say, but for some reason I didn't run. I thought about it though.

I can take what money I have saved up and leave… just

hop on a train and never look back. Nyani would never be able to find me. I can head south and spend my days lying on a beach. Get some kind of bullshit job to survive, and maybe save enough money to go back to school one day. Would I have to change my name? Change my hair color? Who would she send to look for me anyway, her army of whores? Would I always have to watch my back? Will I spend my days looking over my shoulder? No, she'd never find me. She probably wouldn't even waste her time looking. Whatever Hunter said about me ending up like all the girls who've tried to leave had to be a lie. He was just trying to intimidate me…

"Want some of this?" Martin asked me nearly shoving a plate on my lap covered in lines of coke. *Why the fuck not. Maybe this is the shooting star that will give me the inspiration I need to get the fuck out of here.* I was relieved he had interrupted my train of thought at that moment, preventing me from reaching the thought that would inevitably cross my mind… *what if Hunter wasn't lying?*

My eyes began to tear as the burning sensation filled my nostrils. It didn't have the immediate effect I expected, or perhaps needed at that moment. So I just slumped in my chair as Martin chewed my ear off, impatiently waiting for the drug to kick in and trying to control the urge to snort everything he had until I couldn't feel my face. Or at the very least the throbbing pain surrounding my ass hole.

Finally, this guy Martin said something about 'the club' and some 'bitch' not letting him in, and my ears perked up. The conversation quickly became interesting.

"What kind of club?" I asked innocently. There was no doubt in my mind he was talking about Nyani's club.

"A club for men looking for a certain kind of, umm, company," he said with a smirk. "I was tryin' to getta girl for the week, ya know? I mean, it's the only reason I'm stayin' in this hotel. I read about it on the internet somewhere. *What the hell? Nyani advertises this shit?* The girls are clean, like they ain't no hoes. Apparently it's *really* exclusive though. The bitch didn't even care enough to give me a price before turning me down. I got the money! But no, they aren't looking for new 'members' right now. Said somethin' about bein' in the process of relocatin'. *Relocating? What, where?* What kind of business turns down customers? She pointed out a few broads I could pay for, ya know, by the hour. But I ain't into *that* shit." He let his eyes widen as he shook his head hard, as if to say the girls he'd pay for by the hour were far dirtier than the girls he could hire for a week. *I wonder how he would react if I told him they were the same girls.* "I'm not tryin' to get no crabs or herpes or any of that nasty shit. I have twenty grand just chillin' in my room now cuz that bitch wouldn't even give me a chance."

Twenty grand? This idiot will be perfect to fund my ticket to freedom. I quickly turned up the flirt.

"You know, I work for that club as a long-term escort. We *also* charge by the hour."

Martin's smile brightened. "Can you to tell me

202

that?"

Technically there's nothing in the rules that says I can't. "You don't look like a cop to me."

"You've got that right baby." He put a cigarette in his mouth and smiled as he lit it. "So what would a girl like you charge a guy like me for the week?"

"Depends what you're looking for." *Please don't be into anal…*

"Nothing fancy, just tryin' to get my dick wet and have someone to chill wit. I'm not into anythin' freaky if that's what yo gettin' at." I began to notice his speech was slurred, and his eyes were bloodshot and sunken in. This was my chance to take advantage, just enough to benefit myself without turning him off.

"Well, I can do it for three hundred an hour. Cash up front, and no one in the club can find out about our arrangement. Club escorts aren't supposed to take on clients outside of the club. If you like how things go tonight and want to meet up again, I'll give you my personal number and you can text me. I can't guarantee the whole week since we're, uhh, relocating, but I promise at least three nights." I grabbed the cigarette from his mouth and took a drag. There was no way to know if I could meet up with him again the next two nights, but I knew it was what he was looking for. So I lied out of desperation. My price was absurdly high for what he'd be getting, but I'm sure it was a small chunk of change compared to the price

Nyani would have requested. I had to ask for enough money for it to be worth the risk though. *If the wrong people find out about this…* I shuddered at the thought of what could happen to me.

"Well damn," he said taking back his cigarette. "Let's head back to my room then, shall we?" He stood up and reached for my hand. I let him take it, feeling pretty damn good about myself, and followed him inside.

MARTIN'S ROOM STANK of cigarettes and kitty litter. Clothes had been chucked all over the floor or poured out of dresser drawers. It was far too much to bring on a single week's vacation. He muttered an apology as he quickly tossed the clutter from his bed onto a nearby chair. During the few appointments I had with Martin, I never once saw a cat. I also never saw proof that he actually had as much money as he claimed. His hotel room was small, and ordinary. The room I had shared with Tanya was even a little bigger than his.

Martin's attire was always boring, and clearly inexpensive. He continually wore a t-shirt three sizes too big displaying a ridiculous slogan on the front, and baggy jeans with unintentional tears in knees. I always saw him in the same flat-rimmed hat even though there were others scattered around his room. He never told me his back-story, or where he got all his 'money'. During one of our appointments, while he was too high to notice anything but the television screen, I created my own version of his life. I imagined he grew up poor, in some ghetto where he was the only white kid on his block. His grandmother raised him, because his mother had left when he was a baby and wound up being a cracked-out whore. Maybe she was found in a dumpster, or in a gutter. In my story, she was always found dead somewhere. Then on his thirtieth birthday, a man shows up at his grandmother's door. Martin still lives there because she's sick and dying. His life of pursuing his dream as a baller is put on hold while he takes care of her. The man who showed up at his grandmother's door is an old friend of his mother's, and claims to be his father. After hours of 'fuck you for not being there' and 'I hate you', Martin finally breaks down and accepts his father who happens to be a successful doctor or lawyer or something. When Martin's father sees the unemployed bastard son he's created with no high school degree and zero chance of making it in the NBA, he decides the only thing he can do to make up for lost time is to give him a small fortune. In his mind, it's a way to help Martin get on his feet and on his way towards a more successful life. Unfortunately, Martin would rather spend it on a tiny ass hotel room in New York City, a shit ton of coke, and a hooker. So, that's what he does after his grandmother finally passes. The End.

After I had Martin's three hundred dollars in my bag that first night, I let him kiss me. My mouth was devoured by tongue and saliva, and it took all I had in me not to laugh at the poor guy. I could feel his tongue on my teeth and our combined mucus dripping down my chin. Without thinking, I pulled my head back and wiped my mouth off with the back of my hand in disgust.

"What's wrong?" he asked annoyed. I'm sure I wasn't the first girl to wipe the nastiness off their face after kissing him.

"Nothing, I'm just not supposed to kiss clients. I forgot to tell you."

"Oh, ok." And that was it. He moved his lips to my neck and I never had to deal with his drool on my face again.

When he said he wasn't into anything freaky, he wasn't lying. Martin completely skipped foreplay, and was ready to go and searching for a condom within the first two minutes. *This is going to be even easier than I thought.* He kept his enormous t-shirt on, which read 'Hi Haters' on the front and 'Bye Haters' on the back, the entire time. He looked ridiculous when he was down to nothing but the shirt and his long red socks, which he also kept on the entire time. I slid off my panties as he had his back to me, playing around with the condom for much longer than anyone his age should.

"Do you want me to do it?" I asked rubbing his back.

"Nope. Got it."

He climbed on top of me, pulling his t-shirt down probably as an insecure habit. As he pushed himself inside of me, it all became clear as to why he wanted a long-term escort. I barely felt anything as he slid in and out of me. At first I thought he wasn't putting it in all the way, trying to tease me with his cock. I moaned in anticipation for the rest, but instead I got the classic 'oh fuck' cum face. He finished.

As he pulled out, I could feel the condom slip off his dick and dangle out of my pussy.

"Whops," he said and pulled the rest out of me. I let out a small yelp, and cringed at the feeling of my insides coming out. He tossed the condom on the floor among the rest of his shit, and rested his head next to me. "That was amazing."

I was in shock. Yes, of course I'd *heard* about guys who are bad in bed or cum too quickly, and even about guys with cocks so small that they're mistaken for fingers. But this guy was the fucking trifecta. I imagined that most women he was with never came back for round two. He wanted to pay for someone to keep coming back. And I had no problem if that someone was me. *Now what do we do for the other fifty-five minutes?*

I was relieved when he turned on the television, and took out more coke. "Want some?" he offered. *Why the fuck not?*

DAY THIRTY-FOUR

I SLID THE BLACK PENCIL across my eyelid, and took one last look at myself in the mirror. Only, the girl in the reflection wasn't me. It was Hannah. I reached for the clip that was holding my hair up and let it fall to my shoulders with a natural, seductive wave. I had on one of the dresses Nyani bought for me, a strapless grey thing. Looking back to that first day in the hotel when I tried on everything in my new wardrobe, I thought about how excited I was to be part of this club and shook my head at how desperate I must have been. *Desperate for what? Love? Attention?* I used to see cocktail parties and business dinners when I looked at my new dresses. Now all I could see was a future of scrubbing cum stains out of them in hotel bathrooms.

When I left my apartment for what I hoped would be one of the last times, I realized it was the *first* time I wasn't heading out to see Hunter. Instead, I was going to be sent to a random hotel room with a hideous stranger inside waiting for me to sit on his cock because no one will do it for free. As I walked through the summer air, there was no sadness, no pain. I had developed this hardened exterior, suppressing any thoughts or emotions directly related to my new life. It was a new me. In many ways, I got exactly what I wanted.

I barely had the chance to take five steps into the lobby before Nyani was in my face. She slid her arm through mine, and casually directed me towards the elevators.

"There you are, Miss. Hannah. I was just about to come look for you," she said with a profound sense of ownership over me. Without saying a word, I glared at her with intense hatred. *Martin's right. You are a fucking bitch.* "Mr. McPartland is waiting for you in room 2113. No need to go into the lounge." A couple stepped out of one of the elevators, and I was gently nudged towards its entrance. She released my arm so she could use it to keep the elevator doors open. "When you're done, meet me behind the red door with the cash and I'll give you your next room number." She dropped her hand, allowing the doors to close and forcing me to take a step back inside the mirrored cell.

I just stood there with my jaw dropped. Every ounce of my being was overflowing with rebellious energy. It took all of my strength not to open the elevator doors and pounce on that cunt's back, shattering her teeth on the lobby floor. The brief imagery brought a sinister smile to my face, and was enough to suppress my rebellion. *For now.* I pressed the button for the twenty-first floor, and glanced at Hannah's image reflecting off the elevator walls. My eyes looked small, hidden behind dark makeup. There was no life left behind them, they were empty.

As I stepped into the hallway and headed towards Mr. McPartland's room, I felt nothing. Any feelings of regret and shame had faded. Eva didn't exist inside of me in that moment.

"I'm here for Mr. McPartland," I said to the kid who opened the door to room 2113. He did a full body inspection before informing me that his father had to run out and deal with some kind of 'business emergency'. I was invited in, and the kid made it obvious I was to fuck him since his father would coincidentally be absent for the rest of the evening. Everything in me knew this was probably against all of Nyani's club rules, but I peeked over the kid's shoulder and saw the cash on the dresser. *Better than coming back empty handed from my first gig.*

Hannah walked into the room, and scooped up the money. I looked at the kid and he seemed tense. He couldn't have been more than sixteen years old. Beads of sweat were forming on his forehead and his hair looked wet and greasy. We never would have been friends in high school. I could imagine his small clique in the cafeteria all wearing similar preppy attire, pretending to know about worldly issues and discussing future business endeavors over frozen pizza and tater tots. There was no doubt he was a virgin.

"Are you sure you want to do this?" I asked. He nodded yes, so I shoved the cash into my purse and unzipped my dress. Part of me was relieved. The kid wasn't attractive, but I preferred him over his perverted old man. He must have been the result of a second marriage, maybe even third. His father looked old enough to be his grandfather.

The kid just stood there, awkwardly watching me undress. *Great, neither of us knows what the fuck we're doing. This should be interesting.* "Where do you want me?" I asked hoping to get things going and over with.

"The bed is fine," he mumbled. If he hadn't motioned towards the mattress I wouldn't have even understood what he said. The kid's nerves were empowering. I tossed my dress playfully over a chair in the corner, and hopped on the bed. *Over an hour to get ready, and the dress was barely on my back for ten minutes.* I made a mental note to cut down my prep time.

As I positioned myself on the bed, I made sure to keep eye contact and give him my best 'come fuck me' face. He barely responded to it though, only turning his body slightly to face me straight on. *Ugh, come on kid.* I motioned for him to come towards me with my finger, and he started moving at snail pace. *Oh, fuck this…* I sat up, grabbed his wrist and yanked him on top of me.

His heaviness nearly knocked all the air out of my lungs, and I had to push him up until he got a clue and rested his weight on his arms instead. I could feel his cock getting hard on my leg. *Nothing like young testosterone. This is gonna be cake.*

I rolled him over onto his back so I could straddle him. I felt surprisingly turned on by having such power over the kid. I grabbed his hands and put them on my chest. "Do you like how my tits feel, kid?" I asked throwing in a few low moans. His response was nothing less than a look of horror and an indefinable noise coming from his throat. I unhooked my bra and watched his hands tremble over my bare chest. It's very likely I rolled my eyes at this.

"Let's see what we're working with down here," I said as I began unbuttoning his pants. His dick shot through the pee-hole in his boxers, which I carefully began to slide off. I can't lie, I was definitely impressed.

His gaze hadn't changed though, and he gave me no direction so I continued to improvise. "Wow, who would have thought you'd have *that* hidden in there!" I said seductively. "Are you ready to play?" I asked grabbing hold of his cock.

"Wait!" he shouted. "Don't…" but that was all he could get out before warm cum shot all over his baby blue polo and my left hand. *I didn't even jerk it, that was easier than cake. It was like brownies. Mental note, take the guy's shirt off first next time.*

I hopped up and headed straight for the bathroom sink to wash my hand. When I came out, the kid was doing his best to clean up with a cheap box of hotel tissues.

"Sorry," he muttered without even a glance in my direction.

"No worries, kid. It happens to every guy their first time," I lied. My dress was back over my head, and I was nearly out the door when I heard him sniffling. *Shit, is he crying?* After a quick peek over my shoulder, I could see the kid was devastated. *Fuck. Just keep walking…* I couldn't leave him like that though, so I lost Hannah's persona and let Eva come back for a quick conversation. "Don't cry. It's really nothing to get upset over."

"Maybe to you it's nothing!" he shouted. I'm going to be a fucking virgin forever!" He began to sob, and I assumed this wasn't the first time he had the chance to bring the boat into the harbor and failed. The solution seemed simple enough to me.

"Just jerk off next time, like thirty minutes before." I added a hand gesture to go with my absurd suggestion.

"What? Really? That'll work?" He looked at me through teary eyes with such hope but at the same time despair. *I don't have a cock, but in theory this should work…*

"Yeah, sure."

He seemed just as relieved as I was. My relief, however, came from the fact that this conversation was coming to an end and I could leave his room.

"Can you come back later tonight?" I looked at him uncertainly. "Don't worry, I have more money and my dad won't be back until tomorrow. Please?"

"I'll try," I said and left the room. There was no way I wanted to deal with a blubbering kid twice in one night, but maybe I could figure out some way to keep the money from round two instead of handing it over to Nyani. *Now what do I do?*

I headed back down to the lobby and into the lounge. I assumed that most of the girls had an appointment since I only recognized Missy at the bar. She rolled her eyes at me as I sat down next to her. They were glazed over and shockingly red like she'd been crying.

"What do you want, new girl?" she asked me with disgust. I had a feeling that disgust was directed towards herself rather than me, but it still amazed me how much she'd changed since I met her. She was no longer the bubbly, bug-eyed southern belle.

"I just came in for a drink, Missy. No need for the hostility."

"Ha! A drink," she mimicked me. "You're gonna need something a hell of a lot stronger than that to deal with this lifestyle darlin'."

"Like what?" I asked half ignoring her as I ordered from the bartender.

"Like this," she responded pulling a ball of

newspaper out of her top and tossing it on the bar in front of me. I opened it and quickly wrapped it back up, looking over my shoulder as I did so.

"Missy! What are you doing?" My heart quickened at the thought of Nyani coming in the room and finding the coke in my hand. I shoved it in my purse. "Aren't you afraid of what will happen if Nyani catches you with this?"

She looked at me through narrowed eyes, making me feel small. "That's on me. Next time I want cash. Don't waste it, new girl," and she got up with her drink and walked towards one of the few men left in the room. The bartender put my drink in front of me as my mind began to race. Something wasn't right. There was something… *off* about this club. I wracked my brain for answers, but nothing clicked. Every ounce of my body told me to get the fuck out of there, but I needed the money. *The more money I have, the better off I'll be when I leave. Just gotta ride it out a few more days.*

"Hey there, sugar tits." An over the hill balding man with a Santa Claus pot belly peeking out from the bottom of his shirt and Unabomber sunglasses that concealed most of his face approached me at the bar. "Allan Schaener here, and you are?"

"Hannah," I responded with an occupied mind.

"Hannah? What a pretty name! I bet it'd sound even better in the bathroom with you bent over the sink and my fat sausage in ya! Oh Hannah! Oh

Hannah!" He continued to hump the air and smack my invisible ass while moaning my hooker name until out of the corner of my eye I saw Nyani waving me over to the back of the club.

"Excuse me," I muttered leaving Mr. Schaener to continue degrading me with the bartender as I slinked back to my owner like a dog with its tail between its legs. She disappeared behind the red door before I reached her.

"You must *always* meet me back here when you're done with a client, Hannah. Put my money on the table." She pointed to the table closest to her, eyeing me with urgency. I quickly opened my purse and pulled out the cash, careful to avoid the balled up paper containing my gift from Missy. *What would she do if the coke accidentally fell out and onto the floor? I've already broken her rules, and she didn't do shit about it.* The newspaper had come undone a little, and I noticed there was something odd about it. *Later Eva. Later.* I tossed the cash on the table and quickly shut my bag.

"You have fifteen minutes until your next appointment. He's waiting in room 1622. Make sure you freshen up in the bathroom, and use *all* of the items in the basket on the counter. Our clients don't pay for stank pussy." Her voice was harsh, and blunt. I waited a moment for my cut, but after counting the money several times she tucked it all away. *I guess I'll get my money later then…*

THE BATHROOM OF SLAYERS was deserted, as well as most of the bar. I was relieved to see that 'sugar tits' guy had decided to go home... *unless of course he's in room1622 waiting for me.* My stomach did a double flip and almost came up my throat as I imagined him opening one of the doors I knocked on.

Inside the basket Nyani had mentioned were an array of products not normally found in public restrooms, things that only a less-than-fresh woman would consider using. *Or a hooker.* There were feminine wet wipes, old Q-Tips, baby powder, noticeably used razors, condoms, a communal deodorant stick, a hair brush, body spray, and a pair of wadded up old panties. It was apparent that no one had been in there for a while to restock, or more importantly, toss out the clearly unusable items. I grabbed a wet wipe, and headed for a stall. *Wouldn't want a client complaining to Nyani my pussy smells like condoms.* So I let the cold, wet cloth rinse away the grime of my new lifestyle before taking a quick piss.

It hit me while I sat on the toilet why the newspaper article didn't look right. I reached in my bag and pulled out the crumpled up ball. As I unwrapped the coke, I noticed that Missy hadn't just ripped up a piece of newspaper to disguise the baggie. The edges had all been cut. She wanted me to see this particular article, and I knew why as soon as I began to read it.

The door to the bathroom swung open and I quickly shoved the article and the coke back into my purse. After I finished my business, I grabbed a few condoms and quickly left. My head was spinning with theories the entire journey to room 1622, but I knew it would all have to wait.

HE NEVER GAVE ME his name, but I guess names don't matter in this business.

"Wanna smoke first? It helps me last longer."
Great, cuz that's what I want… you to last longer.

"Sure," I said as he handed me the cash. He had a bowl out by the window, and I could tell by the smell of the room that he had already smoked before I got there.

I was surprised Nyani had given me such a young, good looking guy instead of letting one of the other girls have him. But I guess she knew better than I did that the better looking the guy, the harder the work is. And I definitely worked for my money during that appointment. He fucked me for the entire hour minus the five minutes we were smoking and bullshitting. I almost thought he was going to go over the hour, and I'd have to charge him extra… *right? Who the fuck knows.* I didn't have to tell him to wrap it up though. Maybe he was just making sure he got his money's worth, right down to the last minute.

"If I request you again another night, would you be interested in doing… umm… other things?" he asked me as I started getting dressed.

"Like what?" I asked. He came off rougher in bed than I had expected, and seemed to be doing whatever he wanted to do with me already. *What more could you want?*

"Maybe a little rougher? Some choking and slapping?" He was standing by the window in his boxers packing another bowl. *So that's why he needs a hooker. Normal girls don't want to walk around with bruises all over their face.*

"We can make some kind of deal, but it would have to stay between us. My employer would never allow this," I said slipping on my dress, smirking at the term 'employer'.

"Yes, of course. I would never say anything." I trusted him, only because he had a sweet smile.

"Pay me double and you can do whatever you want, as long as there's no blood and it doesn't kill me. Deal?" My eyes flared with greed. I saw the money that was going to come my way between this hot guy and Martin, and my dreams of escape were finally becoming a possibility. Then I remembered the kid that was waiting for me for round two, and I got giddy with excitement. *I'll easily make two grand this week behind Nyani's back.*

"Sounds like a good deal to me," the guy said. *Idiot.* "See you tomorrow then."

As I headed downstairs to hand off the money to Nyani, I checked my phone and noticed I had five text messages. The first one I read was from Martin, asking if I was free that night. *For three hundred dollars, I think I can make time for you.* I held off on responding. It would look bad if I told him I'd be free in an hour if Nyani had five more guys lined up for me. I had a feeling there wouldn't be any more appointments for me since *Slayers* was so empty, but who knows how the appointments were made.

The other four text messages were from Mr. Edison.

"IM SO SORRY EVA."

"PLEASE DON'T BE MAD AT ME."

"WHY AREN'T YOU ANSWERING ME? I HAD TO DO WHAT I DID TO YOU, DON'T YOU UNDERSTAND?"

"YOU HAVE NO IDEA WHAT YOU GOT YOURSELF INTO."

What the fuck is he talking about? He had to knock me out and shove things up my ass? What the fuck kind of excuse is that? My anger over what he did to me overrode any rational thought. I knew I'd gotten myself into some stupid shit, I just didn't know how bad it was yet.

Nyani took my money, and smugly asked how it went. Instead of following my first instinct and spitting in her face, I smiled and said it was 'hot'. She looked disappointed, but she had no more appointments for me and I was officially 'off duty'. I was relieved. The second I stepped into the elevator I texted Martin back saying I would be there in an hour.

WHEN THE KID in room 2113 opened the door, he seemed flabbergasted to see me again.

"I uh, didn't think you'd come back," he said as he moved aside to let me in.

"You asked me to," I shot back. "Do you have money for me?" I wanted to get it over with as quickly as possible. Every part of me was fighting the urge to take the news article out of my bag and read it fully. For some reason, I didn't think it was safe yet. The paranoia had started.

The second the kid's money was in my purse, I started to strip. "Take your clothes off," I demanded. He was still wearing the same cum stained polo from earlier in the evening.

It didn't take him very long to get hard again. I pulled out one of the condoms from the basket and put it on him without actually touching skin. Then I hopped on his cock as fast as I could. *I have no time to deal with the kid's tears again. There's more money to be made tonight.* His dick was enormous for a kid and it felt pretty damn good inside of me, but I tried not to let it show. I rode him slowly at first, trying to prolong the outcome a bit, but it was barely a minute before he was twisting his face and breathing heavier. So I leaned over and fucked his cock until he moaned and cursed in agonizing pleasure.

I giggled with him, and congratulated him on his long awaited defeat before I got dressed and left. Part of me felt guilty for taking away something that should be saved for someone special, but this was what he wanted. This was how he wanted it to happen, and that's what I tell myself every time the guilt of sleeping with a child seeps in. *Child molesters say the same thing, don't they? 'She seduced me!' or 'She wanted it'. Fucking gross.*

MARTIN WAS LOOKING through the selection of movies he could order when I got there. He didn't seem to notice or mind that I was twenty minutes early.

"Can I pay you for two hours, and you stay and watch a movie with me?" he asked handing me a small mirror with a line of coke on it for me.

"Sure, Martin." I said inhaling the line. "Can I just use your bathroom before we start the movie?"

I couldn't wait any longer. I had to read the article. Martin nodded, and I rushed off making sure to lock the bathroom door behind me. Maybe it was all the coke I'd been doing, but I was paranoid as fuck. I searched the entire bathroom for the sign of something… anything that would mean someone could see me. A camera, a peephole, I had no idea. I finally decided that there was no way Nyani could see me in that bathroom. She didn't even know I was seeing Martin as a client, and that bathroom would be the safest place to do what I had to do. I turned off all the lights anyway, and used my cellphone to read the article.

It was titled '**MISSING GIRL FOUND DEAD**', and there in the bottom corner of the article was a picture. There was no doubt in my mind that it was Tanya, my incredibly immature roommate. According to the article, her real name was Lauren Smothers. She was adopted as a baby into an extremely wealthy *(white)* family from the Upper East Side, where she also attended a prestigious private school. One day she didn't show up to school, where she was a sophomore, and she hadn't been seen since. That was about a month ago. Thirty-seven days to be exact. The article didn't give any details as to how she was killed, or where she was found. It was full of quotes from her classmates saying how 'outgoing' and 'happy' she seemed, and they didn't think she would have 'run away' or 'left by choice' like the police were saying. The article ended with a request from the parents for any answers, and the implication of a cash reward. *Cash reward for what? An answer that satisfies your curiosity? That gives you closure? Would knowing your fifteen year old daughter was lured into a world of prostitution really make you sleep better at night?*

I took one last look at Tanya's picture. It was a yearbook photo, showing off her school uniform and braces. She did look happy like the article said, but I knew better. A smile is easy to fake. Anyone can *look* happy if they try hard enough. I ripped up the newspaper and threw it into the toilet before I pissed on it and let it disappear into the New York sewers.

Martin handed me six hundred dollars when I walked out of the bathroom, and I shoved it into my purse before getting in bed with him. He didn't want to have sex right away, so I used the entire duration of the lame romantic comedy he made me watch to let my paranoia consume me.

They killed her, I know they did. 'They' being Nyani and…. and who else? Who is she working with? The other escorts? No, they're her money-makers. But maybe not all of them… some of the girls could be helping out behind the scenes, keeping an eye on us. If that's true, Missy definitely isn't working with them. Why else would she warn me with this article? That's what it was right, a warning? Because I'm next. If I don't start playing by the rules, I'm next. Or perhaps it was already decided. I broke too many rules with Mr. Edison, and it pissed them off. Death for breaking the 'no kissing' rule isn't sensible, but none of this makes sense anymore.

Last time I saw Tanya she was screaming at someone on the phone. Who was she talking to? And why was she so pissed off? Was she trying to escape that night? Is that why she came back to the room in the middle of the night? To pack? No, I don't remember her taking anything. What would I take if I was leaving? Money… maybe a change of clothes. So where did Tanya go wrong? How did she fuck up and get caught?

Every part of me wished I could go back to the night I last saw Tanya and ask her what happened. *Should I be afraid? Am I next?*

DAY THIRTY-FIVE

I WOKE UP WITH the overwhelming feeling that everything would be coming to an end soon, and my new paranoia motivated me to prepare for the worst. It wouldn't be long before my cozy new apartment belonged to someone else. Whatever Mr. Edison and I had was now over, which he thoughtfully pointed out to me in dozens of unanswered text messages. *Will I wake up one day, and all the furniture will be missing? Or will I try to open the door and realize the locks have been changed? Am I going to be stuck with an unpaid rent bill?* I wasn't going to wait around to find out… not *this* time.

However, my mistrust had forced me to fear things much worse than not having a place to sleep at night. My actions and demeanor as I walked around the apartment would appear nothing less than absurd to an outsider. In my head, however, every action was justified by my suspicion that I was being watched. I felt their eyes everywhere. It was like an icicle constantly brushing against the back of my neck, and I couldn't stand it.

There were a few possessions that I wasn't willing to give up. Whether for sentimental reasons or simply due to the fact that I knew I'd need them while I attempted to relocate, these things found their way into my suitcase. It was go time, but I couldn't just walk out of this empty-handed and start my life completely over. *Maybe that's where Tanya went wrong. If I'm obvious about packing and keep a smile on my face maybe they won't think I'm trying to run. Nyani must know things didn't work out with Hunter, she'll think I'm just packing to move back into the hotel… I hope.*

I crawled into my oversized closet, comforted by its darkness. As I hunched over the small stack of cash I had accumulated, using the small light radiating from my cellphone to count it, fear consumed what little sensibility I had left. I'd barely made two thousand dollars as Mr. Edison's escort. Even with the extra money I'd managed to make the night before, I wasn't sure it would be enough.

My heart was racing and it became hard to breathe. I dreaded Nyani and her gang of hoes storming through my apartment and finding me in the closet with all that cash. *What would she do to me? Beat me senseless? Slit my throat?* I took a deep breath, trying to calm myself down. *She can't see you. Relax.* I knew I wasn't safe though, and quickly shoved all the cash into my purse with a trembling hand. It was time to start executing the first part of my plan.

I threw on a bathing suit and the only clean dress that could pass for a cover up before heading out the door. It was time to have a chat with Nyani. I must have gone over the conversation a hundred times in my head as I walked to the hotel and up to the rooftop bar. Every scenario I could think of ran through my mind, and I created a solution for each one. In my head, my responses reached perfection and I delivered each one with a calm exterior. The reality of the situation, however, was that nerves were shooting through my body like fireworks on the goddamn Fourth of July. I needed a drink.

Nyani was nowhere in sight when I planted myself in a lounge chair with the perfect angle to catch the afternoon sun. I sighed in relief, and let my heart find a steady beat. So far, everything was going according to plan. If she'd already been at the pool, I would have had to approach her. It would have been suspicious at the very least, especially with my damn stomach in my throat.

As I'd anticipated waiting by the pool for her as long as I needed to, I ordered a drink immediately. This was a necessary part of my plan, even though I had little money to spare on overpriced cocktails. I needed it to appear like I was relaxing, and not just waiting around for her. Being a little tipsy would also help things go more smoothly. At least I hoped.

The waiter came back with an enormous fruity concoction and placed it on the table next to me. I had no idea what I ordered, but it looked pretty damn good. As I reached into my purse and pulled out cash, he politely denied it.

"I put on Miss Nyani's tab." He had a thick

Spanish accent, but I understood every word he said.
My heart dropped.

"Oh, I'm not here with Miss. Nyani today…"

"She says put all girl's drink on her tab," he
interrupted.

I nodded. "Is Miss Nyani here today?"

"No, not today."

"Okay." I smiled and he continued to stand
there. "Thank you," I added.

He smiled and walked away. *How does he know I
work for Nyani?* I looked around the bar and suddenly
felt like I was in my own Truman Show. No one was
staring at me, or even glancing in my direction. They
were all going about their business, but my mind
wouldn't let it go. *Are they here to enjoy the bar, or are they
here because Nyani is paying them to watch me?* I continued
to gaze around the bar for over an hour, sipping on
my drink and searching for anyone who was paying a
little too much attention to what I was doing. No one
even looked at me twice. *This is fucking ridiculous.* I
sighed. *Why would Nyani hire people to watch me? Why
waste the money?*

It was after four, and Nyani still hadn't shown
up. None of the girls had shown up to hang out by
the pool that day. I stood up, accepting defeat, and
left the hotel. There was no Plan B. Of course the
idea that Nyani might not show up had crossed my

mind, but I was too busy figuring out how to react to every other possible scenario to actually come up with a Plan B. *I guess I can go back tomorrow and try again. And if she doesn't show up again? No, it's too risky. I have to put everything in motion as soon as I can. I'll have to alter the plan and talk to Nyani tonight.*

HOURS OF WRACKING my brain while I showered and prepared for Round Two of America's Next Top Slut, and I still came up with nothing. It didn't matter that I had no Plan B though, because Nyani wasn't there to give out room numbers that night. In her place was a man I'd never seen before. He appeared to be much older than Nyani, with the same smooth caramel complexion. Only his was slightly distorted by the dark scar that crossed his right cheek and continued just above his eyebrow. He was dressed in a nice black button down and introduced himself as Jim, Nyani's 'business associate'.

"Nyani is taking the night off to prepare for the party this weekend," he said casually.

"Party?" I blurted out without thinking.

"Uh, yeah. A party we're hosting for potential clients. The limo will pick everyone up Saturday night out front and take you to Nyani's." *Does this party mean a night off or free samples?* I shuddered as I answered my own question. He spoke with grace and intelligence as he presented me with the details of the party. Every word was a lie, but nothing about his demeanor gave it away. There was no sign of my cut of the work I put in the previous night as he gave me my only client for the night. It was the hot pothead with no name that offered me double to do some freaky shit. I was relieved it was a slow night.

The guy in room 1622 was being modest when he said he was into some 'light slapping and choking'. I undersold myself. It started immediately after we smoked. He pushed me onto the bed with one quick motion, and I found myself losing focus on my surroundings immediately. I rolled lazily onto my back, trying to control my stoner giggles. He glared at me with such intense desire as he pulled his shirt over his head and climbed on top of me. His abs screamed for me to touch them, so I reached out and slowly brushed my hand across them in a way an artist would run their hand over a Jackson Pollock – gently, and wide-eyed. He smacked my hand away, and restrained my wrist against the mattress. I began to extend my other hand, and he grabbed that wrist also. Throbbing pain shot up my arms as they were crushed under his weight, before they began to tingle with bloodless veins. My eyes lit up as I felt him get hard against my thigh. The roughness of his grip unexpectedly turned me on as his teeth sunk into my neck.

Finally, my arm was relieved from his mass when he released it to bring his hand between my thighs. I could hear the sounds of my wetness as he forced his fingers inside of me. My eyes rolled back in my head as I let out a small gasp.

"Mmhhm," he moaned. "You like how that feels, slut?" He took his fingers out of me and forced them in my mouth. "Do you like how that tastes? That's right, make sure you clean my fingers real good."

I went along with it and sucked his fingers, using my tongue playfully. He smacked me across the face, and flipped me onto my stomach. Black spots clouded my vision as my hand instinctively reached for my cheek.

"Get on your knees," he demanded.

This was the moment when I got that familiar feeling of déjà vu. Mr. 1622 was unknowingly bringing me back to that night in Hunter's room. The way he spoke to me was remarkably similar to the way Mr. Edison expressed himself as he beat and tortured me. I tried to push away the memories, but it was harder than I thought with the pain still lingering from the incident.

I did what I was asked though, and brought my knees up towards my chest. He immediately pushed up my dress exposing my bare ass. I could hear him moaning softly as he caressed my curves. He began smacking it with the palm of his hand, gently at first. Then harder and he did this over and over. Each time his hand came down on me, I let out a small yelp. Over time the pain became overwhelming, and I desperately wanted to tell him to stop. I didn't though… even after twenty minutes passed and tears were rolling off my chin, I let him continue. *Just wait it out, you need the money. He won't do this the whole hour.*

Fortunately I was right. He didn't.

Mr.1622 stood off the bed, and pulled down his jeans and boxers.

"Open your mouth," he said as he pressed his member against my lips in encouragement. I did as he said and didn't protest when he ripped my hair back and fucked my mouth. He wiped the tears from my face as he choked me with his cock and tore strands of hair from my head.

"Open wider bitch. Take my whole cock in your mouth."

I gagged and coughed until he pulled it out of my mouth and smacked me across the face.

"I said open wider!" he yelled and hit me a second time. His blows were unintentionally painful. I imagine he could have done a lot more damage if he put effort into it. Every second of his abuse brought me closer to leaving the room with an extra three hundred dollars in my pocket, and I refused to give up. So after the dizziness passed, I opened my mouth wider and tried to control my gag reflex. He fucked my mouth until I felt his warmth hit the back of my throat, and I exhaled in relief.

"I'm sorry." He sounded ashamed. "I didn't mean to make you cry," he said as he wiped the tears off my face. He appeared legitimately concerned. *Concerned for a hooker? Why?*

"It's okay," I muttered. "It's what you paid for."

"Well, don't go anywhere just yet. I still have ten minutes left." I looked at the clock on the bed stand, and groaned. He was right. "Don't worry, I'll be gentle." He pushed me down on the bed slowly, kissing my neck and dropping his weight on top of me. I held my breath, preparing myself for ten more minutes of his presence. Mr. 1622 had an intoxicating smile, and even though I was certain his mind was full of sadistic fantasies that far surpassed what I'd just experienced, I still felt safe with him.

He lifted my dress up, and put his head between my thighs. At first I was amazed that he would dare to venture between the legs of a prostitute. However, after the initial shock passed I was able to lie back and enjoy the movements of his tongue. It didn't take him the entire ten minutes to make every inch of my body explode. I pulled my dress back down in a fit of giggles, and buried my head into the mattress.

"Now I don't feel so bad for making you cry," he said joining in on my giggling.

"Umm, thank you."

I was more than slightly awkward as I wobbled out of room 1622 with trembling legs, as I didn't expect to get pleasure out of paying customers. Not on purpose at least.

After dropping off Nyani's share of the money with Jim and pocketing my half, I stopped by Martin's room. It was my new safe place. The only location I knew I wasn't being watched. I could relax, do a few lines, and clear my head long enough to come up with a new plan.

"Who is it?" I heard him grumble from the other side of the door after I knocked for the third time.

"It's Hannah."

"Are you alone?" I rolled my eyes.

"Of course I'm alone Martin." He opened the door a crack, and peered down the hallway before opening the door just enough for me to slip inside.

"Did anyone follow you?" He was high as fuck, sweating through his t-shirt and double locking the door like someone would be along any minute to bust it down.

"No, no one followed me Martin," I said firmly hoping to get his eyeball out of the peephole. "I just thought you might want some company tonight."

"You almost missed the beginning of the movie," he said finally stepping back from the door and stumbling over towards his bed. He opened the nightstand draw and pulled out that fancy Bible that comes in every hotel room. Stuck between the pages were all hundreds and fifties. He pulled out six hundred dollars and handed it to me without asking if I could stay the two hours. I could, of course. The guy still could have asked though.

"I don't like my money wrinkled," he said to explain why he kept it in the Bible.

"Oh," I replied with an amused grin. "Me either. Maybe I should try the Bible thing."

He handed me the handheld mirror he usually did coke off of, and I helped myself to a few lines. I justified it in my head as the only way to escape my paranoia. In reality, it was only making it worse. The movie started, and so did my brain. I needed a sensible plan that would allow me to get away from this mess. The party at Nyani's was two nights away, so I had one more night with clients; one more night to squeeze as much money out of them as possible.

Half way through the movie, Martin asked me to climb on top of him. I was annoyed he had interrupted my thoughts, and frustrated that I hadn't come up with a solid plan yet. As I lifted up my skirt, I felt his hands turning my waist so he could get a better look at my rear.

"Woah, what the fuck happen' to yo ass?" He extended his arm in attempt to examine what I assumed had become massive welts and bruises. I quickly pushed his hand away.

"Don't touch. I fell. Down the stairs earlier." I started sliding off his pants, avoiding eye contact and hoping the bruises disguised any marks resembling a hand.

"It looks really bad Hannah." He was concerned

about me. *Two guys in one night, concerned about me… a prostitute.* I couldn't hide my smirk.

"It's fine, really. It doesn't hurt too bad." Then I sat on his tiny cock to shut him up, and as usual it was over before it began.

"That was amazing," he whispered in my ear as he pulled me down to the bed and wrapped his arms around my waist.

"Yeah," I said rolling my eyes. *He can't actually think that was good.* "Do you want to do another line?" He released me from spooning to grab the coke. *Hookers don't spoon babe.*

I spent the rest of my time with him staring blankly at the television screen, and coming up with a strategy so full of holes I couldn't even call it a plan. It was more like a possibility, if I *happened* to end up in the right place at the right time. *Well I hope the right place is Nyani's house and the right time is while everyone is too distracted by the festivities Saturday night to notice me leaving.*

DAY THRITY-SIX
PART ONE

IT WAS THE DAY before the party and I'd decided to spend it walking around the world's greatest city. I let myself get lost in the faces of the crowd as my head spun with morbid and terrifying thoughts of my near future. Everything inside me told me I was going to die soon. Even if I did manage to get through this, I thought I should at least take the opportunity to enjoy the city one last time. Who knew if I'd ever be able to come back.

So I walked, everywhere and nowhere. I did everything I dreamed I'd do when living in the big city was never a possibility. Ate a street vendor's hotdog, walked around the Met, got lost in central park. It wasn't until I decided to browse through a street fair I randomly came across that I noticed her following me. Her bright blonde hair stood out like Hitler in heaven. We made eye contact for a brief moment, but that instant was all it took for her to draw me in.

Missy didn't let me get closer than five yards behind her, but every thirty seconds or so she'd turn around and make sure I was still there. Her eyes looked red and puffy, but from a distance I couldn't tell if she'd been crying or just doing too much coke. We walked block after block in silence. *Is she leading me to them? To Nyani and her whore gang? Is this when I die?*

Without warning, she ran across the street and ducked into a coffee shop. I tried to catch up to her, but when I saw the 'DON'T WALK' sign flashing red, I hesitated… and then it was too late. My heartbeat quickened as I stood at the crosswalk, impatiently counting the seconds until the light changed. *Come on, come on!* Missy had already been inside the cafe for a good three minutes before the sign finally told me to 'WALK'. I swiftly squeezed myself through the crowd, trying not to draw too much attention to myself. Whether she knew something I didn't or she'd gone crazy with paranoia, I was positive Missy also thought we were being watched.

When I walked into the coffee shop, I half expected to catch Nyani out of the corner of my eye with a gun pointed at my damn head. *Farewell cruel world.* Instead, I was calmed by the cool breeze of an air-conditioned lounge and the delightful smell of espresso. The front of the café was overcrowded with couches and small tables where a few people were sipping their tea, and reading the paper. No blonde hair stuck out from behind the few laptops in the crowd. The line for coffee was rather short, and once again Missy was nowhere in sight.

I walked through the place keeping my eyes peeled, knowing she had to be in there somewhere. There was no panic at the thought of losing track of her. She wanted me to find her. Then, in the back of the shop, nearly hidden by the shadows of the corner, I spotted a doorway. Above it, a handwritten sign read 'Internet Café'. *Maybe she's in there.*

Her blonde locks bobbed above a computer in the very back corner, hidden by rows of deserted computers.

"Can I help you?" the clerk asked, poking his head up from behind a Sports Illustrated magazine.

I shook my head. "Just looking for someone."

She looked up at the sound of our voices. I began walking cautiously towards where she sat, searching her face for any sign of immediate danger. However, as I approached her she stood up and walked in the opposite direction. I paused in confusion. *Ugh, where is she going now?*

Missy looked back at me, and nodded towards the computer before scurrying out of the room. I took her gesture as an invitation and quickly sat at the computer she'd been using. *This is it. The truth is going to finally come out.*

Instead of the word document I expected with a lengthy explanation as to what kind of bullshit I got myself into, a website was up on the screen. *What is this?* It was for an escort service… *our* escort service.

She had directed me to a tab titled 'Meet The Lingerie Girls'. My hooker name and a small photo of me in a tight dress were at the top of the page. *Where the hell did Nyani get that picture of me?* I clicked on my photo and a video popped up. It was forty seven seconds of my worst nightmare. A 'preview' of what you could get if you bought an hour with me... clips from moments I'd thought were private and never imagined were being videotaped. These clips included my spastic pole dance, playing with my vibrator during that video chat, having sex on my kitchen table, and of course, me being tied up and raped.

All of these things had one thing in common... Mr. Edison. *He's in on it! That fucking shit! He's one of them!* Tears were rapidly falling down my face, and my stomach felt tight as I replayed the video over and over. It was obvious by the different angles that not only were there cameras set up all over Mr. Edison's hotel room and my apartment, but on more than one occasion there had been some kind of hand held camera. It was perfect for the close ups. 'Full Length Videos' were also available for a fee of 'Only $29.99 a Month!' and platinum members can even make 'Special Video Requests! Better Hurry Though! There's Only One Day Left!'. *This is porn... I'm in fucking porn! People are paying a membership to a porn site, and requesting to see me do all this shit, I can't believe this! People all over the world can fucking see this!* [The Douchebag] *can see this...my parents can see this! And what the fuck does this mean 'Only One Day Left'?*

Included in the list of my full-length videos were the three-way with Nyani and Jerimiah, and *every* single time I had sex with Mr. Edison. Each private moment had been transformed into its own edited thirty-minute film that I couldn't watch without first putting in my credit card information. I scrolled through the other girls' videos and saw that a few of them had also fucked Mr. Edison. Nyani's business partner Jim that I'd met the night before was also the lead in a few clips. Even Nyani herself got down and dirty for the sake of this website. It appeared most of them also only had 'One Day Left' for video requests. I let my head fall into my hands and sobbed. It was all a scam. I wasn't working as an escort, I was a goddamn porn slut.

A noise came from the front of the room, and I quickly reminded myself that I wasn't alone. *Stop crying like a bitch, and get your head together.* I took a deep breath and collected my thoughts. *So a few piece-of-shit human beings came to New York and created this elaborate scam to make a decent amount of money without having to pay their staff much. They decide to recruit desperate women as escorts, and have them sign a lengthy contract that none of them will actually read since the option to leave at anytime has reassured them that things couldn't possibly go wrong. Surely somewhere in that contract they're agreeing to be filmed and put on this disgusting website, but without them knowing about it Nyani can get away with only paying them for escorting. They've found girls who have close to nothing and lure them in by providing a roof over their head, and a man who claims to care about them. Then they threaten to take it all away if they don't follow the 'rules'. This control allows them to force girls to fuck for money on their terms, and even convince them that they'd owe the club a great deal of money if they choose to leave. In the end, they manipulate these girls into thinking a life in the club is better than living on the streets. I mean, that's why I'm still here right? That's why I haven't left yet. I have nowhere else to go.*

My mind continued to race. *Since 'Nyani' has been running the escort service, there has to be someone on the inside at the hotel. Someone to make sure the 'escorts' get free rooms, and someone to lie about what kind of club was really having regular meetings in the hotel bar. Maybe someone to discreetly advertise the club's services to certain guests. Someone like a hotel employee.*

I did a quick Google search for the hotel I'd been frequenting, and quickly found their staff page. To my disbelief, Mr. Edison's headshot was under the title of 'Hotel Manager'. His name wasn't Hunter… not even fucking close. *Hello Joseph Claytone. That's probably not your real name either.* Under him were photos of two men I recognized from his 'business dinner', both labeled as staff managers. I quickly searched for the other members of our dinner party, and found most of them. None of them shared the same last name, so I could only assume Mr. Edison paid them to act like man and wife for the evening. Their lack of intelligent conversation now made sense.

So, how long before the act is up? How long do they stick around before they decide they're pushing their luck and take this scam somewhere else? Because something like this can't last forever. The girls will all find out eventually. This must be why Tanya was freaking out that night… she found the website. And now she's dead…

I switched back to the escorting website and

combed through it for more answers. Most of the pages had denied access without a credit card. There was a phone number to call for 'dates' if you were in the New York City area. I punched the number into my phone and hit save, but a message popped up saying I already had that number stored...*what the hell*... I hit send. Nyani's name came up on my screen and I quickly hit end before the call went through. *Shit.*

A window popped up on the computer screen saying I had sixty seconds left of my internet session and to see the clerk if I wanted to pay for more minutes. I quickly saved the web address in my cell phone as an unsent text message. *Just in case.*

When I exited the café, I allowed the anger that had been building up find me again. Missy was long gone but I frantically searched the crowd for her anyway, hoping she'd waited for me so I could grab her by the shoulders and demand that she tell me more. I began to envision everyone I knew stumbling upon the website, and recognizing me. My father, grandfather, uncles, guys from high school, Jerimiah... all watching me stick my own fingers up my ass. I wanted to vomit.

By the time I found a bench to collapse on my rage had subsided, leaving room for self-hatred and absolute embarrassment to reach the surface. I was ashamed that I'd fallen for all the bullshit Nyani threw at me, believing she was my friend. Even more, I was humiliated for falling for Mr. Edison. I'd trusted that he cared about me, but he was just buttering me up for my big cameos in his films.

I wanted to scream until my voice failed me, and the blood vessels in my eyes burst. Mr. Edison had to pay for what he did to me, they *all* did. I pulled out my phone and made the impulsive decision to text him.

"**Meet me for a drink tonight away from the hotel.**" *He won't ask why.* I didn't have to wait long for a response.

"WHERE AND WHAT TIME?"

I told him I would text him when I was finished 'working'. It was time to head back to my apartment, and get ready for Round Three.

AS I GOT READY for my evening, I could feel the intrusive eyes of my new fans burning holes in the back of my neck. For all I knew, there was a live feed going on the entire time I was living there. So, I skipped the shower but I didn't want to act too much out of character. When it was time to slip into my uniform, it took all the courage I had not to change in the damn closet. Or better yet, not change in the apartment at all and just take the dress with me. *I could probably change in the bathroom in* Slayers *really quick…* Panic spread across my face when I realized I was hesitating. I threw off my clothes, and started to change like I normally did. *You fucking idiot, they could be watching right now! Stop acting like a dumbass! They can't know you know about the cameras! Are you trying to get yourself killed?*

Red blotches invaded my neck and chest as anxiety consumed my body before I managed to hurry out of the camera's view and into the hallway. The numbers below the buttons in the elevator came in and out of focus as I attempted to hit the one labeled 'Lobby'. My breathing was out of control and I nearly burst into the city streets, gasping for fresh air. I didn't feel safe in there anymore, and even though I was off to prostitute myself for money I would never get to spend, I was relieved to leave my apartment.

My paranoia of being watched had been justified, and I was straddling the line of sanity. Every step towards the hotel was a challenge not to look behind me. I was sure that I was being followed, but I couldn't let them know I knew.

Nyani was back to hand out 'assignments'.

"Hey," she said casually as I walked through the big red door. "Nice dress."

"Thanks," I muttered. I could have smacked her.

"Mr. McPartland is waiting for you in 2113," she said casually looking over her notebook. I would have loved to see how many appointments were made throughout the day, and calculate how much money she was stealing from all of the girls. I'm sure it was chump change compared to the money the website brought in though.

"Did you need something Hannah?" I was lingering.

"Yes, actually." I waited until she looked up at me before continuing. "Have you spoken to Mr. Edison recently? I'm afraid he's no longer interested in keeping me as his escort, and he has asked me to move out of the apartment," I fibbed.

"Yes," she grinned smugly, "he mentioned that things weren't going to work out. So?" I wanted to beat the smile off her face.

"Well, I was just wondering if I'm on my own for finding a place to live or if I could move back into the hotel?" I was playing the concerned prostitute role very well considering everything I'd discovered that afternoon. Desire for revenge had turned me into quite the actress.

"Oh," she stared at me as she pondered for a moment. "You'll move back into the hotel. I'll make arrangements for you after the party tomorrow."

"Okay, thank you so much Nyani. I was starting to worry I'd end up on the streets!"

She continued to glare at me with that sick smile she produced so frequently. The bitch was proud that I seemed to finally realize I couldn't survive without her. So I decided to wipe the smirk off her face in another way.

"It would actually be great if I could move back in with Tanya. Does she have a new roommate yet?" I couldn't help myself. "I know she drove me crazy a bit, but I'm actually starting to miss the girl. Have you seen her around?" Nyani's face went dark immediately.

"No," she said looking back down at her book. "I'll do the best I can about your sleeping arrangements. You should go see your client now."

"Yes, you're right! Wouldn't want to keep him waiting!" I waved, my face beaming as I gave her my best fake-friendly 'see you later!'

Strolling up to Mr. McPartland's room, I couldn't help but giggle a little. It was fun to see Nyani squirm a bit. I wanted so badly to be inside her head at that moment. *Was she wondering what I knew? Scared that I noticed Tanya was missing? Trying to tell herself she's just paranoid and that I don't know anything?* It probably wasn't the smartest idea to mess with her, but it was all going to be over soon enough.

I was surprised to see the actual Mr. McPartland open the door instead of the kid. Maybe even a little disappointed.

"We meet again!" I wanted so badly to roll my eyes at his cheesiness. Instead I walked into his room, and greeted him politely. *Hopefully he's just as easy to get off as his son was.*

He handed me the cash, and we immediately got

to business. Mr. McPartland was definitely a tit man. He was hypnotized by my breasts, releasing them from my bra like they were grenades that might explode if he wasn't careful. I moved over to the bed, and he followed me with his hands glued to my chest. It was like he'd never seen a woman's breasts before. *Maybe it's been a while.*

After sitting on the bed for what felt like an eternity of listening to him moan as he awkwardly touched me, I started to get bored and went straight for his junk. Not nearly as impressive as his son's, but it was hard enough to throw on a condom and sit on it. His face contorted into a crimson masterpiece instantly, putting his eyes on display as he let out a low horse-like grunt. He spent more time drooling over my chest than he did inside of me. I sort of felt bad for the kid as I stood up to get dressed. His future in the sack wasn't looking good if he took after his father.

Mr. McPartland remained in bed chuckling as I let myself out. *You're welcome, dick.*

"Did you enjoy that, slut?" It was the kid. He was sitting outside the door, glaring at me with disgust. I wondered how long he'd been there... how much he'd heard.

"Don't be a twat. This is my job, you knew that." I was cold and arrogant as I turned my back to him and hurried towards the elevators. *How dare he call me a slut! I did that little shit a huge favor, and this is how he repays me?*

"Of course you liked it! You're a whore!" He paused. "So, was he better than me?" Without turning around, I knew he'd gotten off the floor and was closing in on me. I sped up, hoping to reach the elevators before he caught up to me. No such luck. He snatched my arm, and aggressively pulled me towards him.

"Answer me whore! Was he better than me?" His eyes weren't looking at me, but through me. Maybe this wasn't the first time daddy fucked a girl the kid was into.

"Let go of my arm," I said firmly. It didn't matter though. He wasn't listening to me. The kid pinned me against the wall, and started kissing my neck roughly.

"Did he get you off, huh? Did he?" I struggled to get him off of me, but he was too strong. He spun me around, shoving my face into the wall as he pressed his body against my back. I felt my dress being lifted, and began kicking and throwing elbows.

"Get the fuck off of me, kid!" He laughed and pressed his body harder against mine, restraining me with his hand on the back of my neck. I could hardly breath as I felt his other hand gliding over my ass. He found the front of my thigh, and pulled on it until my legs were forced to spread. I struggled to throw him off me, but it was useless. He was too strong. I cringed as I felt him slide his fingers over my wet pussy, searching for my clit.

"So, my father made the slut wet. Did he make

you cum as well bitch? I bet he squeezed the shit out of these," he said as he let go of my neck and grabbed my tit with his left hand.

"Please, stop!" My pleas were lost in the wallpaper.

"Oh, please stop!" he mimicked. "What, I can't have you if I don't pay for you? Fucking slut!" He brought his right hand back to my ass, gently pinching and fondling it. "I bet you like it dirty." I felt his fingers sliding back and forth between my asshole and my cunt, spreading the wetness as he did so.

"No! No, please don't…" I started, but it was too late. He shoved his fingers up my ass, and I screamed as loud as I could as I felt old wounds reopen.

"Shut up bitch!" he yelled knocking my head against the wall with his free hand. Everything turned black.

THE NEXT THING I remember is being poked in the shoulder.

"Is she dead?"

"No, her eyes are opening!"

"Run!"

When my eyes adjusted, I spotted two small girls running down the hallway nearly spilling over in amusement. *Great.* The kid was nowhere in sight. I assumed someone or something startled him, and he fled. My head throbbed as I realized my dress was still pulled over my waist, exposing the goods to anyone who happened to walk by. *Real classy.* I quickly adjusted myself, and let out a low groan as I stumbled to my feet. The hallway was spinning, but there was no time to rest. I had to get into the elevator and see how long I'd been knocked out. If I was more than a few minutes late after the hour with the client, Nyani would surely be suspicious. And after our last conversation, that was the last thing I needed.

I used the wall for support, and made it to the elevator at turtle's pace. When I tumbled inside, I was relieved to see that the clock read 7:48. Mr. McPartland's hour wasn't up for another twelve minutes. The reflection in the elevator doors showed no sign of my struggle, but I thought I'd play it safe and check myself out in the bathroom before dropping off the money anyway. *Wait… the money! No way that fucking kid would have the guts…*

A wave of panic fell over me as the elevator descended to the main lobby. I ripped my purse open, and was thankful to see that the cash was still there. Either the kid was really stupid, or really smart. If he stole the money, who knows what Nyani would have her people do to him… or to me for that matter.

In the bathroom mirror, I noticed a small amount of blood drying under my nose. My makeup was also in dire need of a touchup, but nothing I couldn't have pulled off as the result of a rough session with a client. I let my fingers comb my scalp, searching for some kind of wound. Luckily all I found was a small bump that my hair did a good job at covering up. I took a deep breath. *I'm okay.*

"Your next client's in room 3245," Nyani muttered as I handed her Mr. McPartland's money.

"Thanks," I said sarcastically and started to walk away.

"Hannah?" Nyani's voice was small, and uncertain. I turned around almost concerned. *Almost.* "I'm sorry things didn't work out between you and Mr. Edison." Her words sounded sincere and almost apologetic.

"Thank you," I replied and continued to stare at her curiously for a moment before exiting the lounge. *What the fuck was that about?* I didn't have time to analyze her words, and demeanor. I knocked on the door of room 3245 two minutes later, and a woman opened the door.

"Oh, I'm sorry." I looked up again at the room number. "I must have the wrong room."

"No you don't," she said quickly before I could walk away. "Come in." She closed the door behind me, and I immediately noticed the array of sex toys spread out on her bed. "I've never done this before, but I assume I give this to you first." She held out a stack of cash for me, which weighed more than the usual three hundred. *Thanks for the heads up Nyani... fucking bitch.*

"So, what exactly are you looking for?" I could tell I was in over my head before she opened her mouth. She was probably middle-aged, but life's stress made her face look tired and worn out. Even her smile seemed energy consuming. Her body, however, seemed to have taken the brunt of it. It appeared that she'd given up on trying to attract a sexual partner a long time ago. She hadn't even bothered to change out of her work clothes for me.

"I've just always had a fantasy about being with another woman. I'm *very* new at this, so I don't have anything specific in mind." She was tense and shifted her weight, unsure of her next words. "I bought a few toys that I thought might be fun," she said motioning towards the array of shit on her bed. She was fidgeting with her fingers, perhaps a nervous habit.

I walked over to the bed and smiled curiously at the items she'd purchased. *This might actually be fun as hell.* I dragged one of the hotel's chairs to the most spacious part of the room.

"Sit." She didn't hesitate to do as I said. The chair I chose was without armrests, its fabric appearing worn and stained. Not exactly the kind of chair you'd expect to find in the kind of hotel that brags about the number of stars it has. But I guess it's what you get when you request the cheapest room available. I could only imagine that when the budget allowed for them to buy new furniture they put it in the suites, demoting the old pieces to the room priced directly below its current location. The best of the worst ended up here, in a room that no doubt cost more than I could ever afford on a hooker's budget. Especially when I currently wasn't getting my cut of the money.

I had a rope that I found on her bed in my hand, and proceeded to tie her to the chair. Not tightly, but snug enough to ensure she had little control over what I was going to do to her. I tied it around her shoulders and waist, pinning her arms down to her sides. The rope didn't seem like the kind you'd find in your local sex shop. She'd obviously gone out of her way to a hardware store, or found it buried in her garage. It was rough against my hands, the splintered surface finding its way into my skin. Either she got off on the sensation of rope burn, or she didn't properly think this through.

I kissed her neck as I tightened the rope behind her. She let her head fall back and moaned softly. On the bed were several pairs of handcuffs. And by several, I mean at least six. Why she thought so many sets of handcuffs were necessary was beyond me. I snatched two and got on my knees in front of her, removing her shoes. They stank of sweat, and hard work. A smell I could never accept if it were my own. I handcuffed one of her ankles to the leg of the chair, and the other to the leg of a nearby desk. This kept her legs spread wide enough for me to get in there even if she tried to resist.

My lips slid over her stockings and up her thigh. I could feel the heat coming off her as I put my head up her skirt and teased her with my lips. Her legs shook in desire, but I wasn't ready to give it to her just yet. From my little experience being with girls, the best strategy that I'd picked up was that it's all about the tease. Without the tease, there's no begging for it. And I wanted this bitch to beg for it.

I directed my attention back on the bed, debating on what I should use first. They were all pretty much the same toys. Different colors and brands of vibrators, but they all served the same purpose. She didn't even have a variety of sizes. I grabbed a green one, simply because I like the color green.

As I approached her, she was squirming under the thick rope and I was introduced to a new desire. I craved the feeling of my palm striking her cheek, but I held back. *Mr. 1622 with the spanking fetish is rubbing off on me! Probably not the best idea to get too dominant with a paying client.* Instead, I dropped the vibrator at her feet and let out my aggression by ripping open her blouse. She gasped at the sound of her shirt tearing and its buttons hitting the carpet.

"My blouse!" she shouted.

"Fuck your blouse," I sneered. I couldn't help it. It was my turn to play this role.

I yanked down her bra, exposing her chest and roughly pinched her nipples with a look of disgust. They were rough, and tattered. Maybe she had a kid,

255

and breastfed the thing. They hung low, even with her fancy bra still fastened around her desperately trying to fight gravity. I slid my hand across her chunky stomach, and under the waistline of her skirt. She yelped as my hand brushed over her underwear. *I gotta get these damn stockings off. Why the hell would she even wear them?* I yanked them down to her ankles, putting a few holes in them on the way. *Whoops.*

My hand rested on her knee as my mouth made its way to her chest. It pleased me to see she had soaked her thighs with anticipation. Without warning, I pushed her panties aside and engulfed my fingers compelling her to squirm and moan in approval. My lips reached her thighs. She tried to resist, pressing her knees together. I forced them open wider with my free hand, and lifted her skirt over her hips. Her pussy lips spread so I could see her clit perfectly. My mouth brushed against it, making her legs quiver eagerly.

"How bad do you want it?" I asked, allowing my tongue to tease her.

"So bad," she moaned.

"Beg for it."

"Please, please…"

"Please what?" I demanded.

"Please eat my pussy! Please, please, please!"

So I did, with a smile on my face. Her moans got

louder and heavier, and then she began to squeal. Her insides were pulsing as her wetness spilled out of her. I assumed that was an orgasm, but I wasn't done with her yet. And being a female myself, I know better than to assume. The vibrator was down by my knee. I gave her a few seconds to breathe before turning it on and shoving it inside of her. It slid in easily, making her cry out in tortured pleasure.

She made all sorts of noises, I couldn't tell what were orgasms and what weren't. I began to sympathize with men. No wonder they're so lost in the bedroom. They're either asking a hundred times if they're 'doing it right' or too overconfident about their 'skills'. There's nothing better than telling that asshole (or that *douchebag*) who thinks he made you cum a dozen times that they actually didn't make you cum at all… not even once. Their cocky smiles immediately fade, and after the initial shock wears off they become determined to prove to you that they can do better. So after twenty excruciating minutes of them showing you they know what they're doing even though they couldn't find a clit if it glowed in the dark, girls do what they do best. Let out their best fake moans to get the guys face out of their damn crotch. But now I understood first hand why guys get so confused. All the sounds coming out of this chick's mouth sounded the same.

I didn't want to be like the guy who kept going on a useless mission and forced her to fake it, so I gave her ten minutes with the vibrator before I decided to change it up. As I took a second look at the toys on her bed, a strap-on caught my eye. I picked it up, and examined it for a second. *How the hell…* I had no idea how to put it on. *Whatever, I'll wing it.* I stood behind her so she couldn't see what I was doing, and after a few seconds of struggling with the toy, I was stripped down to nothing but my bra, heels, and a nine-inch cock.

Her mouth fell open before forming a lustrous smile. I released her from the chair, and shoved her face first onto the bed. Her ass was at the perfect angle for me to slide my new rubber accessory inside of her. It was extremely empowering having her bent over the bed while I tore into her like a man. Her squeals were hardly muffled by the bed. With each thrust, she clawed at the comforter like it would save her from my furious pounding.

I grabbed her curves, as she almost looked ageless from my angle. It came to me slowly, like a bad headache. Except this was no headache, it was one of those mind-blowing orgasms that started in my toes and rippled throughout my entire body, teasing my every nerve before finally exploding into unimaginable amounts of gratification. The pleasure caused me to tremble uncontrollably, freeing my mind to do nothing in that moment other than relish the feeling of pure ecstasy.

I fell onto the bed, paralyzed and in a fit of giggles. She took that opportunity to climb on top of me, and start exploring my body with her hands. She brought her hands over my chest, rubbing my nipples over my bra. The shy woman I'd met earlier seemed to have disappeared. I felt the strap-on being slid off my legs, and her fingers between my thighs.

I glanced at the clock, and saw that our time together was almost up. For some reason, I felt like I had to make her cum one more time… just to make sure she got her money's worth. So I grabbed the nearest vibrator and held it against her clit while she continued to fuck me with her fingers. It was completely sexist of me. If she were a man I would have left a half hour ago, after the first orgasm.

She finally moaned and screamed 'I'm cumming!' so I knew I was doing something right.

"So, was that close enough to your fantasy?" I asked while zipping up my dress. I couldn't help but be the 'did I do it right' guy. Better than the cocky guy thinking I made her cum a dozen times.

"No," she replied bluntly. I'm sure I gave her a look identical to the one given to me by *[The Douchebag]* so often in the past when I'd hinted at his lousy love making skills. "It was much better than any fantasy I could have come up with. Thank you."

I smiled, letting out a sigh of relief before leaving her room, satisfied in every sense of the word.

After I dropped off the money and Nyani informed me I had no more clients for the evening, I texted Mr. Edison asking him to meet me at a bar a few blocks over. He said he'd meet me there in twenty minutes, so I hit the streets and began the short hike. Butterflies filled my stomach at the thought of seeing Hunter again. My heart wanted him to give me some incredible justification for all of this, an explanation good enough to make it okay to still love him. My heart may have been aching for him, my head, however, wanted to slit his throat and watch him bleed out in front of me. Watching him choke on his own blood would almost make up for what he did to me... almost.

I checked my phone during my walk, and saw that Martin had been texting me pretty much nonstop for over an hour. He wanted me to come to his room, probably watch a movie and do lines. I rolled my eyes and told him I'd be there in about two hours just to get him to shut up. *This is going to be a long fucking night.*

DAY THIRTY-SIX
PART TWO

SO, THERE I WAS. Sitting in some lame-ass sports bar, sipping on a beer with a stomach in knots and a bump on my head that pulsated with my quickened heartbeat. My strategy was to let Mr. Edison do most of the talking, and try not to let him in on what I knew. It was a shitty plan, I knew that. I just needed him to slip up during our conversation and give me something I could use. There were still so many unanswered questions, and if I was going to come up with a decent revenge plan, I knew he'd be the one to inspire it. So I sat and waited, looking at the door every time I saw someone move a damn arm or leg out of the corner of my eye.

Thirty minutes later, I sent him a text questioning where he was and ordered another beer. A beer that I couldn't afford, but the bartender had cleared my empty glass and to sit in a bar empty handed and alone is unbearably awkward. It definitely wasn't the right night to start my sobriety anyway.

For the next forty minutes or so my mind rotated emotions as Mr. Edison kept me waiting. My thoughts started off heated, sounding something like *where the fuck is this asshole? How dare he make me wait for him this long!*. Eventually my anger turned to concern as my old feelings for him resurfaced. *I hope he's okay… maybe I should stop by his hotel room and check on him.* Then I reminded myself who this guy *really* was, and my paranoia came crawling back. *He's probably waiting for me to give up on him and leave. He'll be waiting outside and 'accidentally' bump into me on my walk home. Of course he'll apologize for running late, give me some bullshit excuse. Then he'll convince me to take some back alley 'shortcut' where he'll shank me and leave me for dead. Fuck that!*

I checked my phone one last time, but there was still nothing. This was, in my unreasonable state of mind, a confirmation that I wasn't safe. I decided I had to get the hell out of there, *but how?* Panic rose in my chest. There was no one I could call to pick me up. *What if I text Mr. Edison again to confirm that he's at the right bar, and then name a different bar to throw him off?* It was too risky though. For all I knew he'd already glimpsed in the window of the sports bar and saw me sitting there waiting for him. That kind of text would not only be confirmation that I knew too much, but that I was terrified. *No, scratch that idea. He could be watching me right now.* Besides that, I didn't know the name of any other bars in the area. Not a single one.

"Hey there sugar tits, you givin' discounts for first timers yet?" It was that prick Allan Schaener. *This guy won't give up will he?* I gladly accepted the drink he had in his hand though. It was a nice break from the beer.

"I only give discounts to my regulars Mr. Schaener, you know that."

"Oh, so I'd have to buy you a condo or a car to get at your pussy for a smaller price?" *Obviously if you're buying cars and condos the price is much higher you dumb fuck.*

"Actually you would have to buy me both, Mr. Schaener." I took a sip of my gin and tonic, moving my eyes around the room to show my lack of interest. He didn't pick up on it though.

"Do you accept credit cards? I'd gladly swipe it for you," he said putting his hand on my thigh. *This guy is unreal.*

"You know the rules Mr. Schaener, no touching unless an agreement is made." I pushed his grotesque hand away with a smile. *It's never gonna happen shit dick.* But he ignored my comment, and put his hand back on my thigh.

"Come on gorgeous, let me swipe my card in your ass," he whispered in my ear. *Gag. I'd rather die.* Then I remembered that dying was an actual possibility for the evening. *Assuming Mr. Schaener is who he says he is, just a dirty old man looking to get laid, it's very possible he could help me get out of here safely. Maybe I'm just paranoid, but what if I'm not? It'll be too late by the time I figure it out. Plus, I could really use the extra money.* So I reluctantly changed my mind.

"Well, Mr. Schaener, it appears that my client for this evening is over an hour late, making this your lucky night." I chugged the rest of my drink. *Can't do this sober.* "Shall we go back to the hotel then?"

I was overwhelmed with fear as we walked towards the bar's exit. Adrenaline was soaring through my blood, perhaps the only reason I was standing instead of curled up in a ball crying on the floor. I opted to wait inside while Mr. Schaener's driver made his way to the bar, claiming it was 'too cold'. The black sedan was being parked maybe six yards from where I stood, but it still wasn't close enough for me to feel secure. I walked close to my new client, letting him block the entire right side of my body. For some reason I thought I'd be shot on the spot like it was a goddamn assassination. It was all that coke I was doing. With Allan protecting my right, I kept my eyes alert and ready for anything going on ahead of me and to my left.

My first step out of the bar was terrifying, and I unintentionally held my breath. Each step I took echoed against the hot air. For once the city streets seemed quiet, as I could identify nothing other than the sound of my own heartbeat.

Nothing happened. I didn't see anyone familiar or suspicious. There was no gunfire or bombs going off. Nothing.

AFTER I WAS DONE letting the woolly mammoth fuck me, I had to deal with my apprehensions all over again. The seedy hotel he was staying at was much further from the hotel I did my business in than I would have liked. To walk alone at night, when I was already paranoid about being taken out was nothing less than brutal. Even sticking to main streets, I was quivering like a lost child the entire way. The only thing I could do to keep my sanity was convince myself I would have until the party to live. I thought they'd want me to be a walking billboard advertising their club and handing out drinks, but what the hell did I know?

When I got to Martin's room, I noticed his door wasn't shut all the way. If I were a cop in one of those Law & Order shows, this would have been the moment I whipped out my gun and told my partner to get my back. Instead, I knocked and slowly pushed open the door.

"Martin? It's me… Hannah." It took me a moment for my eyes to adjust to the darkness, but I eventually saw him sitting up in bed. His eyes were wide and focused on the television. He didn't even acknowledge me as I walked into the room. *Fucking junkie.*

"Sorry I'm late Martin. My dinner plans ran longer than I expected," I lied as I closed the door behind me. He had money out for me on the bed stand, the usual six hundred for two hours. "Are we watching another movie tonight?" I tried to put some excitement in my voice as I tucked the money into my purse, but he still ignored me. *Is he pissed that I'm late?* I stood over him waiting for a response. *Nah, he's so high he couldn't have noticed. I wonder if he finally realized what I'm doing all night before I see him.*

I slid my shoes off, and pulled the sheets back. As I climbed into bed with him, I saw his 'coke mirror' sitting in his lap. "Mind if I do one?" I wasn't asking for permission though, I was asking out of polite habit. My nose was already six inches from the shit by the time I finished the sentence.

"What's wrong with you tonight?" I asked getting comfortable in bed with him. "You're so qui_." I nearly jumped out of the bed. His body was stiff… hard as a fucking rock.

"Martin?" My voice was quiet and uncertain. "Martin!" I yelled with more confidence, and waved my hand in front of my face. He was dead.

I sat on the edge of the bed with my head in my hands, gaping at him. There were no tears, but there was a definite sadness forming in my chest. Blood vessels in his eyes were broken, covering anything that should be white with a shocking red. Coke remnants dusted his nose and upper lip. *How could you be so fucking stupid Martin! Did you just sit here all day, snorting this shit?* Of course he did. I knew that's what he did every day, but I was angry he took it so far. *This was my safe place Martin! Now where can I go?*

I picked the mirror up off his lap, and did another line before throwing it across the room in frustration. It shattered against the wall, dropping to the floor in pieces. A cloud of white powder formed for a brief moment before gradually settling on the carpet.

Now what Martin? When the police come they'll see my fingerprints all over this fucking room! All over you! My cum is staining your whole bed because you're too fucking lazy to go out for an hour and let the cleaning people do their damn job! I opened the draw in the bed stand, and took out The Bible. There was no guilt as I flipped through the pages taking out the cash he'd been 'flattening'. *You owe me this Martin. Because you couldn't control your nasty habit, now I have to worry about the police coming after me too! It isn't enough I have a bunch of scumbags up my ass, now the police are gonna get involved! And I thought you had twenty grand in cash? Fucking liar.* After I cleaned out The Bible, I started rummaging through his other draws and piles of clothes, searching for anything useful.

When I left, I made sure the 'Do Not Disturb' sign was still on the door and hoped there were thousands of fingerprints in that room and mine wouldn't stand out from the rest. *They'll see it as a drug overdose and close the case. No questions asked.*

I walked back 'home' to prepare for my performance the next day, making a few important phone calls on the way. My unexpected evening had inspired me, and I finally had a plan. The rest of my night was spent icing my head, and packing for the cameras. I wanted Nyani, or whoever was watching to see I was ready to move back into the hotel, and that I wasn't going to run. Not yet.

DAY THIRTY-SEVEN
PART ONE

IT WAS THE FINAL DAY of the countdown... day zero... D-Day... and I couldn't help but feel like a dead woman walking. I was going to get all dolled up for a party just to meet my end. Death was on my mind, and I just couldn't shake it.

I had attempted to sleep in that morning to avoid the anxiety that would have come with sitting around, waiting in silence. Sadly, things didn't exactly go as I'd planned. Even though I double-bolted my door from the inside and hid my entire body from view with blankets, sleep didn't come easy. The only thing that settled my mind was the fact that having proof of murder on film would just be foolish, and I lived in a damn live studio. *I think...*

Around noon, I gave up on the possibility of sleep finding me again and got my ass out of bed. That's when the thoughts started... the last-day-thoughts. *This could be the last time I get out of a bed... this could be the last time I take a shower... this could be the last time I ever brush my teeth.* Everything I did that day was viewed in a new light. I cherished every detail of that afternoon, even the little bullshit things that were part of my everyday routine. As I sat at the table and gazed into my last cup of coffee, I began running a mental list of the things I would never get to do if my plan failed. I visualized the cities I would never visit, the careers I would never get the chance to begin, the men I would never date. Then I thought of my family... my sister... my parents. I thought about never seeing them again, about how I'll never be able to fix things.

If I die tonight, I'll be labeled as just another prostitute found in a dumpster. A Jane Doe. No one will try to figure out who killed me. There will be no story about me in the papers. No one will give a shit. And my family, would they even find out? They haven't heard from me in years, it's not like they'd report me missing. Actually, no one would report me missing. There's not a single person in the world that would notice if I was no longer walking this earth tomorrow. Not a friend. Not an employer. No one. But that's why Nyani picked me, right? I was exactly the kind of girl she was looking for. Naive and completely alone.

Tears began to form in my eyes, but I forced them back. *This is no time to get emotional. You're not dead yet 'sugar tits'!* I laughed at myself, and took my last sip of coffee. *You'll have another coffee tomorrow, Eva. You're smarter than they think you are. All that coke is fucking with your head and making you paranoid.*

The rest of the day was spent packing as I mentally rehearsed my plan. There were far too many opportunities for things to go wrong, but I couldn't just walk away. Not anymore. Not after what they did to me. Of course the party was black tie, but this time I didn't care that everything I owned screamed 'whore'. There was no one to impress anymore. I put on the most comfortable dress and shortest heels, and headed out the door with most of my belongings either weighing down my shoulder or being dragged behind me. Everything was kept separate. Hannah's things were stuffed in an enormous suitcase on wheels that I had brought with me from home. Eva's things were tucked neatly into a decent-sized tote bag, which had room for only the essentials; a pair of sneakers, four t-shirts, two pairs of jeans, yoga pants, a sweatshirt, miscellaneous undergarments, a toothbrush, some makeup, the toiletries a girl just can't live without, my letter to [*The Douchebag*], an old flash drive, and a wallet which held the hard earned cash of a retired escort. Anything else was left behind.

Leaving that apartment for what I knew would be the final time, I didn't get to take that one last glance back. There was no opportunity for me to create that mental picture of a place I once called home. No opportunity to make sure nothing was forgotten or to say goodbye to the things that couldn't come with me; a ten year old photo of me and my little sister, [*The Douchebag*]'s old sweatshirt that still held a hint of his cologne when I held it close to my nose, Jerimiah's *Scarface* DVD... nothing valuable yet all irreplaceable.

I took the long way to *Slayers* that night, which was where I was told we were all meeting. Two blocks over, however, someone else was waiting for me, and that's where I went first.

"Tom?" I asked as I approached the husky young man in what I assumed was his uniform. He was leaning against the driver's side door smoking a cigarette. The limo was more expensive than a town car or cab, but no one else was willing to do what I needed done.

"That's me," he said flicking his cigarette to the ground. Tom was a stereotypical New Yorker, with his Brooklyn accent and 'fuck you' persona. I didn't want to trust him, but I didn't exactly have a parade of options to choose from.

"The man I spoke to last night said he would explain to you what I need done, did he do that?"

"Yeah, he did." Tom gave me a suspicious smirk. I could tell he was excited to be a part of what I assumed he imagined was an Ocean's Eleven type of heist. It's amazing what people will do for the right price, and Tom's price was steep as fuck. I went over the plan with him one more time just to be sure, and handed him a wad of Hannah's cash before tossing Eva's bag in the backseat. *He'll do it… he'll do it for the money and the curiosity of it all. He'll hope I slip and confess my troubles to him, giving him the opportunity to press me for more answers. He'd be asking the wrong questions though.*

"See you later then," I said and scurried away, Hannah's suitcase still dragging behind me.

There was no limo waiting for us outside of *Slayers*, just a cab with a pissed off driver. I had a feeling he'd gotten suckered into the long drive to Long Island.

"How are we all going to fit in one cab?" My question was directed at Missy, but she didn't acknowledge me.

"It's just going to be the four of us," Lacie said as she tossed her cigarette to the ground and walked around the cab to sit in the passenger seat. *Just the four of us? Where the hell is everyone else?* Missy, still without even a glance in my direction, hopped into the back of the cab.

"What's wit that?" Carmen asked nodding towards my suitcase.

"I'm moving back into the hotel tonight," I said casually as the cab driver took it out of my hand so he could toss it in the trunk. I walked towards the back door with the intention of sitting down next to Missy, but Carmen cut me off.

"'Scuse me!" she hollered as she threw herself into the cab before me, forcing Missy to scoot over. I tried to keep an emotionless face as I climbed in after her, but the mistrustful thoughts started to consume me immediately. *Is Carmen just a cunt or did she do that intentionally to ensure Missy and I didn't sit next to each other?* I glanced in her direction, and received a smug smile in return. *Intentionally.* I answered my own question.

The car ride was long, and tense. No one spoke except Lacie who occasionally gave the cab driver directions. It was becoming obvious to me that Lacie and Carmen's arrogant attitudes might have something to do with the fact that they knew more about this lovely club than Missy or I did. At least they *thought* they knew more. Nyani's scheme would have been too risky without someone on the inside to ensure none of the escorts caught on. Suspicion can be contagious. There had to be someone around reassuring the girls that there was nothing shady going on. *So which one of you is it? Or is it both of you?*

Twenty minutes into the drive, my concerns began to grow about this 'party' I was attending. *What if there is no party and they're actually taking Missy and I to some deserted area to shoot us in the back of the head and bury our bodies in shallow graves? Or we get to Nyani's house, and no one's inside? Where the hell are all of the other girls anyway? At the party already? Or are they fucking dead?*

I tried to grab Missy's attention and clue her in on my suspicions, but she intentionally kept her eyes out the window in a daze. I imagined she was wishing she never left that farm in Ohio or Idaho or wherever the hell she was from. All I knew was that my plan would go to shit if we weren't taken to Nyani's house. That scenario hadn't even crossed my mind until then, and I began to wonder how many other situations I hadn't considered.

I was eventually put at ease when I began to recognize several landmarks I'd noticed during previous trips to Nyani's house. *At least we're headed in the right direction.* When we pulled up Nyani's driveway, I felt a brief moment of déja vu before I was hit with an intense flashback of the first time I pulled up to that house with Jillian. I think I would have done just about anything if it meant I could go back to that night. As hard as it was to deal with Jillian, I had to admit she was right about Nyani. *And if only I had listened to her... I wouldn't be getting out of a car for the last time in my short, pathetic life.*

I made sure I was last in line walking towards the house, which was easy to do with that goddamn suitcase. Carmen made sure to keep me company though, pausing with my every struggle and keeping no more than a yard's distance between us. *Don't worry Carmen, I'm not going anywhere just yet.*

A wave of relief fell over me when I walked inside to be greeted by the laughing faces of a sea of people, all conversing in small social circles. It seemed like most of the party was outside, but a large number of guests had trickled into the foyer and living room area. I hadn't thought about the possibility of the event being held outside. *That'll make my snooping around a bit more obvious.... fuck. Just another scenario I hadn't considered.*

"What the *hell* is that?" Nyani demanded furiously under her breath as she pointed to my suitcase. She seemed surprised to see me, looking elegant in a long strapless dress with her hair pinned up like she was modeling for a goddam bridal magazine. You would never look at her and think 'yeah, this bitch is gonna scam me out of all of my hard earned money I fuck people for and record my sessions with clients to help get a porn site started'. She just didn't have that kind of face.

"I had to move out of_" I started my rehearsed speech but Nyani held up her hand in frustration.

"I don't give a fuck!" she whispered in a harsh tone. "Just go put it upstairs somewhere!"

"No problem," I said forcing a smile but she had already walked away. I thought for a minute Carmen might follow me, but she chased after Nyani like a puppy trying to catch a frisbee, leaving me to venture on my own. *Dumbass*. I dragged the heavy luggage up the stairs, while scanning the crowd for Missy's golden hair without luck. *Where the hell could she have gone? Carmen and I were only ten seconds behind her.* I couldn't be bothered with it though. My plan *could* include Missy, but I wasn't going to risk going out of my way to make her part of it. She just had to be in the right place at the right time.

I had kind of counted on someone telling me to put my suitcase upstairs. For once things were going my way. It was the ideal place to start my search, and I'd decided only hours earlier that it would be safest to enter Nyani's bedroom first. If anyone came looking for me, most likely I'd have already moved on to another room. Nyani's room was definitely *not* a place I wanted to be caught snooping around in, but I knew exactly where the camera was to quickly cover it up and get things done. *Well, maybe I don't know exactly where it is, but I remember the angle the video was shot from...*

275

I mean, how could I ever forget?

I opened her bedroom door a crack, and peeked inside. The lights were on, but it was deserted. I wheeled my suitcase into the room and tossed it on the bed. As I unzipped my bag, I glanced nonchalantly in the direction I thought I might find the camera. There it was, right in plain sight. Not at all the high tech hidden camera in a lamp I thought it would be, just a regular handheld sitting on a damn tripod. *How the hell did I miss that?* I grabbed it to ensure it was off, and cursed myself for not being more aware. *She must have covered it with a sweater or something… or she just counted on the fact that I'd be too distracted by the porn on her TV and her pussy in my face to notice. Ugh.*

Locking the door from the inside, I silently prayed that there weren't other cameras in the room. *Even if there were cameras with live feeds, no one would be watching them, right? Everyone's too distracted by the party. They probably only turn them on when they know they're gonna have a show for their damn website anyway.* My reassuring thoughts were hard for even me to believe. Nonetheless, I began tearing through Nyani's bedroom, searching for anything of use. I was looking for some kind of paper trail proving that they were responsible for what I'd been through. Bank statements, the contracts she made us sign… something. Then I saw her laptop, just sitting out on her dresser. *I'm sure it's password protected…* it wasn't. I opened a webpage, and it went straight to her e-mail. It really couldn't have been easier. The third e-mail gave me more than I ever could have dreamed of. It was a confirmation for the purchase of four tickets to Heathrow Airport in London. The plane was scheduled to leave at nine o'clock the next morning. *Four? Who else is going? And to London? That's their big getaway plan? Well, they must have bags packed and ready to go if they plan on leaving so early.* I glanced around the room and saw no sign of luggage other than my own. The only name on the e-mail was Jaclyn. *Nyani's real name? So who are the other three tickets for? Mr. Edison…Jim…and who else?*

I skimmed the rest of her recent e-mails, but nothing else caught my eye. The name Jaclyn was repeated in the subject of several of them, so it had to be a name Nyani went by if not her legal name. There was nothing concerning the escorting website in her e-mails. Either she didn't run the site, or they had a separate e-mail account set up for it. I found the site in her browser's history, but when I clicked on it the website appeared to be 'Under Construction'. Their logo was still there, but none of the links were active. It didn't matter though. I already knew everything I wanted to know about my short-lived career as a porn star. Even though my videos were temporarily off the internet, I wasn't relieved.

Now with more direction in my search, it was time to move on to a different room. I took a quick glance around the room to make sure everything was where it should be, got my shit together and moved on. The door to the next room was locked. I didn't have time to play with it, for all I knew it was just a storage closet or an empty bedroom people were fucking in… *or exactly what I came here for. Ugh.* I walked down the hall to the next door, which rested partially open. So I turned on the light and closed it softly behind me. It was a decent sized bedroom, which I assumed by its appearance wasn't being used by anyone. The white walls were bare, and the only furniture in the room was a queen-sized bed and a small dresser. Compared to Nyani's stuffed closet and decorated walls, this room didn't seem to fit. Even the comforter was out of place. It was several shades of green, with the occasional pink or yellow flower. I pulled back the blanket to find two off white feather pillows without covers, and a bare mattress. *She must not have guests very often.*

I opened each of the dresser drawers, but wasn't surprised to find them empty. It was the same for under the bed. I rolled my suitcase over to the closet, thinking it was the perfect place to store it. However, just as I was sliding the bag inside, I heard people coming up the stairs. *Shit!* Instead of following my well thought out plan for what to do in this *exact* situation, my instincts took over and I crouched down next to my luggage. I heard the doorknob to the bedroom turn just as I got the closet door to slide shut.

"Why is this fucking light on?" A man's voice came booming through the room.

"Just relax, baby. You're wound too tight. This time tomorrow we'll be far, far away from this place."

It was Nyani's voice, only sweeter and more sensual. I heard some kissing noises, and giggling.

Who is she with? I heard them moving around the room, talking at an inaudible volume.

"Just get on your knees already and lets get this shit over with." The man was Jim, her 'business associate'. *I guess they're more than just partners in business.*

As I listened to her unzip his pants and start slurping on his cock, I couldn't help but be furious with myself for not sticking to my plan. I was going to pretend to be changing… unzip my dress really quick and have whoever accidentally found me walk in on me half naked. A typical reaction would be to apologize and quickly close the door, which would give me the time I needed to quickly cover up the fact that I was snooping if I needed it. But no, I had to jump in the fucking closet and get stuck squatting in a dress while listening to Nyani get this guy off.

"Come on, fucking take the whole thing in your mouth! Prove to me I did the right thing choosing you over those other two sluts!" *Choosing her?*

It sounded like Jim was fucking her mouth, making her choke and gag on his dick. Then I heard a loud smack, followed by Nyani yelping and a thud. "Watch the teeth you stupid bitch!" My heart pounded when I realized they weren't role-playing.

"Get the fuck up, and bend over the bed! I'll fucking do it myself, you useless whore." I could hear Nyani sniffling, probably trying to hold back tears.

"Why the fuck are you crying?" I heard another

279

smack, and Nyani cried out this time before she began to sob. "This is what I pay you for, so you better do it with a fucking smile. I took your nasty ass in off the streets. Appreciate that bitch! Now bend over."

I tried not to imagine what he was doing to her, but the sounds were too disturbing. Thankfully it didn't last long.

"Clean yourself up, you fucking disgust me." I heard the door open and close. Nyani was crying uncontrollably, muffling her sounds with what I could only assume was the mattress or that nasty comforter. *Shit, I got it all wrong. Nyani's stuck in this world. Just like me.*

Nothing made sense anymore. All this hatred I had built up for Nyani suddenly felt undeserved, but my desire to get my revenge still overpowered the instincts screaming at me to flee. Nyani got up after only a minute or two, turning the lights off as she exited. I stayed put in my hiding spot, not wanting to risk running into either of them in the hallway. *What a mess I've gotten myself into…*

"How the *fuck* do you not know where they are?" I could hear Jim's voice clear as day from inside the closet. It apparently shared a wall with the room that had been locked. *I guess it's not locked anymore.* The second man responded, but his voice was too low to understand. I pressed my ear up against the wall.

"Well, then look for them! Is that Missy? Right

there! Outside on the deck?"

"I'm not sure..." It was Mr. Edison's voice.

"Well go downstairs and fucking get sure! That bitch has been talking to the cops! And find that slut Hannah too!" *Me? Why are they looking for me?* "Weren't we supposed to take care of that cunt last night?"

"She never showed up," he said defensively. *Take care of me? What does that mean? He was gonna* kill *me?*

"Well I don't blame her after that beating you gave her! You were hired to get these idiots to fuck in front of the camera, not to tear them a new asshole," he chuckled. "Although, I did enjoy editing the footage of that!"

"Well your *girl* screwed me by telling her all that bullshit about me being married." *Bullshit? So it's not true?* "How else was I going to get her in bed?" Mr. Edison sounded like he was desperately trying to keep his anger under control.

"Yeah, well you're not the first man to beat the piss out of a chick just to save his own ass. Find the sluts so we can finish what we've started. We're running out of time." I heard the door slam, and Nyani questioning him in the hallway before they descended the stairs together.

My heart pounded as I desperately listened through the wall, wanting so badly to hear Mr. Edison's voice one more time. Part of me wanted to reach through the wall and wrap my arms around him. A much larger part of me, however, wanted to tie him up and shove everything within arms reach up his ass. I heard him sigh a few times before he left, the sound of his footsteps disappearing down the stairs. One thing I know I *didn't* hear was Hunter closing the door behind him. *Jackpot.*

I slid the closet door open quietly, and felt my way around in the darkness. The hallway was silent, so I opened the door just enough to peek in either direction. *All clear.* I barely took a step out before I realized I had forgotten something in my suitcase. *Ugh, shoot.* Closing the door softly, I felt around in the dark to get back to the closet. I needed to get my damn purse. It was in a front zipper compartment, purposely made easy to grab. Then I made the trip in the dark one last time back to the door, and finally into the hallway.

The purse was kind of bulky considering there wasn't much in it. It also didn't match the coral cocktail dress I had on at all but it was a good size for what I needed it for, which was to be full within the hour. Entering the previously locked room, I was instantly panicked by the large computer screen sitting on top of a desk displaying the feed from six different security cameras. *Six cameras? That's it?* I studied each room that was on the screen, all packed with people from the party. *There must be a way to change what's on the screen...*

It had a regular keyboard and mouse, so I fucked around with the buttons a bit. *I wonder if this is all being recorded? No,* I answered myself. *If that were the case, Mr. Edison could have easily watched the video from the moment Missy and I arrived and found us instantly.* I finally figured out how to change the display to a different camera. It turned out there were ten different cameras around the house, all at obvious angels to prevent burglars. None were in the bedrooms like I thought they'd be. My mind had created an image of an entire house full of hidden cameras, always ready to record the sexual encounters that occur. *Maybe they just aren't these mastermind criminals that I thought they were. Maybe I'm giving them too much credit. But if Mr. Edison was in here watching the cameras, how is it possible he didn't see me come up the stairs? Or hear me try to open the door to the room he was in?*

I looked over the security videos one more time but saw no sign of any luggage I was looking for. The clock on the surveillance screen read a little after eight o'clock. *Shit. I'm running out of time, and I've been missing from the party far too long.* I changed the screen back to how it was when I walked in, and started to leave when a filing cabinet caught my eye. *Just a little more snooping can't hurt.* The last thing I wanted was to be caught up there. They don't say 'curiosity killed the cat' for nothin'.

Most of the files had already been emptied, and occupied three garbage bags, shredded beyond recognition. The bottom draw hadn't been finished yet, and I quickly ripped them out. *Bingo!* It was a handful of the contracts signed by escorts, my own included. I rolled my eyes as I noticed that I had foolishly signed my real name. There it was scribbled on the bottom of the last page, in perfect cursive, Eva Palmer. I wanted to tear it up immediately, and get rid of any proof of my humiliation. *And if they kill you? It would be a huge clue as to what happened to you if they found it with your body.* I skimmed through all of the contracts, and I realized I wasn't the only one who had signed their real name. *For all the girls who couldn't be here tonight…* and I quickly shoved the contracts into my purse. *Now it's time to make an appearance at the party.*

DAY THIRTY-SEVEN
PART TWO

AS I REJOINED THE festivities, I soon realized how much I stood out in the crowd. All of the women wore long elegant gowns, and had their hair off their shoulders in a formal up-do. My dress, on the other hand, was barely long enough to cover my ass cheeks. And my hair, well, it definitely was *not* up. I probably looked more like a hooker that night than I ever did throughout my journey working for that club. My appearance was finally catching up to my mentality.

I grabbed a glass of champagne off the tray of a server walking by, sipping on it as I squeezed through the sea of people. It was difficult to ignore the not-so-few disgusted glances pointed in my direction as I searched for a familiar face. *There is no way these people are here as potential members of an escort club. Almost every man in the room is well into their sixties, and they all brought their wives. No chance. What the hell is going on?*

I walked outside just in time to catch the very

285

end of what appeared to have been an emotional speech given by a stocky bald man I didn't recognize. Everyone cheered and wiped tears from their eyes as he raised his glass in honor of the crowd. Behind him was a huge banner that read 'Children of the Future Benefit'. *Children of the future? What the hell is that?*

"Hello, Eva."

I spun around to be greeted by the enemy. Barely six inches from my face staring at me with such intensity with those heart melting grey eyes.

"Mr. Edison," I replied coldly with a slight nod in his direction.

"Ouch," he responded taking an over exaggerated step back. "I guess I deserve that."

"No, Mr. Edison. You deserve much worse." My words were spoken to the air rather than to him. I avoided eye contact by focusing all of my attention on my drink, making it a bit easier to keep up the cold front. As much as I hated him, I still enjoyed his attention.

"Come with me somewhere to talk. Please." I glared at him but he just gazed back at me with sincerity. "*Please,*" he begged.

"I don't trust you. For all I know, you're going to take me somewhere out of sight so you can rape me again you sick fuck. And where is Missy? Or did you kill her already?" My voice was angry and my tone

286

was brutal.

"Shhh," he begged. "I've never killed *anyone*, I swear! I'm just the manager of a stupid hotel who was dumb enough to be tempted by a shit ton of money and a few pretty girls."

"Oh, please…" I rolled my eyes in disbelief.

"Please, Eva. They paid me to 'turn a blind eye' to anything happening around the hotel related to the club. So, I let them hold their meetings in the hotel bar, simply because people don't go into *Slayers* when it's nice enough for the rooftop bar to be open. A few weeks after I agreed to that, they came to me asking if I would be interested in more money. I admit it, I got greedy." He looked down as if to show me he was ashamed. "So they asked me to act as an interested client, and have sex with a few of the girls for some website. I really didn't think any harm would come of it! The money was just too good to pass up. I swear I didn't know what kind of people they were! These girls were picked up off the streets, for God's sake! It never occurred to me that perhaps I was getting in over my head, and I *certainly* never thought I would meet someone like you." He reached for my hand.

"Stop messing with my head, Hunter!" I nearly screamed, and stormed off in any direction I could to get away from him.

"My name is Joe!" he shouted after me. "Joseph Claytone!"

My legs stopped moving. I recognized the name immediately from the hotel website. *No, he's just being manipulative. He must know I saw his picture on the website… Missy must have told him something. No… what the hell am I saying? That makes no sense!* I turned around to face him, and saw that he was near tears.

"Please, Eva. Just give me five minutes to explain." People were starting to stare, so I closed the distance between us to ensure our conversation would once again be private.

"Prove to me I can trust you."

He took this as an invitation to grab my arm and lead me towards the house. I tried to place my empty glass on a table along the way, but he was moving faster than I'd anticipated and the glass fell to the ground with a loud shatter. We didn't pause though. The place was packed, and the air was full of laughter and conversation. I hoped it was enough to suppress the commotion caused by my clumsy error, at least from the ears and eyes of my dearest 'friends'. Almost everyone had ventured outside by that time, making it easy for us to sneak through the kitchen and down a deserted back hallway.

"Here," he said gesturing towards the furthest door. He opened it, and led the way down a narrow stairway. From the bottom of the stairs, the room looked like a stereotypical storage space. It was consumed with the perfect amount of darkness that allowed for minimal sight and smelled of mold and rot. There was shit everywhere.

"This house is a popular summer rental," 'Joe' said pointing to all the junk. "The landlord puts everything that gets left behind down here. It's one of the few rooms that can't be seen on the security cameras." He casually gestured towards a few cardboard boxes stacked near the bottom of the stairs. "Any of that look familiar?" I glanced at him curiously before peeking into the one on top. An abundance of bright pink lace lured my hands towards the box, encouraging my fingers to caress this found treasure. The box contained dozens of corsets, identical to one I had pulled out of that dresser drawer my first day in the hotel.

"Where did it all come from?" More were stacked against the walls.

He shrugged. "Stolen, I'm sure." I moved on to another box and continued to admire each piece, cringing at the memory of wearing some of them. "I can't promise they're all unworn." I lost interest in the lingerie instantly.

"So, tell me more," I encouraged as we made our way through the maze of garbage. "What's going on upstairs?"

"It's a fake charity or something. You know that guy who was making a speech just now?"

"Yeah. The bald one, right?"

"Yeah, well we call him Mr. Reed. He's the 'co-founder' of this charity. I gave him the mailing list for all of the hotel's big fundraisers so they could hold this event. Just a bunch of old rich folks with nothing better to do with their time and money. It just happens that the money raised tonight will be going into Mr. Reed's pocket," he smirked. "Well, not all of it. I'm sure it'll get divided someway or another. I already got my share."

"Share for what exactly?" I asked cautiously. Part of me didn't want to know how he was involved in the whole thing. I still wanted to be able to think of him as Hunter, the man with sexy eyes that swept me off my feet just a few short weeks earlier.

"My main purpose is to ease the minds of anyone questioning the ethics of the club around the hotel, including the police. Ever since one of the girls was found dead in an alley, they've been questioning my staff regularly. There's not enough proof to press charges, of course. These people aren't stupid."

I nodded and waited for him to continue.

"Then of course, they also paid me to act as an interested client to get the girls to do particular things in front of the cameras. Customers pay extra for, um, special request videos."

There was a long silence before I decided to continue.

"So why was Tanya killed?" I knew what his answer was going to be, but I wanted to hear him say it.

"She knew too much... and to them, you're all disposable. As soon as they get what they need on film, girls start to disappear." And that was exactly what I needed to hear to confirm the paranoia I'd been feeling. "How did you find out about the website anyway?"

"I never said I knew anything about a website." I glared at him hard with mistrust. He just rolled his eyes at me. *He knows.* "Missy showed me," I replied suddenly depressed.

"Yeah, Nyani fucked up. You're not like any of the other girls she chose for this, umm, project. Nyani was supposed to recruit girls off the street, but she really screwed up when she got you and Missy involved in this. She screwed up with Tanya too. That girl's parents have enough money to keep an investigation going until *someone* eventually goes down for their daughter's murder. But I can pretty much guarantee none of the other girls even suspected foul play. As long as they got paid enough to keep up their drug habits, they were happy."

"Maybe Nyani didn't screw up. Maybe she chose us because she wanted everyone to get caught and finally put an end to it all."

"I never thought of it like that." He looked off in the distance as if in deep contemplation. "It would make sense though. She was just another girl off the streets who got mixed up with the wrong people. Not much different from you." There was a long pause, as he seemed to continue making the connection.

"What happened to the other girls?" I seemed to have interrupted his concentration, and he nearly exploded with an answer.

"I didn't know he was gonna kill 'em," Joe shouted as he turned me to face him. "I swear, Eva, I had no idea that was his plan until it was too late! I was in too deep, and I didn't see any way out. Jim, see, he would tell me to bring a girl to his place to record a video there. I'd wake up the next morning and I'd never see the girl again. I swear he must have drugged us or something! After that happened twice, I caught on. What could I do though?" Tears fell from his eyes, and I could tell he'd been dying to get that off his chest.

"Shh, it's okay." I tried comforting him by brushing his cheek with the back of my hand, but he wasn't having it.

"No! It's not okay!" he said pushing my arm away. "Last night, they asked me to take *you* to his place! I knew you'd end up dead in some alley if I took you there, so I acted like you told me to meet you at *Slayers*. For hours I just sat there and pretended to wait for you, while inside I was dying to see your face. I wanted to tell you so many times about the people you were involved with. When you came to my room accusing me of being married and renting everything for you, I didn't know what to do. I panicked! If I didn't get some kind of sex on tape I thought they'd kill me, I swear! I know what I did was unforgivable... I just didn't see any other way. I'm so sorry, Eva!" He got on his knees and sobbed at my feet.

I let my fingers run through his tousled hair. *Wait, what am I doing? Ugh, there's no time for this right now!* I bent down and pulled on his collar until he finally rose to his feet. His eyes were puffy and his cheeks stained with tears.

"You can't fall apart on me now! We'll have plenty of time to discuss this later. I need you right now." I tried my best to soothe him with my voice as I held his hand and he nudged me to continue our trek through the rubbish. We walked the rest of the way in silence, Hunter with his eyes glued to the floor. I couldn't tell if he was ashamed of himself for his actions during our brief history together, or just embarrassed that he was so vulnerable in front of me for a moment. It wasn't the time to overanalyze this though. As we reached the back of the basement, I saw a small doorway in the corner and my heart stuttered. *I trust him… I have no choice but to believe Jim isn't inside that room waiting for me with a goddam hatchet.*

"Here it is," Joe muttered as we paused at the doorway.

"Here *what* is?"

"Your reason to trust me." My heart thudded as I took those last few steps.

I was relieved to be confronted with an empty room. Jim wasn't hiding in a dark corner, crouched down in attack mode.

"I don't understand," I said as I stood near the doorway, still petrified of what I might find if I walked further into the darkness.

"Well, I met them here one night to pick up money they owed me. Jim was blazed out of his mind, and foolishly let me come down here with him." He walked to the back corner of the room, where a wall safe was hidden in the shadows. "I still remember the combo."

My jaw dropped as the safe swung open revealing a small mound of cash, begging me to take it. As I got closer, I noticed loose bills were floating towards the ground. Benjamin Franklin's face was fucking everywhere. I immediately rushed forward and greedily began counting… *three hundred… four hundred…*

"Just leave enough so that it's not terribly obvious they've been robbed. I doubt they keep track of it well enough to notice a few thousand missing though."

I nodded in understanding. "Where did it all come from?"

"I believe Jim's exact words were 'we hustled some white folk down south'. What exactly were you doing upstairs, Eva? I saw you snooping around on the security cameras." Joe asked me as he leaned his back against the far wall, watching me with little amusement.

"It's part of my plan," I mumbled as I continued to count... *fifteen hundred... sixteen hundred...* "Do you think anyone's looking for us on the security cameras right now?" *Thirty-two hundred.... thirty-three hundred...*

"Doubtful," he muttered allowing himself to slide to the floor. "Camping out in the security office was my gig tonight. At least it was until I failed to hand you and Missy over to Jim. Now my gig is to get you both back to Jim's hotel room tonight, drug you, and leave you for dead. Interested?"

I smirked at his sarcastic tone. "Aw, you made a joke." *Sixty-nine hundred... seven thousand...*

"So, what's your plan anyway?"

"I don't trust you with that information just yet, *Mr. Edison*," I said teasing him with my eyes as I mimicked his bogus name. "It'll all come together when you show me where everyone's luggage is." *Ten thousand... ten thousand one hundred...*

"Luggage?" The tone in his question caused me to stop counting immediately.

"Yes, for your *getaway*... to *London*." Joe continued to stare at me blankly, so I explained further hoping to refresh his memory. "I found Nyani's laptop in her room, and in her e-mail was a confirmation for *four* plane tickets to London leaving at nine o'clock tomorrow morning." He shook his head and shrugged, looking at me like I was talking crazy. "You're not going with them to London?" I practically demanded.

"Nope. I guess they forgot to invite me," he said with a sarcastic smirk on his face. I wanted to smack it away.

"So you don't know where their luggage is?" I asked near panic.

"No clue." His short answers were really starting to piss me off. I understood that he was in the middle of some sort of emotional breakdown, but I just didn't have the patience for it.

"Well, we have to find it! So snap out of it and tell me where you *think* they might be!"

"I don't know, Eva. Maybe upstairs in Nyani's room?"

"Wow, at least put some effort into your brilliant suggestions." My irritation encouraged me to pick up the cash at an incredible pace, but I was no longer counting it. *I'll just grab as much as I can stuff in my purse. I can't fucking believe my plan is falling apart with so little time left.* But I could believe it. I can even say I predicted it.

"Okay, smartass. If you only discovered earlier tonight that they bought plane tickets, and that there's a possibility their packed luggage is laying around here somewhere, what exactly was your plan before you got here? Come in, guns blazing?" *Dick.* "And how do you know who to direct your retaliation towards when you obviously don't even know who's running the show? Do you even know who's asses are gonna be sitting in those four seats tomorrow? For all you know, it could be a diversion from the cops and the luggage you're looking for doesn't even exist. So what's Plan B, Eva? Cuz helping you out isn't exactly going to please Jim, and I'd like to leave here with my balls intact. So lets do what you came here to do and fucking bolt."

I was still digging around inside the safe when he finished his little speech. He was right though. I had no Plan B… I never even had a solid Plan A. My only idea was to snoop around a bit, see what I could work with, and stay alive long enough to catch my ride out of here. Maybe send an anonymous package to the local police department holding all of the contracts I found with a lengthy letter explaining the ins and outs of this club. I'd been so focused on getting my revenge on Nyani, I hadn't really thought things through. Everything was so screwed up, I didn't even know if Nyani was the right person to direct my hate towards anymore. I really thought I had found something though when I stumbled across those plane tickets. But without their pre-packed luggage and my targets planning to leave the country, everything that weighed down my suitcase wasn't worth shit. It was time to go. Time to give up, and just be thankful to get out alive.

"Jim's hotel room," Joe muttered.

"What are you talking about?"

"The luggage. It's in his hotel room." He stood up, and began helping me collect money.

"How do you know?" I asked suspiciously.

"He told me. When he told me to bring you and Missy to his room tonight, he said something like 'we have to get our bags anyway'. He must have been talking about their luggage, right?" he asked as he stuffed a handful of cash into my purse.

"How do I know you're not just trying to get me to go there to have me killed and save your own ass?" I asked unwittingly. As the words came out, I barely recognized my voice. It was shaking with the sounds of a frightened toddler. Making adult-like decisions doesn't make you an adult, and my voice was only showing my true self.

"Eva! You have to trust me! If you want, we can just act like we made up and we're gonna go to the hotel and instead take the first train out of the city. I don't give a shit! In fact, that's what I'd rather do. I'm just trying to help you with your dumbass plan."

"Fine," I muttered getting to my feet. He was right, I had to trust him if I really wanted to do this. "I have a limo waiting for me at the hotel. We'll take a few minutes to search Jim's room for their luggage. I owe it to the other girls to do that much at least. Then we'll take the limo to the airport." I started to walk out of the room.

"Wow, so you *do* have a plan, Miss Eva!" He

grabbed my hand, and pulled me close to his chest. My stomach turned in surprise as his lips came closer to mine. It was almost like he never knocked me unconscious and sodomized me until blood was dripping down my thighs.

"Shit," he said abruptly pulling away from me. "Someone's coming! Hide!" he whispered.

He closed the safe and bolted ahead of me into the other room, leaving me in a state of alarm. I scurried after him into the clutter, and mindlessly crawled behind an old door that was leaning against a stack of boxes. The door was painted white, and still had the manufacturer's stickers on it to indicate that it had never been used. It didn't *look* new though. In fact, it looked more like a forgotten project from the eighties. Kind of sad. The door probably looked exquisite in its prime, but unfortunately its destiny was to sit in a moldy basement and rot for several decades. *Is that my destiny also? Am I going to die in this house, and be left here to rot in the land of the forgotten?*

"Where the fuck is she Claytone?" Jim's voice came booming through the basement sending a shiver down my spine.

"Where's who?" *Good, Hunter, keep calm. Please don't sell me out...*

"Whad'ya mean who? That slut Missy!" I released the air slowly from my lungs, relieved that he wasn't looking for me. Piles of junk came crashing down as I heard Jim tossing things out of his way. "I fucking saw her come down here!"

"I don't know Jim, I haven't been able to find her all night. Hannah is willing to come to the hotel with me though. She's, uhh, waiting for me upstairs."

"Ha! You got that bitch to talk to you after you shoved that shit in her ass? What a fucking twat, she deserves what's coming to her." I cringed as a man I hardly knew talked about me with such hate and malice in his voice. "I saw that other whore come down here though, help me find her!"

My entire body began to shake in fear of being discovered. The room sounded like it was being torn apart, and my only hope of getting out alive was to stay hidden until he gave up on the search. The door I was taking shelter under vibrated from nearby movement, and I knew it was only a matter of time before the pile of shit it was leaning against gave out. I scurried out of my nook, to a new spot under a collapsible table. From there, I had the perfect view of Jim and Hunter attacking the opposite side of the room. *Joe…ugh, that name sucks. I'll never get used to calling him that.* I could tell *Joe* was scrambling around in a panic, searching every nook and cranny in hope to find me before Jim did. *Calm down, sweetie. You're gonna give us away!*

"You know, I've been down here looking for her a good ten minutes and I didn't hear anyone come down the stairs except you. Maybe you saw *me* come down here?" Joe suggested, his voice teetering between hysteria and desperation.

"Nah, I know it was her!" Jim was taking his frustration out on the items left behind by throwing them across the room. I swiftly ducked my eyes out of view as he turned around to throw a vase in my direction. It hit the wall behind me, shattering into hundreds of pieces. "MOTHER FUCKER!"

My eyes found the peephole again, and I saw Jim standing there with his hands on his hips. His shoulders heaved up and down as he tried to catch his breath. That's when I saw her. Out of the corner of my eye, I saw a little blonde head pop up and down. It was a brief moment, but I knew it was Missy. *Shit.* The whole time I'd been sitting there with my heart in my stomach thinking Jim had seen *me* coming down the stairs, wondering if he was suspicious of Mr. Edison helping me. Hoping he didn't decide to open the safe and start counting his money. But it wasn't at all that complex. He really had seen Missy come down to the basement.

I saw her head pop up again a little further back. *She's heading for the stairs...*

"Why don't we go back to the security room and look for her on the monitors? I don't want to keep Hannah alone long enough for her to change her mind, ya know?"

They were both standing in the middle of a small aisle that had been cleared out by the few people who dared to trek through the garbage. Jim looked defeated, almost ready to give in. But Missy didn't see the look on his face. She didn't know how close he was to going upstairs. And she fucked up. She had crawled as close to the stairs as she could while still being able to remain hidden, but there wasn't enough junk at the foot of the stairs for her to stay concealed. It was only a few yards, so I could see the appeal of making a run for it. She was surprisingly fast in her white cocktail dress, and three-inch heels… but Jim was faster. *Should've taken off the shoes…*

Missy made it up maybe five stairs before Jim closed the distance between them, grabbing her by the hair, and dragging her over the railing. She fell to the cement floor, bouncing like a rag doll. My eyes were glued to the scene, as I sat on my knees and trembled in fear. Missy was screaming and crying on the ground, struggling to get up. Jim raised his foot over her body, and brought his heel down onto her chest with enough force to ensure she wouldn't get up again. He walked away, leaving her twisting and moaning in agony. I knew he could have brought his foot down harder, and probably killed her immediately. But the sick fuck wanted to play with her.

When Jim came back into view, he had something in his hand. *What is that? Part of a lamp?* Whatever it was made a sickening crunch as he brought it down on her head over and over… and over. Missy never begged for her life… never told him he'd go to hell for doing this to her… never said a damn word. Her screams just died out, and all that was left was the sound of metal meeting the cushiony substance that had once been her skull. Silent tears were streaming down my face, and I had lost complete control of my bladder. I glanced at Hunter and saw his eyes focused on the back wall. His back was to me, but I wouldn't doubt it if he was crying too.

"Help me move her," Jim commanded. Mr. Edison didn't hesitate to assist him. They carried her right past me, practically under my nose. Jim at the front under her shoulders and Hunter at her feet. Blood soaked through her white dress, reminding me of paint on an unprimed canvas. Her head was misshaped, and her face was gone… caved in. There was nothing recognizable as human left from the neck up.

They put her in the room with the safe, and Jim led the way back upstairs. I sat there in a puddle of my own piss for what felt like an eternity, finally able to let out the sobs I'd been desperately trying to contain. It was only the urge to vomit that forced me to get out from underneath that table, stretching myself out on my hands and knees as it splashed all over the concrete. *Get up, get up, get up, get up.*

My purse was still in my first hiding spot under the door, knocked over and spilling out. I crawled over to it and quickly scooped it up. *Shit, what do I do? Wait here? Go upstairs?* My legs stopped shaking enough so that I could stand up, and walk into the other room. It's sick, but I couldn't help myself. I wanted to take a closer look at her body.

It was even more grotesque up close. Her skull had definitely been cracked open, and chunks of what

I could only imagine were a combination of skin and her brain lay stuck in her gorgeous blonde hair. Next to her body was the murder weapon… *it was the pimp, in the basement… with the candlestick.* I took out my cell phone and started taking photos. A close up of the murder weapon, the body, and what was left of her face. I didn't know yet what I was going to use them for. Proof I guess.

Finding a rag among the junk pile was too easy. I used it to clean off the piss dripping down my legs, the vomit on my hands, and my tear stained face… not in that order of course. *It's time to go Hannah. Your driver is waiting.*

DAY THIRTY-SEVEN
PART THREE

THE PARTY WAS STILL raging outside, but it seemed like more guests had ventured indoors. Of course Hunter was nowhere in sight when I walked through the foyer. I couldn't wait for him long. Panic set in at the thought of the limo driver giving up on me and leaving. *Just go upstairs and grab your suitcase. If he doesn't magically appear in five minutes, you'll just call him from the street. It'll all work out.* I hurried up the stairs, not wanting to draw too much attention to myself. There was no doubt that my face was a hot mess from all of the crying and puking.

My bag was right where I'd left it. I shoved the oversized purse back in its designated spot, now plump with goodies, and headed back towards the stairs. *Maybe just a quick glance in the mirror...* I paused in the hallway and noticed that the bathroom was unoccupied. The entire upstairs area appeared deserted, so I leaned my luggage against the wall and took advantage of the opportunity to make myself semi presentable. *The driver can wait a few more minutes.*

He won't leave, not without the second half of his pay.

Black makeup was smeared across my face, and my eyes and cheeks were pink and swollen. A small portion of my hair was soaked with vomit. I quickly took a tissue to wipe the makeup away, and threw my hair up in a messy bun. *I'll just have to deal with a puffy face until I get to the car where my makeup is.*

"Are you okay?" Nyani was standing outside the bathroom door analyzing my face in the mirror.

"Yeah, I'm fine. Mr. Edison and I got into a little, uh, argument. But I'm sure we'll work it out," I said quickly thinking on my feet. All fear and anger towards her had disappeared, replaced by pity and disgust.

"Oh," she paused. "Are you going back to the hotel with him tonight?" I stood there staring at her for a moment, trying to interpret her demeanor. *She knows. She knows what Jim will do to me if he finds me in that hotel room. I wonder how many girls she's watched him kill... girls that she personally lured in off the streets. How many times did she help him drag their bodies to some back alley or dumpster? Was all the guilt finally catching up to her?*

"Yes," I said finally and turned my back to her so I could wash my hands in the sink. *Fuck her. Let her feel guilty.*

"Here," she said reaching into her purse. She handed me a small compact. "It's a little darker than your natural color, but it might help tone down the

306

redness."

"Thanks," I said taking it from her and spreading the powder across my face. She was right, it wasn't my color. But now instead of looking like a sobbing mess, I looked like a member of the Jersey Shore cast with a drug problem.

"Much better," I said with a smile and handed it back to her. As she took it out of my hand, she abruptly rushed towards me with her arms outstretched. I flinched in surprise before I realized she was hugging me. Returning the embrace, I could feel the wetness of her tears on my shoulder. And just as abruptly as it started, the hug was over.

"Perhaps we'll run into each other again one day, Miss Hannah." And she was gone. For a brief moment I considered running after her. I desperately searched my mind for the right words to say to inspire hope and some form of self-worth, but my mind was a vast desert. The moment passed, and for some reason I was left with a profound feeling of sadness that Nyani was being left behind. *It's not like you could have invited her to take a ride in your secret limo back to the hotel where you're executing a revenge plan against her and her 'business associates', one who happens to be her lover. Abusive or not, murderer or not, I can't trust that she'll be so eager to switch sides. Perhaps in another life... under different circumstances, we could have been great friends. Not this life however, and certainly not under these circumstances.*

As I stepped out of the bathroom, something in Nyani's bedroom caught my eye. Rolling my crap behind me, I headed towards her door with the intention of only taking a quick peek. *You really don't have time for this!* However, the sight of four suitcases lined up against her bed immediately changed my mind. I scurried into the room and locked the door behind me. Directly in front of each suitcase were four identical carry-on sized duffle bags, along with a passport that slightly stuck out of each bag's side pocket. It looked like something straight out of a damn catalog. *Well someone went through a lot of trouble to make sure there would be no problems at the airport.* I dropped my bag and snatched the first passport, excited as hell.

It belonged to Jim, *or should I say Mr. Jonathan Abrahms. I wonder if that's even his real name. Let's see who Jonathan Abrahms is traveling with.* I picked up the next passport. It belonged to the bald guy who was running the 'charity'. I thought I heard someone coming up the stairs and froze. No one came. *Maybe I should speed this up a bit.*

My heart continued to thud in my chest as I reached for the third passport. It quickly dropped to my stomach, however, when Hunter's picture was staring back at me. *He lied.* I didn't know if I wanted to cry or throw a bitch fit in front of all the guests by shoving his passport down his throat. I couldn't believe I'd let him manipulate me again. Nothing he'd said in the basement could be trusted, and I began to question how involved he really was in the death of the other girls. *Maybe it's not Nyani who helps clean up Jim's mess. I mean, why risk her not being able to lift the bodies when the strength of a man is at your disposal? Mr.*

Edison's strength. 'Got drugged' my ass! And here I was, going back to the hotel room with him... fucking moron. I allowed a single tear to roll down my cheek, but it was all I had time for.

The last passport belonged to Nyani, aka Jaclyn. I shuffled through it quickly, curious to see if she had actually ever been to Paris like she told me. Every page was blank. There wasn't a single stamp in Nyani's passport indicating that she had ever left the country, but it didn't matter. None of her lies mattered now that I knew Jim controlled her. I wanted to hate her, but after everything I heard from inside that closet, I just couldn't.

I rested my luggage on the floor and unzipped it. There among the nicest wardrobe I will probably ever own, was enough of Martin's cocaine supply to ensure a few people wouldn't be getting on a plane in the morning. The stuff probably would have only lasted Martin a month or two at the rate he snorted it. Sadly, it wasn't even his entire stock. He had much more than the large amount I had taken, but I had to leave enough behind for the police to find with his body.

The coke was already separated into six softball-sized bags, and all I could do was hope that was enough. I started with Mr. 'Children of the World's bag. I unzipped the top of his suitcase, and let one of the bags of coke plop inside. Hidden well enough just in case he decided to throw in a last minute t-shirt or razor, but a guarantee he wouldn't make it through security. *That's for making those people think they're donating their money to an actual charity.*

Then I reached for Jim's bag. A sick feeling came over me as I rummaged through his things. His clothes were all folded neatly, shirts separated from the jeans. Even his boxers appeared to have been ironed. I ran my hands over his clothes. *So normal… nothing in here says who he really is.* I don't know what I expected. Certainly not an array of murder weapons, or blood stained clothes. Just something out of place… something to show what a monster he was. *Well if you didn't pack anything scandalous, don't mind if I help you out a bit! Two bags of coke for your suitcase, and one for your duffle. That's for calling me a slut, and treating people like possessions.*

I emailed the photos of Missy's body to myself and used Nyani's laptop to print them out. As they printed, I grabbed the stolen contracts out of my bag and started sifting through them. Anger boiled through me as I read name after name. There were a dozen more contracts than girls I'd met, and it sickened me to look at the dates and realize how long they were getting away with it all. There, mixed in the pile, was 'Nyani's contract signed with her legal name and dated almost four months earlier. I doubt I would have believed it existed without seeing it first hand. There was something preventing me from keeping her contract with all the rest, so I put it to the side instead.

I began to slide the contracts into Hunter's bag, but quickly realized how pointless that would be. *He knows my plan. He'll check his luggage. Fuck me and my mouth.* Just in case he didn't realize I found the bags, I dropped the remaining bags of coke into his suitcase, knowing they'd probably be discovered. My only hope was that Mr. Edison assumed I gave up on my plan and left the party unsuccessful. *I can't let him take this away from me.*

Before I made a run for it, there were a few more things I had to do. I rummaged around the room for a piece of paper and a pen. I finally had the words for Nyani... and a few more for the security at JFK airport.

Two minutes later, I was hauling my soon-to-be-abandoned luggage down the street towards freedom, and towards the actual location I had the limo driver waiting for me. Two blocks over. Fortunately I'd been smart enough to fib about that.

I had spotted Hunter stuck in a conversation as I quietly floated down the stairs towards the exit. I thought he was too busy charming a tall blonde to notice me slip out the front door. But I was wrong. As I paused by the door to take one last look at him, we locked eyes for a brief moment. I found that I could see him again as I did before. Not as Mr. Edison, and not as Joe. For the last time, I saw him as Hunter. And I could tell Hunter knew exactly what I'd found upstairs, and that the coke in his bag would never make it to the airport. We exchanged quick smirks, and I felt confident that he'd keep my little scheme a secret from everyone else. *Don't worry, Mr. Edison. I won't forget about you. You'll get what's coming to you soon enough.*

DAY THRITY-EIGHT

NYANI TOSSED HER duffle bag onto the seat next to her, a seat she was relieved to know would remain unoccupied for the duration of the flight. She rested her head against the window, exhausted and still in disbelief over the morning's debacle. After six hours of police questioning, they finally allowed her to get on a plane.

They specifically catechized her about a website that had recently been taken down. The web address was scribbled across the top of one of the legal documents they'd found in her companion's luggage. They also questioned her about photos they'd found in Jim's luggage. Nyani was honest. She told the police she recognized Missy's blonde hair. On the back of one of the pictures was the address to the house Jim had rented scribbled in hurried cursive, leading the police directly to the body. Nyani sneered. *That sneaky bitch.*

"Who wrote this?" they'd asked.

Eva! "I have no idea."

Nyani told the police her own definition of everything, and in return they assured her she would be safe from Jim.

"That's all I get?" she demanded. "A promise? That won't stop him from finding me." Her demeanor turned cold and distant as it became obvious they weren't going to do more to eliminate her fears. They let her go under the condition that she remained in the country, suggesting she stay with a relative. So four tickets to London became two first class tickets to Miami, and seven hours and thirty-seven minutes after her first plane was supposed to take off, she was finally leaving New York.

While the police found nothing suspicious in her luggage, she noticed a few extra items the minute everything was dumped out on a table in front of her. Just over $8,000 in cash, for one. The police hardly questioned it since she held a one-way ticket out of the country. Then there was the contract, something she had essentially forgotten about. The police recognized it immediately, and confiscated it as 'evidence' saying it was exactly like the 'others'. Nyani didn't object. She wasn't ashamed of her decision. In her mind, she did what she needed to do to survive.

Finally, there was an envelope with her name on it. The police had opened it and read it without her consent, but swiftly moved on to the other contents of her bag without a second glance. Perhaps they didn't think what was written in the note was significant. Nyani, however, was dying to know what it said. The curiosity had been lingering in the back of her mind for hours before she finally got the opportunity to read it. Seconds after the flight was done ascending, and the seatbelt signs were turned off, Nyani tore through her duffle bag in search of that envelope. She already knew who it was from. With Missy dead, there was only one girl left, and she had listened to Jim berating Joe all morning about how 'Hannah' managed to disappear. On the outside she was sharing his rage and helping him tie up the loose ends, but on the inside... she was amused... almost proud. And now she knew it wasn't a coincidence that Joe forgot something in his hotel room last minute and never met them at their airport.

Nyani's fingers trembled as she wrapped them around Eva's note, dreading what she had to say. She was curious why instead of the illicit materials found in the others' luggage, there was a gift of all that cash. Why not let her go down with them? Nyani had never had so much money on her at one time in her entire life. She grew up poor and hit the streets when she was only fourteen. After she met Jim, he'd always held on to her earnings, giving her an allowance as he saw fit. The only explanation she could come up with for Eva's actions was that Eva thought she deserved much worse than the few years in jail the others will get. And Nyani would be lying if she said she disagreed.

The envelope was on familiar stationary. Eva hadn't bothered to seal it shut, and had scrawled Nyani's legal name on it with a rushed hand. She took out the note and read:

'For that trip to Paris you never got to take.
- Hannah'

Nyani smirked and let out a sigh of relief as she reread the note several times before carefully tucking it away in her bag.

About The Author

Born and raised on Long Island, Rose Burke didn't fly far from the nest when she enrolled in the six-year-plan at Hofstra University, eventually graduating with a degree in Fine Arts. She sort-of writes a blog based on a bucket list of fifty things she's never done before. Even the small tasks challenge her to step out of her comfort zone and embrace her awkward tendencies. Not-so-shockingly, the most noteworthy moments of her childhood often included the Scholastic Book Fair, in particular the day Jon Scieszka signed her very own copy of *The Stinky Cheese Man and Other Fairly Stupid Tales* and labeled her his 'favorite stinker'. This is her first novel.

Visit the author's website at www.roseburke.com

Made in the USA
San Bernardino, CA
17 May 2014